Out of His League

caroline richardson

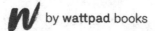 by **wattpad** books

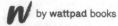 by wattpad books

An imprint of Wattpad WEBTOON Book Group

Copyright © 2022 Caroline Richardson. All rights reserved.

Published in Canada by Wattpad Books, a division of Wattpad Corp.
36 Wellington Street E., Toronto, ON M5E 1C7

www.wattpad.com

First W by Wattpad Books edition: April 2022

ISBN 978-1-99025-906-7 (Trade Paper original)
ISBN 978-1-99025-907-4 (eBook edition)

Library and Archives Canada Cataloguing in Publication information
is available upon request.

Printed and bound in Canada
1 3 5 7 9 10 8 6 4 2

Cover design by Elliot Caroll
Typesetting by Sarah Salomon

For my father
Thank you for a lifetime of steadiness and support

chapter 1

A bright flash of metal caught Gretchen's eye as she plunked down on the closest unforgiving airport terminal seat.

She did a double take as she realized the flash of metal was a Rolex watch, and trailed her eyes up the well-toned arm it cuffed, to the tight sleeves of a white Toronto Sixers baseball polo. Moving up from the shirt, she locked on to a very familiar face that was hidden behind signature Ray-Bans and a well-worn Sixers cap.

A face—hell, a whole man—she'd never met in person but had cheered for on TV and at home games as much as she could.

Gretchen's heart thumped audibly in her ears as she took him in. Joshua. Joshua Malvern, the left fielder for the Sixers, was walking toward her in the airport. A tall, fit, and dangerously handsome major league baseball player, at her gate, the last one on the concourse. Puzzled, she checked the date on her phone.

He shouldn't be here; he should be at batting practice. He should not be getting on a plane to Las Vegas.

Then she noticed the slump in his shoulders as he sagged into an empty seat three down from her, his carry-on duffel dumped beside him. He took off his sunglasses, and she caught his faraway stare as he ran a tired hand over his face, the weight of the world etched across his features.

Oh. Oh no. Not again. He was being sent down. The club likely wouldn't bring him back—he was out of options. Her heart fell, heavy at the thought. It happened all the time to the best of players. But this time it sucked.

She had her team cap with her, and she rummaged through her laptop bag for her fine-tip Sharpie. It was red, but what the heck, it would show up on the white brim of the hat. She wanted to remember him as a player from her favorite baseball team. Her favorite player—period—since his rookie year in Boston.

She hesitated. Would he want to be bothered? He had a "fuck off" vibe she could sense even from where she was sitting. Crushing the cap in her hands, Gretchen bit her lip, debating on the merits of doing it anyway, and quickly stuffed it away. An autograph wasn't appropriate given his obvious mood—he needed a pick-me-up, not a crazed fangirl. She got up, grabbed her carry-on, and strode to the coffee bar in a fit of spontaneity.

She knew how he liked his coffee; she'd read about it in a fluff piece from the *Toronto Star* online sports news. She also knew his batting average and RBIs, his favorite meal and color—basically all the normal tidbits that a celebrity doled out about themselves on social media. Joshua wasn't on any of that publicly—he was a pretty private guy compared to some on the team—but his fans certainly were and loved to share. Celebutainment reporters would take any nugget of information and throw it to the fans like they were a hungry pack of dogs too.

A few minutes later, she presented him with the coffee silently, trying not to wimp out and back away, and he looked up, confused. She wiggled the cup slightly.

"Two cream, no sugar," she said, her voice wavering, ready for him to call security and tell her to get the hell away from him.

Instead, he gently lifted the coffee out of her hand, one eyebrow lifting in apparent amusement. Phew.

"Thanks," he replied quietly, peeling the tab back on the lid. "Have a seat."

"Are you sure? I don't want to be a—"

He patted the chair beside him as he took a sip, letting out a groan from his throat, closing his eyes.

"You looked like you needed it," she offered quietly, slowly dropping into the chair, gripping her own cup to keep from shaking like a leaf. This was by far the most daring thing she'd ever done. She was quite sure she was out of her element in the moment.

"I do. Today sucks," he replied and leaned back. "You know who I am, obviously."

"Yes, I do."

"Has it hit the sports news yet?"

"I don't know," Gretchen answered, relaxing slightly, understanding the implied news of his being sent down. "Is it temporary?"

Joshua shrugged and looked out the window, then swiveled back to her. He had serious eyes, but she knew that if he smiled, they would suddenly hold mischief. There was none of that now. Holding his gaze for a moment, her face heated and she looked away, self-conscious as she blushed.

"I don't know," he replied, taking another sip of his coffee, sighing. "You're right. I needed this."

"I'm—I'm sorry. You'll be missed while you're in Vegas," she stuttered, not really knowing what to say. "But you'll be back."

She wasn't sure what made her do it, but she reached out and touched his leg when she said it. Maybe it was her compulsion to comfort people, or maybe it was just something in the way he looked at her. He was defeated, and her heart went out to him.

The jolt of warmth and the feel of his muscle under her palm was not what she'd expected. Nor was his reaction. His eyes widened a moment, and he covered her hand with his before she could pull away.

"Thank you."

It was a heady sensation. Two strangers, touching in a crowded airport, drinking coffee, and the heat from his hand was zapping her composure to ashes. Shyly, she pulled her hand away as he released it, her heart beating hard in her chest.

"Where are you headed?" he asked suddenly, breaking the awkward silence.

"Same place you are, apparently." Gretchen tried to regain her composure. "I'm attending a wine competition."

"A wine competition?"

"I'm a sommelier. I'm headed to Vegas to observe the competition and take back the results for my clients, update their wine lists, and advise buys. That sort of thing."

"That sounds really relaxing compared to my weekend to come," he replied.

"I doubt that," she said, hoping to deflect his train of thought. "I'm hoping to see my best friend and spend some time with her too. Maybe we'll road trip down to the California coast and I can help her do some bulk vintage buying. She's a sommelier too; we went to college together."

The steam from her cup wafted up into her eyes while they drank, and she took that moment to mentally deep-breathe. Being bold had now netted her a chance to talk to her favorite baseball player, and here she was, babbling on about things he likely didn't care much about. She bit her lip to gain some control over her pulse, which was hammering away with excitement, and peeked at him. Was he humoring her? She sounded ridiculous.

"Wine buying. Sounds decadent," Joshua said. His voice rumbled enticingly, the way he uttered the word *decadent* both sexy and tempting.

The announcement for their gate startled them, and Gretchen gathered up her bag, tipping the remains of her coffee into the garbage, her stomach too keyed up to actually drink it.

"I didn't get your name," Joshua said as he stood as well.

"Gretchen," she replied, holding out her hand. "Gretchen Harper."

"You are a very sweet woman, Gretchen," he said, grabbing her hand. Instead of shaking it, he lifted it and ran his lips over her knuckles. She stifled a gasp, and when he looked up, he finally smiled, stopping her heart. Dear God, he was stunning.

Her knees went weak and her toes tingled. She ducked her head, her cheeks so hot she was sure she was crimson. She heard him chuckle almost to himself and caught her reflection in the polished chrome on the edge of the seats. *Yup.* She was blushing like an idiot.

They walked toward the gate together. Gretchen stopped off to one side and rummaged for her boarding pass as Joshua queued up with the other first-class passengers. He looked around at her when she didn't follow him into line, and he beckoned her over.

She joined him in line, her nerves jumping.

"Sit with me. The plane's not full." He gestured to the line in front of them.

"Oh, I—"

She looked down at her boarding pass. Despite being financially stable, she had to be practical—which she was, all the time. Practical, boring, solid, dependable Gretchen. The Gretchen who never took risks like buying coffee for gorgeous professional athletes in airports.

But at that moment, she wanted to be that alter ego she had momentarily discovered because the look in his eye was enough to make her abandon all restraint.

"Don't argue. Let me repay you for your kindness, at least," he said, interrupting her thoughts as they reached the gate. Joshua charmed the attendants, and they very happily added her to the first-class list. With a hasty "thank you" over her shoulder, Gretchen was swept past the attendants and into the breezeway toward the plane.

As she looked over at him, taking in his profile, a hand came and rested on the small of her back. *Dear God*, she thought, *what was I thinking, bringing him a coffee? Because now I can't breathe.*

' ' '

Josh had walked into the airport feeling sorry for himself, carrying a mood he was having a hard time classifying as anything other than shitty.

The dark cloud hanging over his head at another boot back to the minors was maddening. His batting average was still hovering at a respectable .210, and he fit well with the team. The fans loved him, and he was a veteran player. An all-star. Why was he now the sacrificial lamb when some younger phenom needed to stretch his legs?

But he knew his batting average was slipping, his spring knee strain and shoulder issue were a factor, and his two errors in the last game didn't help. It was high time that he had some stability to just get his shit worked out. He was tired. At this rate, he'd take anything as long as it was in the majors, even a year-to-year contract. Even if it meant leaving the club to go elsewhere.

Which would suck. He had solidified his career playing with the Sixers since he'd arrived six years ago. He liked Toronto too. The city had been welcoming, he had every amenity a block from his condo without much hassle, and he enjoyed living by the lake. The view from his living-room window was spectacular; he enjoyed watching the planes take off from Toronto Island airport and the multicolored sailboats zipping in and out of the marinas on sunny days.

As he settled into his seat on the plane, he looked across at the reason his terrible mood had evaporated into thin air. Wild, blond, shoulder-length hair framed thirst-quenching blue eyes that just about killed him when he looked past the coffee she'd offered him only a few minutes before. Her curvy body with just the right amount of *oomph* had added to the nearly-killing-him feeling when she had sat down beside him.

She looked like a tiny rock-and-roll firecracker.

Then she had put her hand on his leg, and it was all he could do not to yank her onto his lap. The emotions and endorphins he had rolled through after being pulled into the office that morning might be partly to blame for his seeming overreaction to this woman, but . . . she was mesmerizing.

Normally he wouldn't offer a fan the chance to get close enough to go superfan crazy, but somehow she didn't seem like the type of woman who would do that. She hadn't propositioned him, wanting something he wasn't interested in. He wasn't a prude, and like anyone, there had been times when he'd scratched the itch, of course. But, in the long run, he was careful not to let a woman get too close, and it was easily done because he'd never found anyone that he'd connected with. The consequences were really not so great for his career, and his agent had reminded him of that on occasion, steering him back to the focus. Ball.

She hadn't asked for an autograph or a selfie either. Unless he was doing meet and greets with fans or a kid ran up to him and asked him to sign a ball, it grated on his nerves when fans would slap him on the back as if he were a long-lost friend. They'd muscle in to take a photo, no matter what kind of mood he was in or not even ask for permission before blinding him with their phone's flash.

She'd treated him like a human being, not a commodity. He'd been surprised, that was for certain, and in a good way.

Gretchen buckled her seat belt, looked out the window, then turned and grinned impishly, lifting her shoulders in excitement. "I've never flown first class."

That smile. Holy hell. He wondered how her lips would taste stained by a deep, rich, red wine, and he shifted in his seat. *Don't say anything stupid, Malvern.*

"It's my lucky day to share it with you."

She relaxed back into the seat and turned her head to him. "This is so nice, seriously, thank you. I'm sorry about you being sent down."

He tried not to let his bad mood fight through the distraction of her. The fans and sports commentators weren't happy with the decision last time either. Fighting the urge to punch the seat in front of him, he took a careful, cleansing breath before he spoke.

"It's the way the game is played. It sucks, but I'll be okay. Vegas is a good club, and it's not forever, just a few weeks."

Gretchen pursed her lips and Josh realized she didn't believe his weak attempt at avoiding the subject, likely seeing the tension he'd hoped he had hidden. Obviously not.

When she reached out and put a hand on his leg again, the jolt of energy that coursed from her touch up through his nerve endings made him blink. *The firecracker has a fuse*, he thought as their eyes met. A blush crept back over her cheeks. She pulled her hand away and nervously tucked a lock of hair behind her ear. He wanted to lean in and nibble on that ear. What in fresh hell was wrong with him?

"I'm sorry I brought it up. Let's distract ourselves with ridiculously expensive things in SkyMall," she laughed and reached for the magazine in front of her.

For the next few moments, they leafed through the catalogue, pointing out things like gold anodized poodle doorstops and ten-thousand-dollar toothbrushes. Anything to get away from the topic of baseball or the reason he was sitting in his seat. It was a sweet gesture, just like the coffee, and he let a little more tension go, chuckling over ridiculous tchotchkes and dust-gatherers.

"My teammate Freddie? He has that cell phone cover in bright bubblegum pink. His daughter picked it out for him for his birthday," he murmured when she pointed out a ridiculously expensive Swarovski-crystal-encrusted phone case and shook her head in disbelief.

"Oh," she replied and stared at the page. "I forgot that you and your teammates can afford this kind of stuff."

Of course he could afford that kind of thing; he was lucky to be where he was. She was perceptive and the reality of that twisted his gut because the rehearsed media line he'd fed her wasn't the truth. He wanted to tell her how pissed off he was. Like he hadn't been able to tell his teammates or coaches. He'd just thrown his batting helmet across the club room and stormed out, kicking a trash can for good measure as he did, the entire locker room silent at his outburst. He'd hear about that later.

"My bullshit 'it's the way the game is played' isn't okay," he blurted. "I am angry. Being in the Show is the goal, right? This back-and-forth is killing my confidence. I've been a major league player for ten years now, and I am not ready to give up even though folks say I'm past my prime. But it's a reality, and I'm lumping it. Don't want to."

Her hand was back, this time on his shoulder. Her calm demeanor said it all. With the simple admission of him being angry, plus her touch, his shoulders dropped and the tension left. Regrettably, she moved her hand away again, twisting her fingers together in her lap.

"You'll be back," she stated. "You have to be."

"You seem pretty confident in my abilities."

"You should be too," she replied, then covered her mouth. "Sorry, that was way too forward."

"And bringing a stranger coffee in an airport wasn't?" He laughed, which made her giggle, a sound so pleasing he wondered how he could make her laugh again.

As the plane backed away from the gate, he impulsively twined his fingers with hers, going with this dangerously spontaneous feeling he had. This woman, a complete stranger, had defused one of the worst days of his career with a small act of kindness. He didn't want to take out his aggression on unsuspecting objects. He wasn't so tense his back was cracking. The most surprising thing was how he didn't have to run through the anger-management tricks from the course he'd taken in rookie year. All his agent's players took it. He said it was "good life stuff to know." He'd been right.

It didn't hurt that Gretchen was sexy as hell and had him thinking about things other than baseball. He shook their joined hands and grinned. "Now, let's leave my bad day in the dust. Tell me about this wine thing you're going to."

. . .

Josh had Gretchen in stitches the entire flight—telling her funny stories, asking her somewhat serious questions about wine, charming the attendants for an extra blanket. He hadn't let go of her hand except to grab their wineglasses when the drinks cart came around.

She was pleased they were serving a lovely value-for-bottle red up here, not the normally terrible budget wine on the service cart behind her, and savored it. Being a sommelier meant sometimes you just wanted a good glass of wine without having to analyze or compare it. She'd gotten into wine because she loved it, not because she liked dissecting it. As her career grew, the opportunity to kick her shoes off by the fire and just let a bottle of wine be what it was had become elusive. Her business depended on her being on the ball, so her notebook was always close by, and she tasted every bottle, even the ones she opened by herself on a Friday night alone in her condo.

The reminder of what was important to her, right now, was nice. She needed the wine for other reasons. Her pulse had been racing faster than during one of her boot camp fitness classes, and she was sure her nerves were frayed beyond what they could handle. She was comfortable with Josh, but it wasn't lost on her that she was sitting beside a walking, talking dream man.

As the plane banked, she peeked out the window. Off in the distance were the glittering hotels along the strip. Every time she traveled to Vegas, the city gave her a thrill when arriving later in the day. The lights, the excitement, the people. She wondered if that was why she had bought that coffee for Josh, the energy from Vegas seeping into her even before she had left home, making her spontaneous.

"Where are you staying?" Josh whispered in her ear, his breath on her neck, close as he leaned in to look out the window as well.

"Mandalay Bay. The competition is there, it seemed practical."

She didn't dare turn around and leaned back into him instead. A hand came around her waist and he put his chin on her shoulder. It was such a familiar motion, and they barely knew each other, but she surprised herself at how okay she was with it. And aroused.

She'd never had this kind of connection with a man right after meeting him. Normally she'd have waited until the third date to get this close. The heady rush of attraction was strong and intoxicating. Josh was her fantasy man, good-looking and masculine, always charming when he was interviewed. Today? It took on a whole new dimension.

"It's gorgeous, isn't it? An oasis in the middle of the desert," he said quietly. "All man-made, all for man's pleasure."

Gretchen savored the way he said the word *pleasure* just as much as she had the wine. Which had apparently gone to her head. She was behaving completely contrary to her normal self. Uninhibited and impulsive—her sexy doppelganger.

She hummed and heated when he splayed his hand across her stomach, tiny caresses feathering out the warmth even further. She wiggled, curving into him, and realized he felt it too. His breath hitched, and he cleared his throat several times, tightening his hold on her waist.

He pointed with his other hand out toward the lights. "The fountains are my favorite to visit on hot nights. And the Luxor, there? It has a beam of light that points straight up. It can be seen from space. The elevators go sideways too."

Gretchen decided not to spoil Josh's pre-landing tour—she knew Las Vegas well enough—and let him dole out trivia about the strip as it slowly came into view, sparkling in the late afternoon sun. As the captain announced their arrival and turned on the seat-belt sign, she reluctantly sat up and shifted into her seat. The cold was immediate and she wanted him back.

They disembarked first, and he took her hand as they walked up the breezeway, as simple as that. The sound of slot machines could be heard even before they hit the arrivals deck, and a rush of adrenaline kicked her squarely in the solar plexus. She picked up her stride, the words *carpe diem* echoing in her head.

Boring Gretchen could take a hike right now because this felt amazing.

When she pushed through the airport doors, she breathed in the aroma of cheap perfume, cigarettes, and people, and shimmied in excitement. She turned back to him as they stopped just inside the carpeted area.

"I know this is likely old hat to you—"

He shook his head, an amused look on his face she wasn't quite sure what to make of. "Lead on, ma'am," he drawled and winked.

They wound their way through the terminal slowly in the crush of people, Gretchen's eyes following the familiar jumbled-up carpet patterns. More than once, Josh bumped into her back and put a hand on her waist. A couple of times, he held her to him while a crowd of people would push past. They stood at the baggage claim the same way, waiting for the turnstile to shudder to life and belch out the luggage from the plane.

"Where are you headed?" she asked. She didn't want this to be over, this heady space of time that seemed like a *Twilight Zone* moment. Where everything that would never normally happen to a girl like her happened. Joshua Malvern. Big and solid and sexy behind her. In Vegas. She felt reckless, wanting things she wasn't sure were possible.

"I've got until tomorrow morning to report to the office. Likely a driver is waiting outside right now to take me out to the club apartments beside the field where I'll be staying for the next few weeks," Josh said, his breath once again feathering across her neck, sending goosebumps up her arms.

The carousel squealed, and people rushed to the edge, anxious to be on their way. Gretchen held back, not wanting to break the connection she had with Josh, not wanting the warmth to go away. She knew their interlude was likely over. She twisted around to look at him as a gray-haired woman pushed past them with an overloaded baggage cart.

"Hectic," she murmured.

"Yeah." He swallowed a couple of times.

Their lips were an inch away from touching when a finger

tapped Josh on his shoulder, followed by an excited voice. "Excuse me? You're Joshua Malvern, aren't you?"

Josh turned with an irritated sigh. "Last time I checked, yes."

The young man nattered excitedly on to Josh about how awesome he was, and Josh signed his shirt with the Sharpie that Gretchen had in her bag. Soon another, then another fan approached, so she moved off to get her bags.

She was trying to decide what to do when they parted ways. Should she give him her contact info? Should she just chalk it up to a moment in time she could cherish forever?

Spotting her bag, she hefted the large pink paisley-patterned suitcase over to the lip of the carousel, and as she struggled, a hand came out and lifted it for her. She looked back and Josh was right there, a baggage cart behind him. He lifted her suitcase with ease and placed it on top of two large duffel bags full of equipment, branded with the MLB logo.

"Oh thanks! All done over there?"

The reality of why he was here hit her again. *Right. He doesn't want to be here, not really.* She hefted her carry-on farther up on her shoulder and watched as he bent over to retrieve a large suitcase with a garment bag attached to the side.

"You travel with a lot of gear, sir," she said, smiling, hoping to break back into the ease between them from a few minutes earlier.

"Yeah. I could have shipped it with the rest of my stuff, but what the hey, the club pays my ticket here," he replied, adjusting the pile. "Follow me."

He zoomed through the crowd, pushing the cart ahead of him like a pro, reminding Gretchen that he was a seasoned traveler. He'd likely seen the inside of every major airport in the States. She chewed on her lip. Maybe he had a "friend" in every city too.

Her doubts flashed, watching him manhandle the cart between two rows of slot machines, his arm muscles bunching, pulling his shirt tight across his shoulders. He was in a different category than her in life, that was for sure. Jet-setter, well-off. Seasoned. Her confidence faltered.

But dear God, he is magnificent, she countered to herself. Walking sex. And despite her doubts, despite her knowing they were two totally different people, she wanted him, even if it was just for the night.

chapter 2

Josh saw the sign with the Las Vegas Neons logo on it, his name scrawled in black spiky letters. He waved his hand above the crowd and veered toward his driver.

"Josh!" the driver beamed, his familiar accent reaching above the crowd.

"Hey, Ric! Looking good, my man," Josh said, and the two slapped each other on the arm. "Wife doing okay these days?"

"She's due in a month, can you believe it? I'm gonna be a *papá*!" the man said, grinning from ear to ear.

Josh congratulated him. He glanced at Gretchen, her nose in her phone. He didn't want to part ways here, at the busy airport. He wanted more time.

"Ric. I have a request. This is Gretchen. She bought me a coffee today. I'd like to repay her kindness by dropping her off at her hotel. Is that okay?"

"Whatever you say, boss." Ric winked, and grinned at Gretchen, his dark eyes sparkling.

"Oh Josh, it's okay, I can take a shuttle, really," Gretchen protested, putting her phone back in her pocket.

"No arguing. Just say, 'Yes, Josh, that would be lovely.'" He shushed her with a finger over her mouth.

She laughed, stood on her tiptoes, and impulsively kissed his cheek. "All right, all right. You win. Thank you."

When her lips touched his cheek, he reveled in the feeling of her being so close to him. As she turned to follow Ric, he wanted to pull her to him and do naughty things right there in the airport. Even not touching her for a second was driving him nuts. She felt good curved into his body, and the way her hips moved made it difficult to think straight as she walked ahead of him.

His body was at war with his brain because he didn't do the girl-in-every-city routine like a lot of players and had never had a one night stand in his entire professional life. It was always too risky; his career was more important than a roll in the hay. He didn't want to hurt her, since she was both sweet and nice and not likely to be the kind of girl who would fall into bed on a whim. Or not . . . he had no clue since he really didn't know her at all.

But as she pushed through the doors to the pickup area, he paused. Maybe the idea of a distraction was the best way to look at it. He'd have to be clear on the rules. No strings, right?

He warred with himself as to how to handle this physical attraction with the knowledge it could be just that. Besides, who knew where he was going to end up in the next few weeks? Likely not back in Toronto.

They stepped out into the cool desert night and he took in a deep breath of dry air. It wasn't that he hated Vegas; he loved it here. When he was in the minors, he had played well when his team had visited and had loved playing here when he was originally brought into the farm team system for the Sixers. A particular grand slam one night in the Vegas diamond had been the play to clinch him his spot in the Show, and he was traded to Boston for a draft-round pick.

The general manager, whom everyone called Coach, was a constant in his life who had helped him get to where he was, and in the few stints he'd done down here in the past few years, recovering from injuries or simply taking a breather, he'd clicked with the team and management. Often, he'd work the lineups and critique some of the younger players at practice. But it wasn't where he wanted to be at this stage in his career.

When Josh had arrived at the airport to head to Vegas, he had wanted to be anywhere else but there. And now, as he watched Ric heft Gretchen's suitcase into the back of the team van, he didn't want to be anywhere but with her. Preferably naked. He ran a hand over his face.

He was losing it.

He must have made a sound, because Gretchen turned to him and asked. "You okay?"

"Yeah, yeah. Fine. Tired, maybe."

She walked back to him and looked him square in the eye. "Time to get you out of here, I think," she murmured and pointed. More people had recognized both him and the Neons logo on the side of the van. Autograph requests were headed his way if they didn't get in the van soon.

However, he was rooted to the spot. She was practically

begging him to kiss her with those eyes, but now was not the right time. He wasn't sure when that was. Dinner? Night walk on the strip? Bed? Could that be where this was headed?

"Josh? We're loaded," Ric said. "Let's go."

Josh helped Gretchen into the van and hopped in beside her. He turned on his phone. It immediately started buzzing. As he buckled up and told Ric which hotel to drive to, he saw Gretchen poking away at her own screen again. They had been completely wrapped up in one another and had forgotten about the outside world. He didn't want it to invade now, but he couldn't ignore it. It was his job.

"Frig," he muttered and flipped through his messages to make sure there was nothing important. A few media requests for statements, which he forwarded to the club publicity people and his agent, Harv, to reply to. Likely tomorrow he'd do a quick scrum at practice.

Javier, Timo, and a couple of the other guys had all left texts saying how stupid everything was, how he'd be back, to go have fun in Vegas for a couple of weeks and get laid. The usual bullshit. It was heartening, but he turned the phone off again. He didn't want to think about baseball. He turned to talk to Gretchen instead. She was on the phone, so he relaxed in his seat and waited.

"I see, there's nothing you can do?" she snapped, her shoulders drooping as she sighed. "Fine, thank you. Of course. I'll try that." With an irritated growl, she ended the call, her nostrils flaring. Despite her frustration, it was kind of adorable.

"My turn to ask you if you're okay," he said as she muttered a very soft "fuck" under her breath.

"The hotel doesn't have a record of my reservation." Gretchen gripped her phone like she was about to toss it out the window. "And yay me, there are no rooms left, even though I have the email with my booking. They're full. I'm officially without a place to stay."

"Slight change of plans," Josh said to Ric, "We'll take Gretchen to the Luxor to see if they have some rooms available."

Ric nodded and, humming a random tune, wound his way through the strip traffic, barreling up toward the massive, gleaming pyramid. The lumbering van swayed, and Josh sat back, one hand on the armrest. He had stayed at the Luxor during previous visits with friends who had flown in for the weekend. He was sure he could pull some strings since they had rented one of the suites and dropped some cash that weekend. Plus, she had her booking confirmation for their sister hotel. If they had rooms, he'd try to get her a nice one for the mess-up.

"It's right beside the Mandalay, so you won't have to go far," he said. Ric made an illegal turn on the strip into the Luxor main entrance.

"That's fine. I'm not sure—" she started, looking out the window, her hands braced on the seat. She looked uncertain, and he met Ric's eyes in the rearview as the van jolted over the speed bumps at the entrance.

Ric said, "I'll wait here in case you don't luck out. Milady, we'll take care of you."

"Thank you, uh—"

"Ricardo, but my friends call me Ric."

Josh got out of the truck, helping her down from the sliding door as she shimmied over in the seat. He grabbed her hand, and he wanted to just stay there with her. He was a starving man, and she looked delicious.

They walked quickly through the casino, the sounds and lights a cacophony of noise assaulting them. Everywhere people were laughing, talking, and smoking. The airport had been busy, but this was a different kind of crowd with less purpose and urgency. Through the groups of partiers, you could see the people that hadn't moved in hours, their cards on curlicue bungees attaching them to the machine, empty food wrappers and glasses littering the floor under the chair.

He enjoyed Vegas, but this part he hated: the part that ruined lives. Sometimes even players on the team would fall for the lure of the big win, their paychecks drained onto a card table in one night. He supposed he was practical and boring, but he never had time for this side of living here and always stayed away. Too much was at stake, and baseball was always the focus anyway. He wondered if Gretchen liked gambling, and he wanted to know what she thought about it. He wanted her to hate it as well, to find something in common with her.

"It is a bit crazy, isn't it? I'm not one for that kind of stuff, really," Gretchen offered, reading his mind, squeezing his hand. "Waste of money."

The relief washed over him again, and he towed her toward the desk.

. . .

Gretchen was officially in a dream.

She was no longer awake, and soon she would jolt upright in her economy seat, the fantasy in front of her simply that. She pinched herself, then bit the inside of her cheek to make sure. Nope, not sleeping. Not dreaming. She palmed her open makeup bag, having rummaged for some lip balm, and took it all in as she set it on the desk. Dear God, the room was big. Too big for one person.

"Holy shit," she whispered, turning slowly, stopping to marvel at the view, the soft brown hues and Egyptian-themed decorations paling in comparison to the lights below her. The towers of the Excalibur Hotel beside them shimmered red and blue, and the strip peeled away from them in either direction, a ribbon of moving light.

A thump behind her made her turn, and there was Josh, putting her suitcase down, phone to his ear, talking a mile a minute to someone. He flashed a smile and then strode to the desk. She watched, transfixed, as he scribbled something down on the paper pad beside the phone, said thank you, and ended the call.

She'd never acted this boldly in her life. She assumed it was the wine, exhaustion, the steamroll of sensations coursing through her, and No-Regrets-Vegas headiness conspiring to turn her into this strange version of herself. But they had been dancing around this for hours now—she wanted him as much as he wanted her.

"All set?" he asked, stepping to her, looking down into her upturned face. She gestured around her, flummoxed that he was able to get such a room for a decent rate.

"This is too much, Josh! I mean, it's beautiful, but—"

"They've comped you the same rate, right? Why not? The view is really great, it's in the tower so you don't have to take those ridiculous sideways elevators either." Josh's smile got deeper, and Gretchen stopped talking, her mouth dry. She wanted to trace his lower lip with her tongue, and her eyes shifted to his mouth. Steadying herself from attacking him like a hormonal teenager, she decided, as he let out a soft man-groan and pulled her to him, that she was okay with this tactic.

Her senses sparked in all directions as he bent his head, lips hovering over hers, his arm holding her to him by her waist, and she could have melted into a puddle right then and there. Oh. My. God. Josh Malvern was going to kiss her. FINALLY.

"I have been wanting to do this," he murmured, and then kissed her.

She opened up to him, her hands exploring his muscled body, letting the sensation of his kiss travel the length of her. He was not gentle but not rough. She liked that. His teeth grazed her lower lip, and she growled, grabbing his shirt. It seemed he brought out her inner bad girl.

She was okay with that too.

He broke away slightly, both of them breathing hard, and put his forehead to hers, his nostrils flaring as he took a deep breath.

"Jesus," she whispered, peeking up at his closed eyes, his jaw clenched as he tried to regain some control.

"Hmmm?" he mumbled, opening his eyes and quirking an eyebrow.

"That was the best cup of coffee I have ever bought," she blurted.

He snorted a laugh and stood back from her, control suddenly back in place, twirling her in mock dance, making her even dizzier. She wanted more. Much more but realized he likely did not have the time for it, his ride waiting in the drop-off, the summer ball schedule in full swing and demanding his time the minute he landed. But if it could be one night? She wanted to make it amazing. She was being selfish.

24

"Have a late dinner with me," he blurted out before she could. "Say yes."

· · ·

What demotion? All he could think about was how goddamned good her lips had felt when he kissed her.

"Josh? You want me to take you home? Or do you want me to turn around and take you back to the hotel where you left your brain?"

Josh broke out of his thoughts and turned to Ric, who was driving the van through stop-and-go traffic, weaving and jerking as they made their way out toward the team apartments. Ric was grinning ear to ear, his hands drumming on the oversize steering wheel to the background pop music on the radio.

"What?"

Ric's entire body shook from laughter and he waggled a finger. "I see the way you look at her, my friend."

"And how is that?" Josh countered, peeved at being transparent.

"Like a hungry man," Ric chuckled. "I don't blame you. She looks sweet enough to eat. A good distraction for you."

Josh looked out the window at the lights and people. Maybe he was looking to distract himself from what was really the problem, which was his career. But was distraction what he needed right now? He should be laser-focused on getting back to the majors. The resolve he'd had in her hotel room was wavering.

"Jesus, Ric, I just met her. But thanks for the offer," he deflected, then laughed. Ric arched his eyebrow, side-eyed him, and then cut three people off to get to the exit he needed.

Ten minutes later, Josh turned the key to his assigned villa unit and sighed as he set his bags down. Swedish furniture, cookie-cutter art, galley kitchenette, a low-to-the-ground queen bed, and a stand-up shower. He missed his apartment in Toronto already, with the massive jet tub and California King Posturepedic mattress.

Awesome. Just awesome. He thought about turning around and heading right back for the Luxor and blowing a pile of cash staying there for the duration, but if this stay was prolonged, he would have to think economically. He was well-off, but he wasn't Alex Rodriguez rich. Besides, he could walk to the field from here, and the jogging was first class in the early mornings in Vegas—the weather was always perfect.

A shower was in order. He poked at his phone, sending a text to Timo and Javier that he'd arrived safely, and spent a few moments checking his email again, sitting on the edge of the couch. He needed to report in tomorrow morning by ten for batting practice.

A text buzzed in from an unfamiliar number and he flicked over to it.

Seeing friend @ Aurora. Meet there when u r able to get back?

A friend? She would likely know people coming into this wine thing and had said she wanted to spend time with her best friend. He immediately quashed the jealousy that threatened to seep into him; she wasn't his. He just wanted her to himself for the night, if nothing else. That was all it was.

Sure. Showering. Be there soon.

He set the phone down and it dinged again. He picked it back up, expecting a simple okay and he immediately got a shot of arousal.

That was a mental image I can hold on to until I see you.

He'd never showered faster.

26

chapter 3

Gretchen spotted her best friend sitting at a high bar table and waved, watching as Sharla's face lit up when she spied her. It had been far too long since they'd seen each other. Gretchen momentarily forgot she was wearing a slinky sequined dress and stilettos and promptly stumbled into an old man. After he had gotten a good look down the front of her dress, she made it to the table Sharla had claimed.

"Look at you, honey! All dressed up!" Sharla said as she reached the table, laughing. "Wow. All for me? Are we headed out on the town?"

Gretchen made a face and did a penguin-waddle turn. "You like it? Is it okay?"

"This is so not for me, is it?" Sharla sighed, "You have a date. You are blowing me off for a date. I knew it! Who did you bring with you?"

She could never keep anything from Sharla. They lived an ocean apart, but their bond was as strong as ever. Facebook and Skype helped with that, of course. They'd met in college and had worked their first few gigs in Toronto together until Sharla had moved home to Niagara to help at her parent's vineyard and Gretchen had struck out on her own. Gretchen missed Sharla's influence on her to loosen up, relax, and spend less time working. It had been a year since they'd been in the same city at the same time, with Sharla concentrating on her fancy new job in the UK.

"I do," Gretchen replied impishly. "I met him on the plane coming in. He's meeting me here."

"And you won't be spending long here. I imagine you'll be riding the elevator right back up to your room wearing those fuck-me shoes."

"Sharla!" Gretchen admonished, laughing. "Seriously though. I don't know what has come over me. I'm not normally *this* bold, am I? I saw him at the gate and bought him a coffee, and it went from there. We just clicked!"

Sharla tried to pump her for more details as drinks arrived, but Gretchen remained mum—she wanted to see what her friend thought of Josh without knowing anything about him, to see if her instincts were right—and Sharla wouldn't hesitate to let Gretchen know her opinion.

"If I don't like him, I'm tossing my drink at him and taking you out on the town myself. We are not wasting that dress tonight. Deal?"

"Deal," Gretchen said, smirking, because how could anyone not find Joshua Malvern anything but perfect? Well, maybe not everyone. Sharla had long perfected her eye roll when Gretchen would casually slip him into conversation, relaying his latest play or how nice he'd looked in pictures from some fundraiser. She teased Gretchen that she'd likely faint if she ever actually met him face to face.

Which she hadn't, funnily enough.

She stopped herself before she let her nerves take hold. Tonight she was different. Tonight she was bold, flirty, and about to have a one-night stand with the big-time baseball player that she'd met on a plane. Her life was straight out of a romance novel.

"What are you up to these days? Did you find that bottle of 1945 Romanée-Conti that the earl missed out on at Sotheby's?" Gretchen asked to change the subject and keep her train of thought from derailing.

"No, dammit, it's still in the wind. Some collector in Morocco is being selfish. That's old news. The past two weeks I've been on His Lordship's yacht, touring some Mediterranean wineries," Sharla replied, picking up her drink. "His Lordship is spending a lot of time there too."

Gretchen bit her lip and looked at her friend in mock serious-ness. Sharla had lucked into a job as the wine advisor and buyer for the Earl of Rathwell, or Kevin, as he preferred to be called. His was a rather new title in the peerage, as he was only the second earl, having inherited the earldom from his father. The first earl's sister had married into the royal family and earned her brother the title as recompense for their parents having predeceased the good fortune.

Sharla had been seduced six months ago by the fact that he was willing to pay her a ridiculous salary plus expenses to simply help him build his wine investment portfolio, critique wineries for said investments, buy wines for his homes and estates, and basically be his personal taster. He wanted to build one of the best cellars in the world. The earl loved wine and was considered one of the smartest investors in the industry. Sharla had jumped at it, given she was going broke where she was, slinging wine in her parent's vineyard tasting room.

Gretchen was mildly envious. Sharla got to jet-set and spent a lot of time at fancy European vineyards and tastings, negotiating huge orders. Kevin was also very much single, and highly recognized as one of the UK's most eligible bachelors. It was quite a plum post.

"Oh, he is, is he?" Gretchen took a sip of her drink. "Anything you can't tell me, but will anyway, because if you don't, I'll never speak to you again?"

Sharla masked an unreadable reaction, then laughed and hit the table with her hand. "I expected that reaction from you, Miss Nosy! No. He drives me nuts! All nitpicky and work, work, work. I'm just winding you up."

Gretchen wasn't sure she bought it but let it go. Suddenly Sharla stopped, mid-sip, her eyes widening at something behind Gretchen.

"Oh my God," she whispered. "Do not look, but your favorite baseball player just walked into the bar. For real. Not shitting you."

Gretchen put her hand to her chest and pressed her lips together to freshen her lipstick. *Here we go.*

"Really? Where?" she asked innocently while Sharla flailed for her arm.

"Oh my God. Don't freak out, okay? He's headed our way! He's—he's looking right at us. He's—"

Gretchen decided to turn at that moment and there he was. Josh was gorgeous in a dark-blue shirt unbuttoned at the collar, his hair slightly messy, his eyes not wavering one bit from hers.

He bridged the distance to her in three steps as she stood, grabbing her hand and kissing her knuckles. She felt a bit unsteady as she caught the scent of fresh soap and man.

"You look—" he started, then stopped, eyes not leaving her face. "Wow."

Sharla's noises of shock echoed behind her, and Gretchen turned back to her friend. "Sharla, please meet Josh. Josh, this is Sharla, my best friend. We went to school together."

"Are you kidding me? He's your date tonight?" she asked incredulously as she shook Josh's hand. "That must've been some coffee!"

* * *

The dress was purple. Or at least it sparkled purple in the dim lighting. What was more distinct was how it hugged Gretchen's hips and stopped midthigh. And it was lowcut in the back with this lattice-thing holding it together, dipping almost to the dimples above her rear. She was wearing heels that added at least three inches, and he traced the curve of her calf with his eyes, his hand twitching to do the same.

Josh's breath caught in his throat. He—a thirty-two-year-old professional baseball player who had stepped to the plate with two outs in the ninth, had pushed through whatever life threw at him, and had mastered controlling his emotions—needed a moment to compose himself before he could speak. She had turned, seen him, and he'd simply forgotten where he was. The front was low-cut too. Christ almighty.

"Drink?" a waitress asked as he sat down with them. He politely declined and refocused on Gretchen and her friend. Gretchen's hands flew about as she talked to her, the bond between them evident. He put a hand on her thigh under the table, and her smaller one slid overtop, sending shots of energy up his arm.

"Okay . . . now you're playing ball here? Why?" Sharla asked as she pulled the strawberry off the glowing toothpick in her drink.

"I am. Temporarily. Until they figure out whether I go back or move on. We have option years that get used when this happens," he replied.

"Explain to me what this option year thing is. A club has, like, passes on how many times you can go back and forth?"

"Sort of," he said. "It gets complicated with waivers and veterans' rules and stuff, but basically, my option years are likely going to be used up with this move. I consented to go because I knew if I said no, they'd cut me from the roster immediately and I need to be able to sign somewhere else. Better negotiating power that way. I'll likely be more informed on Monday."

"I see. Men and their love of obfuscation. Kev—err, His Lordship makes all his paperwork complicated like that. Drives me crazy!" Sharla laughed.

"You work for a lord? Sounds old-fashioned. Doing what?"

"I buy His Lordship's wine," Sharla explained.

"I have to meet with the new DuBoeuf rep in the morning. Do you want to tag along or meet for lunch after that, before the first round?" Gretchen asked Sharla.

"Of course. I get the hint. It's the third wheel's time to go." Sharla drained the rest of her drink as elegantly as possible. She was a ballbuster, this one.

"No, no—" Gretchen argued, but Josh stopped her by pulling her to her feet.

Sharla and Gretchen hugged. Sharla said something low in Gretchen's ear, and then looked at her friend like she had three heads. "Josh, you are approved. I don't think I'll need to rescue my girl here, will I?" she threatened, hands on her hips.

"Rescue? I might be the one who needs rescuing," Josh joked.

They walked away to Sharla's laughter, and out the door of the club, Josh's arm around Gretchen's waist, feeling the fabric shift as she moved. She had delivered on the sexy Vegas dress, that was for sure. He wondered where the zipper was to get it off, mentally undressing her.

The minute they were out in the main area of the casino, he pulled her behind a massive tree and kissed her, holding her face still because it was that or be indecent by planting his hands on her perfectly shaped ass. She moaned softly and he was immediately aroused, the idea of skipping dinner going through his head as she arched into him. He ran one hand down her back, rumpling the sequins on her dress, the heat of her radiating through the fabric.

She was all soft and warm and female and he wanted her. Now. Badly.

"Where are we having dinner?" she murmured when he finally broke from her, stealing back some rational thought. Dinner. Food. A good idea.

"You've likely gone before, but I got us a table at Aureole," he replied, hopeful she would approve. "I've never been and I thought it might be fun to learn a bit about wine from you."

She looked at him, and he couldn't quite tell what she was thinking. She wasn't upset; she actually looked impressed.

"I think that's a perfect choice," she said simply. "Lead the way."

chapter 4

Their meals sat in front of them, half-forgotten as Josh and Gretchen spent most of the evening just talking. She couldn't have eaten much anyway, her nerves shot to hell in anticipation. They talked a lot about Toronto, comparing their experiences living in the city.

Gretchen swirled the big glass of red in her hand, watching Josh's face as he tasted the same wine in his. "This is really good," he muttered, raising his eyebrows as he placed the glass back on the table. "Tastes very expensive."

"But it's not really. Part of my job is finding the best wines for the best price. Hidden gems, underrated wineries—that sort of thing. I buy for restaurant groups. Value for bottle is super important."

"How on earth did you get into wine? I would never have picked something like this, and I love it."

"My mom was a caterer. I spent a lot of my youth in the kitchens at events. She wasn't great with wine; she had a friend who would give her recommendations. I loved how rich and inviting the tables would be with the bottles sparkling in the lights, watching the staff trying the leftover bottles at the end of the dinner and hearing their comments. I worked alongside my mom a lot growing up."

"Inspired by your mom? That's cool," he said.

"I started out in culinary management, following in Mom's footsteps—that was where I met Sharla. We had a lot of fun, the two of us."

"I can only imagine. I remember college, and the stupid stuff my buddies and I got up to. Sometimes I wonder how we survived," he chuckled. "I went in for business at Clemson because they had a good ball program too. Why aren't you running your mom's catering business now?"

"I found out, after I graduated, that the organizing end of the catering world wasn't as glamorous as I remember it being when I was a kid. Sharla convinced me to take the sommelier program with her, and a year later, I took the certification."

"So you became a sommelier, and the rest is history, as they say? How long have you run your own business?" Josh asked, changing the subject.

"About three years now. I branched out on my own; working for restaurant syndicates wasn't getting me where I wanted to go," Gretchen said, trying not to sound too boastful. "I was able to gain ground quickly because I'm a certified sommelier with feet-on-the-ground expertise."

She was shy to share more with him, and steered the conversation back to safer ground: him. She knew so much about his career, but now, all of the trivia and MLB information had come to life, fleshing him out as he talked about it both on the plane and now.

"What was it like to come to Toronto? Had you spent much time in Canada before?" she asked.

"Only ever visited to play ball. It was a big change, moving there. I almost didn't come to Toronto, actually. Deal nearly fell through. They wanted this other guy, he was a home-run machine from Atlanta, but he wanted too much money. The contract negotiations fell through; my agent caught wind and pushed me forward. I was originally headed to Milwaukee."

"Were you happy about that?" she asked. He looked serious when he'd shared that.

"I liked Pittsburgh well enough, but the coaching on the team was in flux and I was thinking a move might be what was best for my career. Harv, my agent, he agreed."

"I'm glad you found your way to Toronto," she replied softly. "You've been a good player for the team."

"If I were to pick a bottle to go, what would your recommendation be?" he asked abruptly, looking away from her. He opened the wine book. "Red or white? If you were to blow a boatload on a wine, what would you buy?"

The thought of drinking wine with him, in bed, or surrounded by fragrant bubbles in the massive tub in her suite was fuel to the fire already smoldering between them.

"What about champagne?" she suggested. "Or a really nice, deep red, like a zinfandel. That's a lovely varietal to sip by the fire."

The heat of his eyes hit her as he leaned across the table and brushed a knuckle over her cheek. "Or other activities, I think."

Holy hell. She wanted to grab the collar of his shirt and yank him over the table. She had never been this turned on in her life. She cleared her throat and bowed her head, positive it was showing.

"Or other activities, yes."

Josh waved at the waiter, making a signal for the check, and within minutes, he had the 2013 Joseph Phelps Insignia she'd spied on the list under his arm as they headed back toward the Luxor. They took an elevator down to the main concourse level, his hand on her back, warm and solid. If not for the three other couples in the space, she would have reached for him and kissed him senseless.

"Gretchen Harper, do you like to dance?" he asked as they were walking briskly through the casino close to the lobby of the hotel. She was having to take two steps to his every one to keep up with him, her shoes clicking as they hit the tile of the lobby. Her legs and stiletto heels were no match for his long, ground-eating stride.

"Yes," she replied, breathless, "but I haven't in—"

Josh stopped and a mischievous look stole over his face. He caught her up with one arm and lowered his lips to her ear. She shivered, her entire body wanting to plaster itself to him and never detach. She could feel his breath, the heat from him, and she put her arm around him to steady herself.

"Wait here," he whispered huskily.

He strode off, and she did as she was told, her entire body thrumming. The wine at dinner, paired with the sex appeal of Josh, was making her head swim and she looked for somewhere to sit. She swayed over to the edge of a column and perched on the lip of the wainscoting.

As he walked back, the way he exuded confidence caught her.

While in Vegas, right? If nothing else, it would be one crazy story to tell Sharla tomorrow, and something to savor when this trip was over and she had to return to being dependable, boring Gretchen.

Who was that Gretchen, exactly? An almost-thirty, solely career-focused woman with only one serious relationship under her belt, who had never dared to contemplate a casual hookup and considered dating sites too dangerous? That normal, basic woman who had managed to put her hair up in a sophisticated twist and wiggled into the daring dress she'd brought for the competition social—but had expected to wimp out and wear her more modest choice—was so far removed from the one leaning against the side of the casino wall that she wasn't sure what to think.

She deserved one night of letting it all go, right? Hopefully Normal Gretchen wouldn't worry too much tomorrow when it was all over.

"I've sent the wine up to your room. Let's go. There is a night-club here that I really like," he reached out a hand. She took it and he yanked her flush against him, pulling her arm up and around his neck, his hand sliding down the length of it, down her side and resting on her hip. Little shots of pleasure zapped through her and she closed her eyes, a small gasp making its way out. They swayed softly together and he kissed her upturned lips.

"I want to see you move in that dress," he ground out and she opened her eyes to see his eyes fierce and full of arousal. She took in a breath, steadied herself, and the last of her reservations left, the buzz from him intoxicating.

"Then let's go," she purred as seductively as possible.

"You should come with a warning," he uttered hoarsely before kissing her again. "You are going to set me on fire before the night is through."

The bass pounded through his chest, but part of it was the woman in front of him, sending his senses into overdrive. She was dancing, her arms up, her eyes closed, completely taken over by the beat. When she opened them again, the *fuck me* look was very direct and very, very hot. He was going to hell for what he was thinking of doing to her later. Or sooner. If she kept dancing like that, he was going to drag her back to her room like a caveman.

She had pulled him out onto the dance floor the moment they got into the club, her eyes lighting up, laughter bubbling out of them both, and they had stayed there. The firecracker, at that point, went off, and he felt it as he let the beat take over, enjoying her body as it moved.

She angled over to him, slid up as far as she could, then ran her hands up her body as she backed up again, her eyes boring into him. Jesus. Okay, that was all it took to make him painfully rock-hard. He couldn't wait any longer.

He grabbed her hand, spun her, and then gathered her up against him, moving with her, his head bent to hover over her lips and catch hot, searching kisses. He wanted more. He wanted to feel her wrapped around him, he wanted to taste her. He'd never been this forward with a woman, and with one shake of her hips, he'd seemingly lost all ability to be a gentleman.

"I want you naked and under me," he murmured, ghosting his lips over her mouth to her ear. She let her head hang back, exposing her neck, shivering. He brushed his lips there too, still moving with the beat. He could have taken her right there, on the dance floor, he was that riled up.

"Now," he added, and she brushed her leg over his crotch. His cock twitched and a wicked look stole over her face.

"Yes," she replied and he practically dragged her out of the club toward the elevators at the main entrance, and then to her suite. They ran, she on her wobbly heels, laughing, stopping several times to kiss. He could not get enough.

He pulled her off her feet and into his arms, wanting her closer, tighter. He was too far gone to care the moment their tongues met anyway.

The doors of the closest elevator opened, and the car was thankfully empty. He walked her in, his lips on hers while he fumbled for her floor button and she flailed her room key against the scanner.

Every part of her he touched reminded him what awaited, as she rotated her hips into him, the impatience mutual. The elevator stopped, and two people decided to take the next one when he stabbed the Close button, glaring at them to stay out.

"I want—" she gasped, and threw her leg up over his hip, her dress riding up her thigh, heel firmly in the small of his back. He turned his attention back to her, not the swiftly closing doors and laughter from the other side.

"Tell me," he whispered in her ear. She shivered as his hand slid over her calf. "What do you want?"

She made a very sexy noise that cut straight into him, and one hand wound its way into his hair, her fingers digging in. He focused in on her eyes, the wicked glint in them setting every nerve ending on fire when she tugged his lip down to hers and purred, "You."

. . .

Gretchen threw the plastic key card on the little side table as they crashed through the door to her suite, feeling him kick the door closed. They stumbled into the foyer of the suite, his hands roaming everywhere at once.

He pushed her up against a wall, kissing her hard, possessing her mouth, and she responded, the ache to have him inside her almost unbearable. She launched her shoes, and they skidded along the tile floor, forgotten, as he picked her up, hands under her as he strode toward the bed.

"Fuck, you are hot as hell," he rasped, his hands on her back. "Get out of this damned dress so I can see all of you."

She laughed as he dropped her onto the bed. She reached behind her and undid the low zipper, biting her lip, as one strap of her dress slid off her shoulder. His hair was ruffled in all directions, a shadow of stubble across his jaw, and his muscles flexed as he lifted his shirt and undershirt over his head in one swift movement. His chest and abdomen were taut and rippled, his features dangerous. He was perfect. Beautiful. She paused a moment to drink it all in. He stopped, sensing her.

"Still okay?" Josh whispered, moving up her body, holding her gaze. She shimmied further out of her dress, pooling it around her waist, while reaching for his belt, undoing it, and popping the top button of his pants.

"Oh yes," she breathed, running her fingers over his stomach. "Just admiring the view."

She ran her hands up his chest, feeling him tense wherever her hands went, and he gently took both her hands in his, shaking his head. "Stop. You'll—"

"I'll what?" Gretchen replied softly. "I want to feel you."

He yanked her dress down in one swift motion down her legs,

throwing it behind him, and kissed her again, lifting off her to hungrily look down her body. He made a sound low in his throat, his fingers tracing the line of her bright-blue lace underwear.

She wanted him. Now.

"Those too."

She hooked her thumbs under the sides and slowly wiggled her panties down, looking up at him, then tracing her fingers to the front, slowly running her hands over herself. "All the way?" she teased.

"Baby, you're *killing* me," he growled and snatched them off her the same way he'd taken off her dress, coming back to kiss up her inner thigh, his mouth covering over her the moment he reached the top, his tongue and fingers exploring every part.

"Oh my God, Josh, stop or I'll—"

"You'll what? I want to taste you," he replied, crawling up over her, playing her game.

She laughed as he did, pulling at his pants, and he slid them off at her insistence. She heard them hit the floor. He followed them, crouched down, then slowly stood back up and there he was. All of him. Ready to go, with a condom held between his fingers. Emboldened, she reached for him again.

"Now, Josh. I want you inside me. I can't wait any longer."

He pulled her under him, his arms above her shoulders, and she raised her leg over his hip, digging her heel in, her hands caressing every inch she could reach. He breathed in and out a few times as he sheathed himself with impressive speed between them. She raised her hips the moment he finished, and he thrust into her, his mouth crashing to hers the moment he did, stifling her cry.

Josh stilled, his eyes wide, and she moved her hips up to him again, raking her fingers across his back. The heat of him sent her nerve endings into overdrive, begging for more. He pressed forward, stretching her, filling her completely, tension and gentleness meeting in the middle.

She lost control of her body from the sheer pleasure of him moving inside her slowly. The buildup to this had been teasing her, and the sensation of an instant orgasm waved through her body, her legs shaking as she came. He brushed hair off her face, leaning in to kiss her, his thumb caressing her lips, gentle and sweet as he continued to rock in and out of her.

"That was beautiful," he murmured, as they moved together, in perfect sync. "Did you like that?"

"Yes," Gretchen breathed, the curl of another climax building the moment he spoke. She wanted him hard and fast, all of him, nothing held back. She sucked his thumb into her mouth, swirling her tongue over the pad, gently scraping with her teeth. He hissed in a breath. *He liked that.*

"Fuck me, Josh. Hard," she added when she let it go.

He let out a moan that was pure animal, pulled her hands up and over her head, holding them, and he thrusted into her hard, picking up the pace, his eyes sharp and dangerous. She met him thrust for thrust, biting his shoulder, licking and sucking his skin. Every graze of her teeth made him twitch and moan.

"Oh," he breathed, raising himself to see her. She left her arms above her as he lifted her by her hips, one hand coming down to stroke her between them. "I feel you, baby. Come for me. Come now."

It was all she needed to shatter like a glass thrown against the wall, arching into him, gasping his name as he tensed and then let himself go with her, groaning loudly. Somehow, through the fog of the most incredible orgasm she'd ever had, and him collapsing breathless on top of her, it registered that she had never, ever felt like that before.

, , ,

The wine was even more decadent than she remembered. She swirled the glass and held it under her nose, taking in the deep, rich cherry notes.

"Does it pass, master?" Josh asked as he finished pouring his own glass and rejoined her on the bed. He kissed her gently, the taste of the wine on his lips.

"Oh yes. A bottle of Insignia never disappoints," she replied. "Thank you."

He slid under the covers, and they sat with their backs to the headboard. Gretchen tucked the sheets up under her and took a sip, sighing happily. This was a wine to sip by the fire on a cold winter night, but it also worked as a rejuvenating draft after incredible sex. She rarely indulged in a bottle this expensive for just her; it was a treat to have one almost to herself and not sharing it with six people. Josh's arm slid around her and they clinked glasses.

"To good wine, sexy company, and a memorable evening," he quipped cheerfully.

"Memorable," Gretchen repeated, amused at the word to describe their encounter so far. "I'll take it."

Josh looked into her eyes, and she caught the smolder of arousal in them. There was a promise of more in that gaze, and she forgot everything for a moment except his big, strong body beside her. He was gorgeous and good in bed. Was this really happening?

"Mmm, this is really good, even better than the bottle at dinner," he remarked as he took another sip. "You don't make many bad choices, do you?"

"My dad used to say my mom could never pick a bad wine with dinner but had terrible taste when it came to buying a bottle for drinking. She was so used to pairing food with varietals that it was difficult for her to taste a wine's individual characteristics. Thankfully, I think I avoided that curse by making wine my career," Gretchen replied lightly.

He sipped again, staring out toward the big picture window, stretching a little as he sighed. "What do your parents do now?" he asked.

"My mom sold the business; she lives in a retirement community now. My dad,"—she stopped, fiddling with the stem of her glass, then setting it off to one side. She hesitated; this was a downer, a mood killer—"he died, three years ago. Cancer. He and my mom weren't together. They split when I was about thirteen."

"We don't have to talk about it," Josh said, pulling her under his arm, his thumb brushing her shoulder.

"Thanks. It's fine. He's the reason I enjoy baseball. It was one of the few things we bonded over."

Josh held her a little tighter and made a sound of agreement in his throat that was sexy and sweet all at once, and she wanted him all over again, just like that. But this was nice too. Wrapped up in bed, postcoital and talking about personal stuff like it was easy. Gretchen wanted to share with him now that she wasn't so nervous.

"Sounds like you were close," Josh said, a hesitant tone in his voice.

"After he left, we weren't. He was a proud, simple man, moved to the interior of BC, didn't trust doctors, and trusted women even less," she mused. "When they split up, he moved for a job in forestry. He loved the wilderness. Toronto was a nightmare for him, I think. My mother once told me that my father would likely fall off a cliff while hiking. I believed her."

"Wow. Yeah, my parents live on opposite sides of the country from each other too. I lived with my mom in Boise and would go see Dad once or twice a year in Upper New York State until I was around sixteen, when summers became part-time jobs and competitive ball."

"Your dad must have been happy to have you closer when you got to Clemson. That isn't too far from where he lived, right?" she added.

"It was a twelve-hour drive from Carolina to where he lived. We didn't see each other much."

"Yeah, that would be long," Gretchen replied. A couple of years back she had read an interview in *Sports Illustrated* where Josh had talked about his parents. He hadn't had the typical Little League experience—being driven to every game, then pushed to be competitive, going to scouting meets and tryouts. She'd admired, when she'd read it, how he hadn't been handed a scholarship to a good school because of his varsity play. He'd worked two jobs to pay for college before he'd been offered grants his sophomore year, given how well he'd played as a freshman. Then it was into the farm system straight out of college. He'd never had a chance to use his degree. Now, watching him and talking to him, the fact that he had taken his rocket to the top in stride and seemed humble about it was icing on the cake.

"I'm not close to either of them. Mom didn't know what to do with me as a kid, and my dad, well, he started another family that I wasn't really a part of."

"I'm sure they're proud of you," she murmured and patted his leg.

"I'm sure they are," he said, and kissed her again gently, sweetly. It curled her toes under the sheet, the promise of more. She drew her legs up and leaned into him, deepening the kiss and he obliged.

"Your parents are proud of you too, I'm sure," Josh murmured, and set his wine to the side, pulling her down to lie beside him, slotted into his shoulder, her feet tangled with his legs. It felt perfect, like they fit, and she cautioned herself, *Don't go there. This is one night.*

"Someday I want a crack at the Master Sommelier rank, but I need more experience first," she replied. Her mom had always said go for it, to reach for those goals, even if she never took a big interest in what Gretchen did.

"Well I'm sure you will get it. You can be very determined when you know what you want, Gretchen. I've had firsthand experience." They both laughed.

"Tell me about the Neons," she said, wanting to take the focus off things she'd rather not think about right now.

"Oh," he said and blew out a breath. "Like what?"

"Are they a good team? I bet there are some players you know already."

"Well, there's one young kid on the team I really enjoy working with, Neptune Gilbert. He's been with them since last year. I really got to know him last time I was out here. He's seriously good. Super fast, good eye. He'd make a great pitcher too. I've brought him up to visit me a couple times in Toronto, special invite for batting practice. We get to do that for prospects every now and then."

"Sounds like you're looking forward to seeing him?" she asked. His expression had softened the moment he started talking about his friend. She sighed and ran a hand up his chest, enjoying the flex of his muscles as he shifted to look over at her.

"I am. I feel like he needs the support too; his family is all back in the Dominican Republic. Between me, Coach, and his billet, I think we've done okay by him."

"It won't be so bad to hang out here while they figure out your options," Gretchen added. He did sound like he was happier to be here than he'd been at the airport.

"This is a good club, the staff care about everyone. The ball is less tense, there's an element here that you sometimes forget when you're up in the majors."

"What's that?" Gretchen asked, her hand now straying downward onto his lower abs. He let out a breath and moved his hand down her leg, pulling it up over his hip. They went nose to nose, and he groaned softly when her hand went lower still.

"That it's fun. Why you started playing the damned game in the first place," he murmured, rolling her into him, his hands finding much better places to be than on her thigh.

"Mmm. Fun, you say?" Gretchen replied shakily as his lips met her neck, and she fisted her hands into his hair, holding him there. "I think I can imagine that."

Josh levered up, eyes flashing heat as he smiled wickedly. "Let's have some more fun, then, shall we?"

chapter 5

Gretchen opened one eye and looked at the clock. Six. Still early. A hand was on her waist, and she pulled the covers up to her mouth, stifling what could only be described as a girly scream of delight. If not for waking up Josh beside her, she would have kicked her legs in excitement.

It was not a dream.

She had just spent the night with Joshua Malvern. Like something out of a fantasy porno. They had done things she had never even dreamed she would do. All night. They'd barely slept.

She stretched and her muscles complained, remembering how his arms had tensed around her when he had her bent over the couch. Or up against the window, the lights of Vegas glittering below them, their outline clearly visible in the glass. His eyes had bored into hers in the reflection, watching her response as he—

"Good morning," a rumbled, husky voice said beside her ear. She rolled over and looked into his eyes as he gazed down at her. "Sleep well?" he added, tucking her further into his warm body.

She ran fingers through his hair, reveling in the few moments they had left together. He would be heading off to the ball field, and she would be getting ready to meet with distributors. Real life was about to interrupt this interlude that she didn't want to be over.

"I did, thanks," she murmured as she purposely ran her hand down his neck, over his chest, and down his arm. She wanted to remember every inch of this man.

The slow, bad boy, all-knowing smirk that followed her hands was irresistible, and she moved in close to him. Just as his lips met hers, his phone went off. He ignored it, moving down to her neck, then her collarbone. As he sucked a very sensitive nipple into his mouth, it went off again.

"Dammit," Josh sighed in irritation and lifted off her. "I really should get that. Likely my agent, Harv."

"It's early," she mumbled.

"I'm normally up and working out by now," he replied before he answered the phone.

Gretchen tugged the sheets back up over her as he stood, his perfectly sculpted ass flexing as he stretched and reached for his pants, still on the floor where they had been flung the night before. He lifted the phone out as it rang for a third time.

"Hello?" he said, groggily as he carefully hop-stepped into his pants, pulled them up, and walked toward the sitting area in the suite, the belt undone and the waist hanging enticingly low on his hips. He sat down on the curved brown couch and began talking to the person on the phone.

Gretchen slowly slid out of bed, wrapping the white sheet around her, and headed for the bathroom, not wanting to intrude on what was obviously a work call. When she reappeared, Josh was still on the phone, facing away from her, random *uh-huh*s punctuating the silence. His shoulders slumped as he rested his elbows on his thighs, his face a mask of calm reflected in the window. Outside, the city was waking up with a desert-orange glow, and she took a moment to catch his eyes in the glass. He winked at her and wiggled his fingers.

"You can pick me up at the Luxor. Yeah. A car? Okay. I have to be there at ten. Yeah."

Rummaging through her suitcase, Gretchen came up with some underwear, thoughts drifting to how to reconcile the heady, out-of-this world sex with how she was currently feeling. She'd never had sex like that before, and part of her was dreading the parting. Perhaps that was the secret of hookups and one-nighters for people who did that kind of thing. It was mind-blowingly good because there were no regrets. No emotion. Just sex. But how many people had sex like that as a one-nighter? *Not many*, she wagered.

"Don't put those on yet," Josh murmured in her ear as she straightened up. His hand came around her waist, his lips on the back of her neck. "You look so fucking good right now. Your ass is perfection."

She shuddered when his hand went lower, brushing her crotch, the other hand throwing her undies into her suitcase, then circling one of her nipples, pinching. He was hard, brushing up against her, and she lost all resolve, letting him hold her up, stroking and pressing.

"Josh," she breathed, spreading her legs as his fingers dipped inside of her.

"I want to watch you come," he breathed in her ear. "I want to fuck you up against this wall, but we're out of condoms. So this will have to hold you until—"

"I'm on the pill. I'm . . . I'm clean," her voice shook, leaning into his touch, hungry for more. "Are you?"

He paused for a moment, and she looked back at him. He had his lower lip in his teeth, his hand gently caressing her hip. His eyes searched hers, heat and hesitancy in them swirling. It was a big question.

"Yes, I am," he replied quickly. "Are you saying—"

"Yes. Fuck me up against this wall," she answered.

His belt buckle thunked as it hit the floor, and with a single thrust, he was inside her, letting her go so she could brace against the wall. He leaned up against her, pressed together skin to skin, his muscles taut against her back. He moved inside her hard, and she reached back for him, the sensation of his skin hot both inside and out.

"More," he murmured fiercely. "I want more of you."

She gasped as he thrust harder, pulling out of her abruptly, turning her.

"I want to see your face when I'm inside you," he said, reaching for her.

She was shaking with the need to have him back and pushed him over to the bed before he could pull her to him. He grabbed her as they fell, and she straddled him as quickly as possible, fingers finding and sheathing him, and his resulting hiss of pleasure was all she needed.

"Oh God, Gretchen. Like that. Ride me," he gasped as his hands gripped her hips. She rocked over him, the sensation of him tight against her unbelievable. Sitting up and circling her waist, he encouraged her as they moved together, lips on each other, her nipping at his shoulder when he tightened his hold.

"Josh," she breathed in his ear. "Come for me. Come inside me."

He pulled back, looking at her with heavy eyes, full of animal arousal, for her. He closed, then opened them again to her, the heaviness gone, piercing need replacing it.

"Come for me," she repeated, thrusting her hips faster, matching him. She wanted to watch him explode, to see him lose control and remember that for the rest of her life.

He let out a groan, hands roaming everywhere, all at once. He was close, she could feel it, and the coil of her own orgasm started low in her belly, spiraling out as he gasped in time with their movement. Her eyes bored into his, their mouths close, lips brushing one another, he moaned as the familiar tension of her own orgasm built.

"I—" he gasped. "Oh God, Gretch. Oh—"

He exploded, shaking, and she let her own control go, not caring how loud she was, their eyes riveted to each other, orgasms perfectly in sync.

That was more than sex, Gretchen thought. They fell sideways to the bed, both of them breathless. She closed her eyes for a moment, trying not to let tears slip out, because the emotions she saw swirling in his eyes as he had lost control were raw, intense, and not at all what she had expected.

They lay there for a few moments, completely spent. His hand on her hip, his eyes closed, she studied his face, taking her time to settle her emotions. She would never, ever forget this. Most people never forgot their first tryst, and she'd had a memorable one, if she was comparing it to the stories her girlfriends had told her of their own.

"That was incredible," he murmured after a moment, his eyes opening to her, looking down her body possessively. "It's been a long time since I, you know . . . went—"

"—bareback?" she finished for him, and giggled. It was a ridiculous description, but her brain was addled and a more sophisticated word hadn't revealed itself to her.

"We'll go with that," he said. "It's still okay?"

"Yes," she said. It was. It had been intimate, raw, and unfiltered. She hoped he felt the same way.

"What time is it?" Josh asked, rolling onto his back, hand running through his hair. "Do we have time to sleep more? I have to tell you, you know how to wear a man out, Ms. Harper."

Gretchen craned her neck over at the clock radio. "It's around seven now."

Josh reached for her. "Come here," he said gruffly. She slid up beside him, and he wrestled the knot of blankets around them, finally giving up and yanking the comforter up, cocooning them underneath it, blocking out the real world with an airy whoosh of fabric.

"Should we set an alarm?" she asked. He mumbled something about already having one set for eight-thirty on his phone, and pulled her closer, his arms encircling her. It was intimate and sweet, and as his breathing evened out, his hand caressed her skin. She melted into him, her heart bursting with the knowledge that saying goodbye was going to hurt even more later.

. . .

"Here. The TV says you'll likely need this, especially after last night."

Josh turned at her voice, and he took the bottle of water she offered. The news was on in the background and the anchor was talking about the weather in Vegas being stupid hot again today.

"Thanks," he said as he cracked it open and took a grateful sip. He'd just taxed parts of his body that would parch almost any man. Willingly, of course.

She had showered with him before they'd finally dressed just after nine, soaping each other up, which had, of course, become another round of the most mind-blowing sex he had ever had in his life. The sheer intensity of her was throwing his mind into chaos, upending the idea of the "just one night" he had promised himself. He was ecstatic and exhausted. Not a good combination for rational thought.

The way they had moved together, the way she had held his eyes as they had come together this morning. The feel of her against his skin, literally all of it. The moment thrummed through him, that instant where he'd seen the wild emotion in her, the utter open and raw need for him. The firecracker had gone off in spectacular fashion.

The suite phone rang, and Gretchen crossed the room to answer it while he stood. Likely that was the front desk saying Harv was here, since his phone had run out of charge. He'd called earlier to let Josh know he had arrived on the early morning flight from L.A. and needed to confer before he went over to the ballpark. It was necessary. He needed help to manage the message he'd give to the press when they spotted him today.

"That was the front desk. Your agent is here. Do you want to meet up here? It's more private. I have to get going anyway."

Josh looked around him at the completely rumpled bed, the jumbled couch cushions, the empty wine bottle, and stained crystal glasses. He noticed the hand and ass prints on the window glass smudging through the sunlight and he shook his head.

"No. Harv likes to eat when we meet. We'll head for breakfast, and we'll drive to my place after."

Gretchen fidgeted nervously. Josh stood up and crossed to her. She was feeling things, too, he reasoned. This was supposed to be goodbye—thanks for the memories and all that. But he knew he didn't want it to be. He wanted to see her again.

"We play tonight at seven," he said, hopeful as he tipped her chin up to look at him. "Come to the game if you can. I'll leave tickets for you and Sharla at the west gate."

She searched his eyes, and he pulled her into a hug, holding her as close as possible. She smelled like strawberries and fresh soap, and it stirred his libido again, despite being utterly exhausted.

But there was something more than just a kick to his sex drive. He liked how she felt, like she fit. The only other time he'd been this confused was the first time he'd been called up to the majors. He'd been a jittery mess—so excited he couldn't contain himself—wanting to yell and scream and jump around like a crazy person, yet scared as hell to mess it up.

"This isn't the end," he murmured to her and kissed her gently before walking toward the door. If he didn't leave now, he wouldn't be able to.

* * *

Breakfast with Harv was sobering. Josh had mainlined coffee, refills every few minutes from the pretty waitress who kept smiling at him. The silver and red of the diner décor was harsh. Josh wished he had sunglasses, and he squinted until the caffeine kicked in.

"They need to market you to other teams. I'm pretty certain Toronto isn't bringing you back, son," Harv finally admitted between mouthfuls of eggs and bacon.

"If you can find me a placement, I can ride out the season in the majors, at least?" Josh asked. Harv hadn't received any calls from other clubs yet, and that wasn't a good sign. Monday would be the day that Toronto informed him of their plans, so he had the weekend to stew over it and for Harv to bombard his network.

"Yes, sure," Harv muttered. "In order for that to happen, you need to get your shit together. Your batting average is tanking, and your swing is shit right now."

Harv, despite his gruffness, was a damned good man, and Josh took the bluntness with a grain of salt. He managed his players a little differently than the usual. Sometimes he acted more like a concerned uncle than strictly an agent.

"Got it. Loud and clear, boss," Josh said, and Harv chuckled as he leaned back, his breakfast done. Josh had kept it light. Poached eggs on toast, a side of granola, a bowl of fruit. He avoided the bacon. Grease would not go over well if he had to lace up and get in some practice this morning.

"Keep your head in the game, son. Like you always do. Never had to worry about you like that anyway, but all the same, I'll say it again."

Conversations like this were why he'd signed with Harv, back when Harv had been recommended to him when Josh was hunting for representation out of college. He'd wanted to stay steady as he got used to the big game, not lose his head and spend all the money he was making.

Josh tossed a few bills on the table, and they made their way out into the bright Vegas sun. It was going to be hot today; Gretchen had been right about that. He shielded his eyes and looked down the street, back toward the strip. His mind was definitely not on baseball yet.

"Want to ride out to the field together? The car's yours while you're here."

"Need to go home. Get my gear first, sure," Josh replied.

When he slipped into the front seat, the water bottle Gretchen had given him was in the cupholder. Harv hadn't asked about why he'd been at the Luxor, nor had Josh offered an explanation. Sometimes it was better not to. Harv would remind him of his priorities and to "quit skirt chasing" as he would so eloquently put it. Not that Josh did a lot of that.

"Thanks, Harv," he said as they stood in front of the apartment building not long after. Harv handed him the keys to the car and he slapped Josh on the back.

"You'll be fine, son. Enjoy some downtime. It'll be good for you."

Josh paused, thinking on that, and then hopped into his car to head back to reality.

chapter 6

The clubhouse was familiar and welcoming, and he was glad for it. He had to make the best of this, and as he breathed in the chlorine smells of the jet whirlpool and competing tangs of muscle rub and sweat, he was thankful it would be here.

"Yo, Malvern!"

"Hey, Josh!"

"*Hola!*"

Josh was greeted as he always was—high-fived and shoved in the shoulder as he made his way into the locker room.

The carpet was still worn in the right places, and he stopped in front of the locker that he'd claimed each time he was here. His name had been placed in the paper sleeve above it, with a note that he needed to come up and sign payroll info.

Josh sat down on the bench and pulled out his cleats, running a finger along a stitch line, thinking about what had to happen now. Harv had arranged for him to have the car he'd picked him up in while he was here, which was one less thing for him to figure out. His was in storage in Toronto, since he didn't need it living downtown. He didn't know where he would land yet; it made no sense to have it driven down. Most of his shit was in storage—his needs were pretty simple in a small condo thirty-five stories up. His life was eat, sleep, baseball.

He was well-off financially and hadn't gone down the path of parties, the flashiness of showing off wealth, or the popularity that had women falling over themselves. He'd never wanted to follow the path of illicit drugs, and he'd never so much as sniffed a steroid, having watched many of his fellow athletes become trapped in that relentless cycle. Harv had steered him clear through that time until he knew himself better, and he was thankful for it.

"Earth to Josh. Yo, man, where'd you get to last night? We came by your place. You weren't there," teased Victor, one of the pitchers for the team, as he threw his running shoes into the cubby beside Josh.

The *oohs* from the other players made Josh try to hide his smile, and he looked up, chagrined.

"I went out," he said. He didn't want to talk about what had happened with Gretchen last night. He needed to keep her, *them*, to himself for a little while longer.

"It was a woman. Ric delivered the laundry this morning and told us. Said he gave her a lift to the Luxor," someone else shouted from farther in the locker area.

More heckles came from that, and Josh just waved his hands at them and continued getting dressed.

"Josh. Can I see you for a minute?"

Josh looked up. Coach, his face stern and wrinkled from years of staring out into sunbaked diamonds, poked his head around the corner of the doorway.

"Yes, Coach. Just let me get my cleats on," he replied.

He liked Travis McGovern, the longtime manager and head coach in Vegas. Each time Josh had been here, the man had treated him with respect and kicked his ass at the same time. He was good at his job, and he wondered why none of the major league clubs hadn't snapped him up in some capacity. But Travis seemed happy here, so who was he to judge?

He stood up, walked down the hall to the coaching staff office, and stepped through the door of Travis's office. Paperwork was everywhere, with random baseballs and trophies scattered on the side tables, holding down more piles of paper.

"Felicia is going to lose hope someday, Coach," he said as he stepped in and shook the now-smiling Travis's hand.

"Naw, she won't. She keeps me organized here and at home. I never worry," he replied and gestured to the worn-out office chair on the other side of the desk. Josh sat, glancing at a picture of Travis and his wife, Felicia—who was the secretary for the club— with their two grown boys.

"Your boys well?"

Travis nodded and gestured to the photo. "Yeah. Both study-ing to become lawyers. You believe that? Two lawyers in my family. I'll never hear the end of it."

They both chuckled, and Josh reveled in the familiarity of the atmosphere. It hit him that this place felt like coming home, even though he'd never settled down in one place long enough to think of it as such.

"Harv says hello. He call you yet?" he asked.

"He called in to talk about a pitcher and mentioned that you have a media scrum before the game, around six," Coach said, then paused, leveling one of his no-nonsense gazes at him. "Gotta say, son, I know you don't want to be here, but it's damned good to see you."

Josh clasped his hands in his lap, studying the man. "I might be here awhile."

"Have you thought about staying?"

Travis asked him this every time. They could use a seasoned, more senior player to help with the rookies. It was good ball and the travel schedule was light. But it wasn't the majors, and Josh wanted one more season at least. He shifted in his seat, looking out through the glass into the coaching desks, the whiteboard with the empty rotation list numbered, waiting to be filled. He looked back at Travis, and he figured indecision was all over his face because Travis chuckled and leaned back in his chair, steepling his hands over his head.

"I know, I know. You are a damned good play analyst, son. We'd be happy to have you for as long as you can stay. But I get it."

"Am I in rotation tonight?" Josh asked, clearing his throat, wanting to change the subject.

"We're putting you in eighth. You'll follow Sparrow."

Ryan Sparrow was a good all-rounder. He got on base more often than not, was a fast runner, and was quick with a ball, hence he made a great shortstop. If he could figure out his batting issues, Ryan would be a perfect guy to follow to drive up Josh's RBI. Ryan had been a rookie when Josh had been here last.

Josh was anxious to get out onto the field to do some warmups and swing his bat. His shoulders were tight, and his hips, well, they were tired from last night.

"I should go up and sign those forms for Felicia before she hunts me down," Josh said and lifted himself out of the chair. He was stiff all over, not just his hips. He winced as he stood.

"Rough night?" Travis asked. "Ric mentioned you met a woman on the plane."

"I did, and Ric has a big mouth," Josh said amiably, again playing it close to the chest. Damn Ric and his easy friendliness. He was a good man, but he could gossip like no one else Josh knew.

Travis left it alone, sensing Josh's reluctance to offer up any further information. He wasn't sure what he was going to do about the feelings inside him whenever he thought about Gretchen. He certainly wasn't going to discuss how quickly they had torn into each other or how perfect it had been.

"All right, son. Get up to the office and then out onto the field. I want the boys to take a look at that swing issue you're having."

At that, Josh shook Travis's hand again and went in search of the ever-patient Felicia.

After he had signed the paperwork for payroll, liability, and travel, and had endured a litany of kisses on his cheek with Felicia exclaiming how glad she was to see him here, he asked her to leave tickets for Gretchen and a friend at the gate. Then, finally, he made his way out on to the field.

The batting cage was up, and he listened for a moment to the rhythmic punt and *thwack* of a bat hitting the ball from the pitching machine, the random shouts, the thud of a ball hitting the palm of a glove. Good noises to distract him from thoughts of Gretchen.

He waved at a few more of the guys he knew and checked in with the batting coach, knowing it was time to get to work.

*   *   *

"Oh my God, girl, you look exhausted."

Gretchen plopped down in the seat beside Sharla and grimaced. "That obvious?"

"Did he let you get *any* sleep?" Sharla admonished, and then shoved a menu at her. "I want frigging details, girl. Is he as hot as you thought he would be? Is he kinky? You don't do kinky. I bet he's kinky."

Gretchen must've blushed pink because Sharla laughed loudly and clapped her hands, throwing her head back. People were staring, and Gretchen slumped back behind the menu, embarrassed.

"Umm, yes?" she squeaked out.

Gretchen didn't want to talk about details of her night with Josh in the middle of a restaurant. She peered around the side of her menu at Sharla and attempted one of her best *shut it* glares.

"I get it," Sharla said, more quietly. "Later?"

"Yes," Gretchen replied, relieved. She wasn't sure she wanted to share the details with anyone. She wanted to keep the experience to herself, to pull the memories out and savor them when she needed to feel as alive as she had this morning. It wasn't that she didn't want to tell anyone who would listen that she, Gretchen Harper, had had a one-nighter with Joshua Malvern, but she had funny, mixed-up emotions about it now and wasn't sure what to do. So, she put it aside and mentally packed it into a little box to focus on what she'd come to Vegas for.

All morning she had met with representatives from different wineries and buying groups, some she knew well, some she wanted to get to know. She had several contacts now to do direct buys through the brokers who managed the Canadian California importer groups, and she had met with the new guy taking over DuBoeuf's sale chain. It had been a good morning. Gretchen had been offered a job working as a rep for DuBoeuf last year, here in the States, but there were plenty of good sommeliers here who could do that job, and her own business had been taking off at home, so she'd passed. It had been a feather in her cap, though, and the new reps had already heard of her beforehand.

"First judging is at one. What are your plans for this evening? More gorgeous Josh?"

Gretchen, pulled out of her thoughts, shook her head. "If you don't have plans, Josh has left us tickets to watch the Neons play tonight."

Sharla lifted her eyebrows and folded her menu shut. "I see it all over you, Gretch. It was more than a night of phenomenal sex, wasn't it?"

"I don't know, Shar," she answered honestly. "I mean, he stayed the night, he wants to see me again, we—"

The waiter arrived at that moment and took their lunch order, and Gretchen worried her lip more. What if it was more? This couldn't work long term. He was likely moving to God-knows-where, and her life was in Toronto. Long distance and travel schedules on his side would make it impossible. But then she chastised herself. Why was she even thinking about a relationship? Jump the gun much, Gretchen? She sighed and Sharla put a hand on her arm.

"It's okay to feel something, Gretch. I mean, he's Joshua freakin' Malvern, for God's sake."

"I know, but—"

"But nothing, honey, I don't want to see you hurt. Be careful. I know he's into you, and—"

"I know, I know," Gretchen interrupted her, and sighed, pasting a grin across her face. "Do you want to come with me or not?"

"Of course I do. He has hot teammates, does he not?"

. . .

Josh looked out through the dugout toward the stands. He'd gotten tickets for Gretchen and her friend in the left field, partially because that way she could sit in the stands right where he was when he was in the field. It felt selfish, but he wanted her close to him any way he could get. It was an odd sensation, thinking of her the way he was right now. A long time had passed since he'd truly wanted to date or get involved with a woman, and something about her had broken some sort of barrier in him.

He hoped she would come. The idea of seeing her again distracted him, but also gave him a nervous energy that propelled him through the warmup, his body recovering from the night before with energy he'd not had in weeks.

"Who you looking for?" someone asked, and Josh turned and grinned as Neptune Gilbert leaned up beside him on the fence.

"A friend. I left her tickets."

"Ohhhh. The girl that Ric said—"

"Did he tell *everyone*?" Josh interrupted, but then let it go. Ric was as harmless as they came, and honestly? Did it matter if he'd told everyone? He chuckled and shook his head, leaning his forehead on his folded arms.

"Nah. I don't think the other team knows yet," Neptune replied, his Caribbean accent soft and full of humor. Neptune patted him on the back, and Josh couldn't help but smile.

He'd taken to Neptune the last time he was here. He was

young, just out of the junior ranks. Scouts had found him playing third-rate ball at a community college, studying to become a
mechanic and working at a local garage so he could send money
home to his family in the Dominican Republic. Someone had
tipped a scout that this kid was faster than Usain Bolt and was a
promising infielder.

They'd brought him in to try out, and he'd been playing for the
Neons ever since.

Josh had helped him sort out some of his batting issues,
namely controlling his body. He was just a kid, he still had time to
grow into himself. Currently, he was doing just fine in the infield.
It had been fun to mentor the kid, reminding Josh of his first year,
working toward getting called up, and the anticipation of it all.
He'd hooked him up with Harv too. Neptune was going places—it
was just a matter of when he was ready.

A lot of the boys were like that. It was a team of transient
hopefuls, all waiting for the call to the big leagues. Only a few of
the boys were longtime players, all happy to have made it that far
in their ability.

He spied blond hair out of the corner of his eye and turned
to see Gretchen and her friend sliding into their seats. His heart
skipped a beat, and he looked at the clock on the scoreboard.
Fifteen minutes to game time.

"Coach. Need a minute. Can I—"

"Go say hi, you big damned puppy dog," Travis said, shooing him with one eyebrow raised. "You've been like a kid at the
Christmas parade waiting for Santa, standing at the fence."

Josh shot back through the clubhouse and around into the
stands, taking the steps up onto the platform two at a time. He
stood for a moment, watching Gretchen look around, pointing,

talking to Sharla. Sharla saw him first; her jaw dropped and she slapped Gretchen's arm, making her turn.

Their eyes met and he was damned glad she was there right at that moment. He strode forward, and she got up and sidestepped past all the people already sitting.

"Hi," she breathed as they met up at the end of the row.

"Hi back," he said.

"I like this color on you," she blurted, then blushed. "Red and black, very sharp."

He laughed at that, realizing if she'd gone to a game in Toronto, she'd have seen him in his Sixers uniform, which was quite different than this. She smelled and looked amazing, and he lifted her off her feet and kissed her. She wrapped her arms around him and kissed back, the perfection of it making him feel invincible. People were looking, and he didn't give a rat's ass. He wanted to kiss her forever.

"When are you batting tonight?" she asked after he gently dropped her back to her feet.

"Eighth in the lineup," he replied, smoothing her hair back down. "And I'm in left field."

"Well, I hope you do great tonight." she put a hand on his chest, looking up at him. "I'm glad to be here, Josh. I don't want to be a distraction, though."

"You aren't. If anything, you make me feel invincible. A beautiful woman in the stands just for me," he confessed honestly, putting a hand over hers and looking down into her upturned eyes. He studied her for a moment, and then leaned in to whisper in her ear. "And later, maybe feel something else."

That made her blush from the tips of her ears down to the V neck of her blouse, and she stepped closer to him, biting her lip suggestively.

"Malvern, get your horny ass back here," came a bellow from the dugout, and Josh sighed. His interlude was over.

"Time to go to work," he grinned, waved at Sharla, smacked a kiss on Gretchen's lips, and leaped away down to the stairs.

"Have fun!" she called.

Hopefully later, they would.

*   *   *

Sharla was asking so many questions about the game that at one point, Gretchen Googled *how to play baseball* and handed her phone over.

"This should cover everything you haven't, but will, ask me."

Her friend laughed and put her arm around Gretchen's shoulders, pushed the phone back to her, and held on to her for a moment. It was the eighth inning and they had been talking nonstop, catching up, and simply having fun with each other. It had been far too long since she and Sharla had really, truly spent time together doing something other than wine tasting. She would have to thank Josh for this gift later. Even though she knew he had ulterior motives, she was happy to oblige them. She got to be here, watching her favorite sport, spending time with her best friend, thrilled at the knowledge that he wanted to see her again, and perhaps repeat what had happened last night.

"I am just trying to get you wound up, you fool." Sharla giggled and tilted her head to rest on Gretchen's. "I'm really enjoying getting to spend some time with you, you know."

"I am too," Gretchen said quietly. "We should do this more often."

"We will, once you marry that gorgeous man down there," Sharla stated and squealed as Gretchen pinched her.

"Sharla!" she hissed, feeling the blush creep back up. "It was one night! A weekend at most! I'll likely never see him again after this."

"Sure. *Bull*shit."

The Neons were batting and the seventh in the lineup was getting ready to take his chances. The opposing team, the Yosemites, had a good closer who was pitching right down the middle, red-hot. So far he hadn't made it easy. If this guy was able to make it on base, then Josh might have a chance to bring him in if he could connect with one of those pitches. Gretchen hoped he would; it would dramatically improve his confidence.

Sparrow, the name across the batter's back, swung wide at the first two, then cracked the third for a base hit. As he ran, her eyes swiveled to the side and Josh was swinging his bat with some weights on it. He looked like he always did, and her heart skipped a beat. His high stance, his tight grip, tall socks favored over the long pants. But as she watched his hands throttle up on the bat again, it took on a whole new dimension. Those hands had been hot on her skin, and her body flushed with heat as he bunched up his muscles, swinging the bat. Those muscles had held her as he—

"You okay?" Sharla asked. "You look flushed."

"Fine, fine. Just a hot flash or something," she deflected, fanning herself.

"Right," Sharla replied, amusement threading her voice. "Big, sexy baseball man in a uniform is flexing his big, sexy muscles. I see right through you."

Gretchen bit her lip and crossed her fingers as he *thunked* the weights off into the circle, the chalk rising in a puff as they hit the ground. Josh stepped over to the plate, flexing his shoulders out, his face a mask of seriousness. He seemed sexier than he had ever been now that she knew him. The way he walked coupled with his fierce stare toward the mound was more intimate to her as she watched him.

Hot flash. *Ha*. She was full-on nuclear, watching him set up to bat and enjoying every minute of it. As she fanned herself again with the program, she reminded herself that she was in Vegas. Her regular, hesitant, risk-averse side could take a hike—and had—considering her reaction each time she laid eyes on him.

"He is sex on a stick, that man," Sharla said, reading her mind, pulling her out of her thoughts of peeling Josh's uniform off him later with her teeth. "Does he taste as good as he—"

"Sharla," Gretchen clipped, covering her face with her hands, her current train of thought now gone. She prayed not too many people around them were eavesdropping—the practical side of her butting in for a moment of reason. "Shut. Up."

Sharla continued to laugh, and Gretchen refocused on Josh as the crowd cheered. It was a big crowd, most of the seats filled for a weekend evening game, which was a good thing for Josh as he debuted back with the team. The draw of the casinos had nothing on a good game of ball, it seemed. She liked the atmosphere. The ballpark wasn't nearly as big as the Dome in Toronto and had the air of an old-time baseball stadium like Fenway.

Josh had struck out all evening, and she felt the tension she saw in him as he stepped up and took his stance. He needed this. She sent up some sort of wish to the baseball gods to give him a good pitch.

The first pitch went high, and he didn't even flinch at it. The second pitch went hard down the center, and Josh fouled it into the stands. He scowled, checked his bat, and reset himself.

"Please, please, please," Gretchen chanted.

The next pitch went straight in, and he caught an edge, sending it high up into the outfield. A pop fly. Josh was chugging toward first without hurry, knowing full well the centerfielder would catch it, but then, incredibly, he missed the catch. Suddenly, Josh was on base, his teammate on second.

"Is this a good thing?" Sharla asked as Gretchen cheered and clapped, whistling through her teeth with everyone else around them. Josh looked surprised, but happy, the base coach running out to talk to him. Then he left, jogging toward the dugout, peeling off his batting gloves and wrist guard while another player went out to take his place. They high-fived as they passed one another, and as tall as Josh was, he had to reach to hit the guy's hand.

The back of this player's shirt said GILBERT. He had shining dark skin and a toothy grin. His hair was a riot of natural curls escaping underneath his helmet, bouncing as he took his lead from the bag. Sharla was looking at her program for the name, puzzled.

"His name is Neptune. Says here he's only twenty. Is that young to be at this level?"

"I have no idea. Josh mentioned him. He said he was a rookie when he was here last. He liked him. Said he's superfast. That must be why they want to put him on. Strange they would do that with the player on second, but I'm not the coach, so who knows."

The next player stepped to the plate and cracked a high ball into left field. The fielder picked it up and rocketed it back toward first, ignoring Sparrow running to third. Neptune, seemingly strolling, made it to second with time to spare.

Gretchen looked back to the dugout and saw Josh leaning on the fence, watching the action, chewing on sunflower seeds.

Beside him was the head coach, and they were talking and pointing with their heads together, identical squints looking out into the lights.

He turned, looking up to where she and Sharla were sitting. Gretchen sensed the relief from where she was sitting as their eyes found each other. He'd gotten the hit, he'd connected with the ball, and she gave him a thumbs-up. His shoulders shook as he chuckled and focused back on the game.

"You are in so much trouble, Gretch," Sharla said in her ear and put an arm around her friend. "That man has plans for you later. He's looking at you like "

"Sharla," Gretchen blushed once more. She most definitely was in trouble, and so was he.

chapter 7

The game was over, and despite the rally in the eighth, the Neons couldn't convert and had lost by two runs. It was hard fought, and a disappointing end, but the team had played well. Gretchen got a sense that this was a good club. She watched Josh for quite a bit—well, no, most of the game—and he was a different player here. It was all business in Toronto, but here, it looked like he was having fun. She understood that this was a different kind of baseball and he'd adjusted his game, just like she altered her delivery when she was talking to a large distributor versus a smaller boutique winery.

Josh looked much more at ease with himself here, and she chastised herself for analyzing a man she'd known for only a day. They had a connection, but it was still new. She wanted to be happy with the exciting night they'd had but knowing it wasn't going to be long-term made her wistful for more time.

When the final out was called, Sharla beelined for the bath-room, and unsure of where else to go, Gretchen walked toward the field and stood along the wall as the last of the fans left the stadium. Bugs gathering around the floodlights buzzed softly in the night air, accompanied by the sounds of the staff putting the diamond to bed for the night. Other than the odd holler or slam from the team lockers behind the dugouts, it was peaceful. Definitely a different atmosphere from the big stadium down-town. Slower, more relaxed. A few of the staff waved at her as she watched them. It was a clear evening, the air cooling quickly.

A nice night in Vegas, for sure.

Josh poked his head back out of the dugout door as Gretchen leaned against the wall, taking in a lungful of air and enjoying the atmosphere. He put down his gear and strode over to her. When he reached her, she leaned on the top of the wall, looking into his eyes. Something about how she felt around him was just so natural.

"Hiya," she said playfully.

He unceremoniously picked her up and lifted her over the wall, then set her down on the turf, dragging her over to the plate, greeting the guy raking all the pitching mound dirt back up into place. He held up a finger and jogged back to his gear, bringing his bat back with him.

"Here," he said, "Give it a try. I know you have a good grip."

Gretchen carefully held the bat, swinging it a little. She liked how nicely balanced it was, and he pulled her toward him, his hands on the end.

"This isn't a Walmart special, is it?" she murmured. The wood felt solid in her hands, heavier than the metal bats she normally swung at monster-sized softballs when she played slow-pitch.

The grit from the chalk rubbed into the tape and was powdery against her hands, but it felt nice compared to the sticky rubber on non-professional bats. It was marked up in places from the weights Josh would stack for his warm-up swings, various impressions from balls where he'd made contact, the dents in the tape where he would wrap his fingers before standing at bat.

It was his bat. One of many, obviously, but she thought this one might be special for some reason. She didn't want to ask. That would sound silly.

Josh positioned himself behind her and adjusted her body along the plate, helping her set up her stance. His body was a solid wall behind her, which she didn't mind at all. He slid his hands over hers, pressing her grip higher on the bat, a knee nudged in between her legs, kicking at her feet gently as he did.

"Plant your feet farther apart. Now, bring your elbow up a little more. Don't worry, you won't jab me."

Glancing back, Gretchen faltered. The wrinkles around his eyes and mouth as he smiled made her want to drop the bat and kiss him instead. His hat was on backward, his sunglasses perched on top. Scratch that. He looked like a fantasy sports hero. She blinked and refocused, his hard muscles shifting around her. She couldn't jump him on a ball diamond. She *shouldn't* jump him on a ball diamond.

"Now, swing," he said softly, guiding her arms down through the arc into the strike zone. He made a sound to imitate a ball hitting the bat with his tongue. Gretchen leaned back into him, lowering the bat, tilting her head up. He looked down.

"I'm glad you got a hit tonight," she said softly, and he brought a hand up to her face, caressing her jaw, his face serious and studying hers. She turned and he kissed her softly, taking the bat from her hands and dropping it as he kissed her deeper. He burrowed his fingers into her hair, taking more, and she responded, hungry for him. She wanted him. Now. She amended her thought—she could *indeed* jump him on a ball diamond, and she didn't care who saw. He was solid and hot and she wanted to climb him like a tree.

"Gretch, we cannot have sex right here, no matter how much I would love to push you up against the backstop and fuck you senseless," he murmured as he broke their kiss, both of them breathing hard.

"Oh. Shit. Sorry," she breathed. "This is kind of your work-place, isn't it?"

He looked down at her playfully, holding her close, and she could smell his deodorant, see a streak of red on his jersey from sliding to catch a runner, and a smudge of dirt across one cheek. He was intoxicating and she had completely forgotten where she was.

She looked around, and all of the maintenance crew were watching, some with their jaws hanging. Sharla was standing at the wall, laughing loudly. She realized that one of her hands was firmly planted on his ass, the other one fisting his jersey and she let go slowly. He was intoxicating, like a fine wine on a cold night.

"Let's go eat. There's a great fried chicken place near here. The guys usually go after the game and I promised I would introduce you," he said, and all she could do was nod—half embarrassed, half enthralled by him.

"Sharla. Come have chicken with us," he called as he headed toward the dugout to grab his things. "Meet us at the west gate. My car is there."

Sharla waved, still laughing, and Gretchen was ushered into

the dugout, then down some stairs, into a hallway. Josh pointed to the door at the end of the corridor. "I'll meet you out there. I just have to grab a couple of things from my locker," he said.

As she made her way toward the door, she passed by what looked to be the coaching offices where the head coach had his feet up on his desk, and a glass of what was likely bourbon in his hand. He saw her and beckoned to her.

"Young lady, come in here a moment."

She hesitated, then stepped through the door, suddenly shy. She felt the need to break the silence.

"Evening. Damn shame tonight, but the rally was good. Their closer has quite an arm on him. What was his top speed tonight, do you know?" she rattled, then stopped, realizing she was nattering on like a fool.

Coach stood up, extending a hand. "Not too sure. Forgot to ask. He's a helluva closer. We could use him, I think."

"It's lovely to meet you, Mr.—" she started, cutting herself off when she realized she didn't know his name. Blushing, she gestured toward him helplessly.

"Call me Travis, darlin'. You must be Gretchen."

Travis gestured to the chair in front of the desk, and she sat. He looked like one of those stereotypical grizzled old baseball coaches, with a natural grimace and wrinkles from experience.

"You know baseball?" he asked.

"A bit. I like to go to Sixers games when I can. My dad and I used to watch baseball together."

Travis leaned forward on the desk. "Good. Good. A man needs a woman who can talk shop with him when he's frustrated about his game."

"Oh, I'm not his—"

"Are you harassing my woman, Coach?"

Josh winked at her. Travis chuckled and leaned back again.

"Ric didn't tell me how you two met," he said, waiting expectantly. Josh shook his head and muttered something under his breath.

"Oh. He was at the airport on his way here, and I bought him a coffee. He looked like he needed it," Gretchen supplied before Josh could speak.

"I did," Josh added. "So I decided to bring her along. Any time a firecracker like this walks by I have to sit up and take notice now, don't I?"

"Indeed you do. I know I did," Travis said.

Josh tried hard to keep a snort of laughter in and failed. "Storytime, Coach?"

"Mind your tone, boy," Travis said, amused. "You know how I met my Felicia? Did I ever tell you that story?"

"No, Coach, you didn't."

"She bought me a hot dog after a game in Poughkeepsie, the year I made it to the draft. I was as grass-green as they come when it came to women. I'd seen her in the stands with her girlfriends, and I never would have talked to her in a month of Sundays, knowing she was out of my league, a true beauty. She marched up to me one evening, put that damned dog in my hand and said, 'Travis McGovern, you're taking me for a proper dinner tomorrow night.' Then she handed me a card with her address and left. I showed up the next night in my best clothes and a bunch of daffodils picked off my billet's lawn, nervous as a chicken in a fox house because she was the prettiest girl I had ever set eyes on, already half in love with her."

"That is such a sweet story!" Gretchen said. "Obviously you had a good first date."

"Indeed we did, young lady. We watched the sun come up the next morning, those damned daffodils in the back seat, wilting alongside a tinfoil swan and two melted candy bars. I proposed to her on the hood of my car as we sat, arms wrapped around each other. She said yes and that was it. One night."

"Jeez, Coach. I never took you for a romantic," Josh said, his eyes twinkling.

Travis grunted and stood, looking at them both, his eyes a little misty. He cleared his throat and let out a breath, signaling they should make a graceful exit from his likely not-normal display of emotion.

"It was lovely to meet you, sir," Gretchen said, standing as well, and offered her hand again to shake. The older man grasped it, and picked it up, kissing her knuckles, just like Josh had just yesterday, and she melted a little.

"Go watch the sunrise, while you can," he mumbled as he sat back down and then ushered them out of his office.

"Oof," Josh said as they made their way out to his car. "That was, uhh . . . interesting. You don't see that side of Coach often."

"It was a lovely story to hear. It would make a fun baseball movie, don't you think?" Gretchen offered.

Josh pulled her over and kissed her gently, a hand stroking her hair as he looked into her eyes. "It might. It was. I'm kind of glad he told me," he murmured, and then they kept going, heading out to the parking lot.

Sharla was waiting, talking to another player who was obviously interested in her. She was flipping her hair, giggling, and he was tilting his head, and looking down, directly at her chest popping out of her shirt.

"That's Ryan. He's a good guy with Iowa farm-boy manners. Sharla might have fun with that."

"Sharla doesn't do good guys," Gretchen replied. "She likes them alpha and aggressive. Which usually doesn't work out for her."

"And what type of guy is your go-to?" Josh asked nonchalantly, but it was loaded, and she wasn't ready to answer that seriously, not just yet. She slipped her hand out of his, into the back pocket of his uniform pants, and pinched his ass.

"The kind that wants to push me up against the backstop and fuck me senseless."

He stopped dead, and she continued walking, purposely swaying her hips, catching up to Sharla and Ryan. She turned as she reached them, because he hadn't followed, and was rewarded by him still rooted in place, slack jawed, hopefully imagining just what her response had meant. His response made her feel fearless and wanton. Like last night, not holding anything back. Normal Gretchen would have *never* blurted that out in the open.

But, if this was her weekend to end all weekends, she wanted to make it epic.

. . .

Josh was losing his damned mind.

He was sprawled on a chair beside Gretchen with the team around them. Sharla was completely immersed in Ryan, and Gretchen had already murmured to him that Sharla was likely going to stagger into tomorrow's wine competition rounds a little tired. Sharla had been taking selfies of her and Ryan, sent one to someone, and then ignored her phone as it practically vibrated off the table. Gretchen's friend was feisty, that was for sure.

Gretchen had been running her fingers up and down Josh's

spine for the last ten minutes and it was frying his brain, making him fidgety. All he could think about was picking her up and taking her into the back so he could have his way with her in one of the bathroom stalls like some sort of freshman punk.

But he was also watching her, learning about her, and it was fascinating. How she relaxed and just went with the flow around her, laughing, joking, interested in his teammates' stories. Her caring nature shone through her in little ways like that. *She would make an excellent team manager*, he thought. It was likely why she did what she did, as she could tease relationships out of people she'd just met, making them feel heard and understood to get deals made.

It had worked on him. Well, that plus her killer blue eyes and soft, sexy curves, which he was aching to run his hands over. And had. And would again if they could get out of here soon.

The boys all clamored for Gretchen's attention, of course, teasing her, calling her "ma'am," asking about her life as a "professional drunk." She laughed and played off what he would have considered an insult. She understood these men were young and somewhat tactless when they'd had a few.

If he'd been a prideful or possessive man, he would have been jealous, but it simply felt good to have a plus one beside him who could keep up in his world, or at least was showing she could. It took a special woman who could understand the boys' club of baseball. Schedules and travel were hard on relationships, and he had a brief, strange thought on how they would handle that. Long-distance relationships were terrible, in his limited experience.

Being a major league baseball player was all-consuming during the season, and in the off-season? You were training for the next one. Relationships had been distractions and after a few failed attempts, he'd steered clear of getting in too deep. He also had never entertained the thought of getting involved with women who propositioned him either, even just for the thrill of it.

Until now.

Which was the other side to him losing his mind. In the space of twenty-four hours, Gretchen had gone from someone to flirt with on a plane, to a welcome distraction, to something more. His original idea was a temporary hookup, but now he wasn't sure he wanted it to be just that. That train of thought made him sit up and clear his throat, shaking off the heaviness. The realization dawned slowly, rippling like a wave. He didn't want this to end.

"You're quiet this evening," José, another fielder, said as he leaned over. "You getting tired on us, old man?"

Josh carefully picked up a strand of Gretchen's blond hair and flipped it through his fingers to deflect his introspection. He was here for a good time, not to play *what if* when there was likely nothing to think over.

"Nope," he replied, causing José to laugh loudly and slap his shoulder.

Okay, maybe he was a bit possessive. Possessive and ready to leave. He wanted to be alone with her.

"Cheers, lads, to a scheduled day off tomorrow!" someone else said, and a bunch of whoops and *hell yeah*s echoed. He had forgotten, and Gretchen turned to him, meeting his eyes.

"What are your plans?" she asked in his ear. The delicate strawberry scent that hit whenever she leaned close reminded him of their slick, wet bodies plastered together as he washed her hair this morning in the shower, his fingers sliding across her scalp as he massaged, resulting in—

"None. I hadn't gotten that far yet. Likely unpack, paint my toenails, binge-watch *Gilmore Girls*," he replied, joking, trying to keep his arousal under control.

It made her laugh, but she went quiet almost as quickly, twisting her fingers in her lap. He'd noticed that was her "tell" when she was unsure of something and that her question had been more pointed.

"You want to spend it with me?" he asked quietly. He could hope, right?

She relaxed immediately. "I have to attend the competition results tomorrow in the morning, and then I'm at the tasting in the afternoon, but—"

"Can anyone go to these?" he interrupted, leaning down to whisper in her ear. "I'll go with you. I'd go anywhere with you."

The look on her face told him everything he needed. She was feeling this connection too. What-ifs be damned. Where she would go, he wanted to follow.

"Sharla? Honey, we're leaving," Gretchen exclaimed before he could, standing and stepping over to her friend. Sharla turned from Ryan and the two of them talked for a moment, Gretchen shaking her head, Sharla seemingly reassuring her. Then Sharla hugged her and Gretchen came back to him, obviously worried.

"She'll find her way back to her hotel. I can trust your teammate, right?" she asked, her hands clasped again, her eyes worried. "I—"

"Yes," Josh said a little louder. "Ryan will take care of your best friend, won't he?"

The grin on Ryan's face was a mile wide. He was the safest of all the boys on the team, so Sharla was in no danger. Likely he'd deliver her back to her hotel and be a gentleman, but the way they had been looking at one another, perhaps not. Josh had already recognized that Sharla could handle herself.

"Okay then," Gretchen said, and pulled Josh up. "Time for bed, old man."

That had the rest of the group howling with laughter, and as they said their goodbyes, Josh only paid half attention. With her hand in his and the way she was laughing, his heart was ready to burst.

What was he getting himself into?

. . .

"I'm just going to stop by my place and pick up a change of clothes," he said as they drove the short distance to his apartment. Gretchen stretched in the seat, a small yawn escaping.

"Okay," she replied sleepily.

He hadn't thought of the fact that they hadn't slept much the night before, and she was likely exhausted, having to work most of the day. How he wasn't was a bit of a mystery. Perhaps it was the time change? More likely it was her. She gave him a ridiculous energy boost. He turned off the car in his parking spot.

"I'll just be a minute."

She slumped in the front seat, closing her eyes. "I'll just nap."

He zipped up into his apartment, threw some nice clothes into his duffel—a pair of jeans, his Neons team sweater, and a T-shirt—grabbed his shoes, chucked his bathroom bag in, and was back down in under five minutes, half a banana already mowed down. Despite all the fried chicken and nachos he'd eaten at dinner, he was starving again for some reason.

Gretchen was asleep.

He stared at her through the glass, her chest rising and falling peacefully. Finishing his banana outside the car, he was as quiet as possible as he climbed inside so he wouldn't disturb her. With the radio off, he headed off toward the Luxor. Her soft breathing filled the car as he let the day wash over him.

He'd gotten a hit tonight. It had been a pop-up, but at least he was making contact. They'd noticed one of his shoulders wasn't rotating properly at batting practice and his knee was acting up—both were sabotaging the follow-through on his swing. Some adjustments, a massage, and some ultrasound were in order, and a brace for his knee would be in on Monday. Honestly, the aches and pains were a normal part of his day now, and he hadn't thought it was physical. He had truly thought he was losing his touch and that it was all mental. It made him wonder how committed the Sixers batting coaches were to him if no one had mentioned anything.

It was a relief, in a way, to know he could improve again, because he didn't want to be done. He wondered if he'd addressed his knee properly, would they have put him on the injured list instead of sending him down, but that was water under the bridge now. He and Harv could regroup on Monday. Harv wanted to meet with him following their afternoon game. They were busing to Bakersfield after that for a three-game series, then to Reno, then back to Vegas for another home stretch of games.

Josh hoped to be back up somewhere by then, but who knew. He ran a hand through his hair, his hat in the back seat, and realized he hadn't even showered yet. He'd been completely focused on spending as much time with Gretchen as possible that he hadn't thought about his demotion much at all. It had been about her, playing ball, and the focus that went into both.

The stop-and-go as he reached the main strip slowed him down and he let his mind wander to random thoughts, rethinking plays from the game, making a mental list to look at some of the tapes from Bakersfield on Monday. He had some analyzing to do since the coaches wanted his opinion on batting order.

In some ways, it felt good to be asked to assist with some of the coaching. He'd always enjoyed that. He liked working with the team to devise options on strategy. Baseball was all about numbers and matching talents for the best results. It reminded him of the business case studies from college. The problem-solving, relief, and excitement when it went right.

His window was down and a breeze wafted through, raising the hair on his arm as it rested on the door. Music from the street performers, traffic noise, and laughter of people walking interrupted his thoughts. The palm trees and lights lent a festive feel and he relaxed fully, feeling the tension ebb away. It was such a surreal world here, all fake and designed to make money. But somehow, when he was here, he felt more himself than anywhere else. He glanced at Gretchen, her face peaceful, the lights creating shadows across her cheeks, the blond highlights in her hair sparkling as they drove.

She was fucking beautiful.

He was the luckiest guy in the world in that moment, with her right there, wanting to be with him.

He pushed a bit of hair off her face, glad he hadn't done what he normally did when fans bugged him, which was clam up. Gretchen shifted, muttered something about buying cases, and went back to sleep.

Josh turned into the Luxor a few minutes later and was able to get a spot in the garage, even though it was late. As he killed the engine, Gretchen roused from her sleep.

"Where are we?" she rasped. "Was I out long?"

"Luxor. A half hour or so."

She sat up, reaching for him over the middle console. She kissed him, then let him go, opening up her door.

He followed her, bag in hand as they made their way to the room. He was still rolling the thought of her in his head—how incredible it was that she was his for the night. She held his hand the whole way. In the elevator she folded into his side, tucking her head into his shoulder, and sighed heavily.

"What was that for?" he asked.

"I feel good. Happy," she replied.

He couldn't answer her, a lump in his throat as their eyes searched each other. There was that damned emotion again, and it nearly undid him when she reached up and ran a thumb over his cheek, palming his jaw.

Jesus. He could fall for her right now and never look back.

They made it to her room, which had been cleaned up except for the butt and handprints on the glass. Those had stayed put.

Gretchen dropped her purse and key card on the table and wandered over to the window, standing with her arms crossed, looking out over the city as Josh dropped his duffel by the bathroom and levered off his shoes.

He crossed to her and embraced her from behind. She put her hands on his arms, holding him there. They stood, silent, the snake of car lights on the strip twinkling and shimmering. A world away as he absorbed her heat, her solidness molding to his.

"I am too," he finally whispered, feeling compelled to tell her how he was feeling right then, how he wanted this to be more. "I don't know what th—"

She turned in his arms, putting a finger on his lips. "Let's not go there yet. I want to be present now, not stew on what-ifs."

Maybe she was thinking of this as more than a quickie romance too. He held her there, trying to decipher what she was thinking, and she cradled his jaw again. He leaned into it and turned, kissing her palm.

"Shower?" he asked, finally, wanting to break the heaviness that had settled on them. He'd tell her, just not right now. Her idea of being in the now was reminding him how much he wanted her.

He'd wanted her all day, dammit, and the lead-up had been torture.

She tugged him wordlessly toward the bathroom, where he proceeded to strip her slowly, kissing each bit of exposed skin as he peeled a layer back. Her shoulder, her collarbone. Crouching, he trailed his lips over her stomach, hands rising up to caress under her breasts, then down as he slipped her jeans off, finally rounding her ass and pulling her to him so he could kiss a hip, sliding a hand to her calf muscle on one leg.

She was soft and warm and he wanted to lift her leg and taste her, but he slowed himself down. He didn't want fast. He wanted to savor every moment he could. Her soft sighs and touches made him as hard as a rock and ready to plunge in, to feel her surrounding him again, tight and hot. The thought of it had him twitching, and he groaned as her fingers found his hair and threaded through it, pulling.

He slid his fingers over the silk of her panties, the heat intense as she moaned and pushed into his hand. She wanted him just as much.

She stopped his hands as he attempted to slip her panties down, and she pushed off the counter, undoing the buttons on his jersey with one hand. He pulled his tech tee over his head and threw it away quickly, and she ran a hand over his chest, kissing where her hand had been, raising goosebumps. Smiling as she licked a nipple, she distracted him as the other hand was undoing the belt on his pants. Before he could tell her to stop, she had dipped in and circled the length of him with her palm, slowly caressing up and down. He sucked in a breath, unable to expel it, the sensation pushing his nerve endings into overdrive. Her touch was featherlight, gentle, and teasing.

All the blood left Josh's head and he gave up holding his breath as she pulled him out, dropped into a squat and took the head of his cock into her mouth as his pants fell, circling her tongue over the top of it, her hand sliding up and down his shaft.

"Jesus, Gretch," he moaned and her lips formed another smile as she continued sucking. He couldn't kick off his pants, his socks holding them to his lower legs, and he was desperate to pull her up and get her under him. If she kept it up he was going to explode right then and there like a teenager.

She pulled him all the way into her mouth, her hands coming around to his ass, grabbing flesh. Eyes glued downward, he moved her hair to one side, holding it back, absolutely amazed at what she was doing to him. The tension in his belly tightened as he tried to maintain control, and he rocked forward as she encouraged him with little moans. It was erotic as hell, but he held himself from thrusting hard, the sucking noises emptying his brain of all thought except how hot her mouth was.

"If you don't stop, I'm going to—" was all he could groan out before she started moving her head faster, her tongue working up and down, and he slapped the wall to stay upright as he exploded into her mouth, his other hand grasping the base of his cock, coming hard and fast. He was lightheaded as she sucked him dry, not stopping.

She stood up, wiped the side of her mouth, and shimmied out of her panties. Reaching past him as he sagged against the wall, she turned on the shower, testing the water with her hands. He rarely came when a woman gave him a blow job, but that was . . . *whoa.* Out of breath, he couldn't move, seeing stars.

"That was fucking incredible," he rasped as she stepped flush with him again, hands caressing him, pressing her breasts into his chest, licking her lips. She knew exactly what she'd done.

"I'm glad," she murmured.

Gretchen stepped into the now-steaming shower, and looked back at him as water cascaded down her back.

"Holy fuck," he swore under his breath and hurried to pull the rest of his uniform off to join her.

. . .

Gretchen stood in the jet of hot water, watching Josh hop awkwardly out of his pants, catching her reflection in the big vanity mirror, unrecognizable. She had just dropped to the floor and . . . damn, she'd never, *ever* done that before. She'd had no idea if she was doing it right until he had reacted. She wasn't as experienced as some of her friends, who shared their secrets after far too many drinks, but she had wanted to please him.

This was not her normal world, and this was not a regular experience. She briefly wondered if sex could be like this all the time, intense and erotic, or if this was once-in-a-lifetime sex, always to be remembered and measured against. She was sensitive everywhere, her skin reacting to the heat of the water, her nipples hard as rocks even though the room was filling with hot steam.

This sex was definitely not as safe and routine as some of her previous boyfriends. There was no resemblance to anything she'd ever experienced before or maybe would again. Closing her eyes, the water cascaded over her, washing away all the doubts she had, pushing all comparisons to other men away. That was in the past, and she was here now.

A hand slipped around her waist, reaching down to cover her crotch, pulling her up and in, and lips grazed the back of her neck. She leaned into it, the slide of his hands roaming over her wet body turning her insides to jelly.

"What you do to me," he murmured and plunged his fingers inside her, probing and rubbing.

She gasped and the wave of an orgasm hit her almost as if he had conjured it from thin air. She rolled her hips into his arm as he held her and stroked, her hand coming to join his, noisily riding the crest of pleasure. He held her up as her legs went boneless, shaking with the intensity. She'd never come that quickly in her life, and it was unbelievably sensual, the hot water pouring over their joined hands, the feel of their skin suctioned together, his strength all around her.

"Go on. Come. Yes, like that," he urged her. He was hard again, pressed into her back as he moved with her, relentless as he continued to tease out the release. She moaned and let go of his arms, bracing on the wall, and he leaned with her, moving his hand over her back, pressing from behind.

"Fuck," she muttered. "Josh—"

"Yes, ma'am," he replied and he pushed into her, burying himself all the way, stretching her quickly. Another wave of pleasure hit, and she gasped, pushing back, wanting all of him at once, grappling for grip on the slick shower tile as he let out a guttural groan and started hammering his hips into her. She wanted it hard, and she held on to the wall in anticipation, the noise from their skin smacking together echoing off the tile.

"More," she rasped, and he slammed her harder. She couldn't get enough, and she turned her head to see him. The effort to keep up the pace was evident across the corded muscles of his neck, his slick hair falling over closed eyes, completely surrendered to the moment. When he opened his eyes, they threw fire, glittering and intense. He moved a hand over her ass, his thumb caressing, spreading wetness over the opening. A small "yes" escaped her lips as the sensation sent a shot of pleasure through her, not caring what he did as long as he didn't stop. She pressed into him as he plunged his thumb inside her, stroking in time with his cock.

She came immediately, fiercer than the last one, bucking into him, screaming his name, slapping the wall. That was a first too. She'd never had someone do that before. She liked it. A lot.

"Oh my God. Josh! Come, come with me!" Spasms rocked her entire abdomen, her hand finding her own nub and stroking to prolong it.

The water sprayed everywhere as he thrust one more time, burying himself to the hilt, his own body shaking with relief. Holding her shoulders as he leaned into her, he gasped her name, the water still hot against both of them. Exhausted and spent, they leaned against the wall for a moment, their breath echoing in the bathroom, competing with the hiss of the shower head.

She'd never be able to forget the look on his face, or how his hands felt pushing and probing, gripping her with more than just strength. It had been possessive and primal. She turned, leaning against the tile, and he pulled her close, the hot water cascading over them, stinging her chafed skin.

After a few moments, they finished showering. Gretchen staggered toward the bed, pulled the blankets back, and fell onto it, her towel falling to the floor. She rolled onto her back, her modesty forgotten. Landing beside her on his stomach, Josh braced his head on his hand and they just looked at each other. It was perfect and simple, and her heart nearly burst.

"You know I've never done that before," she finally said, filling the quiet. Honesty was important, right? He'd been honest with her about the condoms, and now it was her turn.

"What?" he asked, settling in, a hand coming to caress her gently, tracing the curve of her breasts, following down her stomach to her leg, then back up. It was soothing, and her muscles were so tired they just melted under his touch.

"The thing you did with your thumb."

He raised his eyebrows. "No? Was it okay? I'm—"

"I pretty much told you to do it, don't you remember?"

"Yeah, I do." His eyes got dark with desire, and he pulled her toward him until they were completely wrapped together. Somehow, he managed to drag the comforter over them, and she cocooned herself in his arms.

"I think you might have liked it," he murmured.

"I think I might have," Gretchen replied, her eyes drooping. She was exhausted. It was late and she had a full plate tomorrow.

Josh let out a massive, contented sigh, tucked her into his shoulder, and she closed her eyes. She could hear his heartbeat, could feel him breathing, the scent of body wash fresh on his skin.

The thought entered her head again that she was falling in love and there was absolutely nothing she could do about it. She reached out and put her hand over his heart, and his came to join hers. She'd deal with that hurdle tomorrow.

"Goodnight, my little firecracker," he rumbled, as she settled completely safe in his arms.

"Goodnight," she mumbled back.

He said something else that she couldn't decipher, but she let it go as she fell asleep.

chapter 8

The large conference hall of the Mandalay Bay was cavernous, even with the crowd of people filling the space. Sommeliers, winery owners, and buyers milled about with notepads and sheets of wine listings, the echo of conversations filling the air around Gretchen with a nervous energy.

Shining bottles of wine with trophies of etched crystal bristled up on tables scattered around the room, white tablecloths glowing in the fluorescent light. When they arrived, she explained to Josh how there were categories for each varietal and blend. A section for reds, a section for whites, New World, Old World, champagne, even a category for organic.

"What is the difference between Old and New World?" Josh asked. "Aren't they all just wine, based on the grape?"

"Old World is Europe, Africa, Middle East; New World is

everywhere else. Like the U.S., Australia," she answered, pointing to various tables. "The grapes can be very similar, but vineyards in say, Italy, are centuries old now compared to ones from California. The age of the vine can make a huge difference in the grape, as does the generational knowledge of an Old World winery."

"So how does a wine from Niagara even compete with that?" he asked.

"That's why the categories are split. Equal representation, right? Comparing a Chardonnay from France to one from newer wineries wouldn't be fair," she said, gesturing at the results list he had in his hand.

"This is big business, isn't it?"

"A win here can set up a winemaker and vineyard for huge financial gain. Everyone from *Wine Spectator* to Michelin-star chefs take notice."

"Wow. I had no idea," he murmured.

Gretchen continued carefully cataloging all the tables with her phone. With each picture she took, she checked to ensure she got the labels front and center, so she could crop to a picture of the bottle for her customers. Full results with judging commentary would be posted later for her to download from the competition site, but this was a fast way of grabbing results to summarize later.

People wanted a jump on the ordering process, and she needed to be ready with her own selections to fire off by email to her bigger clients. Buyers and reps would be meeting right outside the doors of the hall, wheeling and dealing long before the tasting this afternoon.

"Why are you taking pictures?" Josh asked at one point. Not many others were, most of them scribbling on notepads or holding result sheets, circling their choices.

"Easier than taking notes, and I can fire off a photo to a client from a text faster than an email," she replied and took a spontaneous picture of him. He instantly smiled, reminding her how practiced he was at having his picture taken.

"Smart," he murmured and moved forward to peer at another table.

When he'd asked if he could accompany her, Gretchen worried he would be bored out of his mind wandering a hall filled with hoity-toity wine people, but the chance to let him see her world was too good to pass up. As she bumped into people she knew, he stayed with her, touching the small of her back, asking questions that were surprisingly analytical.

People had noticed him, a few murmured glances his way. Each time someone recognized him, he would shake hands without hunched shoulders or slight frown. It wasn't uncommon for sports figures or celebrities to attend these things; she'd seen her share in the past. She breathed a sigh of relief because he was smiling.

Normally, wandering the results tables at a competition like this was relaxing, but it eluded her today, her nerves zapping every time they touched. As they wound through the crowd, she wanted to stake her claim as other women noticed him. He wasn't hers. She wanted him to be.

Standing for most of the morning was wearing on her and she was anxious to be done so they could go sit and have a coffee and brunch. Sharla would likely insist. Hissing quietly, she stretched her back, her muscles stiff and slightly sore. She swore everyone could tell what she and Josh had been up to in bed.

Gretchen felt like a completely different woman. Awakened, like part of her spirit had lain dormant until this man had come along and broken some sort of barrier in her ability to feel. She'd never expected to have a spontaneous affair, let alone with Josh, and she wondered if she could ever go back to the way it was before. Before him, before she'd been shown how good it could feel with the right person. How many times had she gone through the motions with other men, and it was satisfying but . . . boring? Too many.

Sharla was just behind them, tired and rumpled, arriving just as Gretchen had expected—with the same clothes as the day before and her hair hastily pulled into a bun. Thankfully, she didn't have to impress distributors—they were all eager to do business with the earl. She could hand out cards with orders on them while wearing a sack and they would still ring her up.

She stopped at the New World Pinot Noir table, conscious to catalog the ones that had scored well. All her clients wanted pinots from California. They sold well—sometimes double any other red—especially merlot. But then, cheap shiraz from Australia was normally a better seller than merlot from California, which irritated her. Merlot, when done right, was a far superior grape to a hastily casked cabernet sauvignon and one of her favorites. She tried to ensure at least one merlot was on the menus she devised with her clients.

"Look at this one," Sharla said as she snuck up behind her, pointing to a smaller winery from the Lodi area. "It got a ninety-two. Buy it now, or it's going to triple in price by next pressing."

Gretchen snapped a photo of the bottle. "Are you buying now too?"

"His Lordship wants seventeen cases of the damned stuff. I'll have to try it, but he's demanding I just order it, no tasting. I hope it stinks like plonk."

Gretchen looked at her friend. "Everything okay between you and Himself?"

"Yeah, yeah. Don't mind me. No sleep makes me cranky. I'm hangry too. Food? I see you brought your arm candy along today," she deflected. Gretchen's bullshit meter went off, but Sharla would only share when she was ready, and she let it go.

"Yes. How was your Iowa farm boy this morning?" Gretchen clapped back, changing the subject slightly as they moved down the table to look at some other reds, Sharla scribbling notes as they went. Josh had wandered farther away, looking at something else, and he turned back and flashed a smile at her, halting her thoughts of anything but him. How did he do that?

"Ryan is fine. We both agreed it was a one-night thing. He's a sweet boy. Definitely a bull in the sack, but you know, those farm boys."

Gretchen let out a snort of laughter, and several snotty older people turned and frowned at them. They giggled and moved on. Josh joined them.

"Good morning, Sharla," he said.

"Jesus, Mr. Sunshine. Dial it down. Some of us didn't get any sleep."

Josh raised an eyebrow at her cheeky response. Gretchen braced for tension between them.

"Is my outfielder going to make it to the game tomorrow? You didn't kill him, did you?" he replied. Sharla looked back, her eyes wide, and then let out a huge laugh, earning more annoyed looks from people around them.

Phew. If Josh could handle Sharla when she was hungry, tired, and cranky, he was definitely doing well.

"He's sleeping it off. He's not too damaged," Sharla retorted, then pointed. "One more table, Gretch, then we can go eat. Please? I'm going to die if I don't get some coffee and carbs."

They finished their circuit of the room and left, Josh automatically grabbing Gretchen's hand as they made their way out into the hallway beside the main conference room.

"Tastings start at four," Gretchen said, looking at the itinerary. "It's only ten."

"Food. Now," Sharla grouched.

"I know a great breakfast place," he said. "Come on, ladies."

She had to talk to him, but had no idea when she could, given their schedule was a bit packed on the last day of the competition. Maybe she could stay a few days or travel with him to Bakersfield or give herself a mini vacation down the coast while he was away. She played out the scenarios in her head as they walked. None of them were ideal, but she had to find a way.

"You okay?" he asked. "Need a minute?"

"I'm fine, just need coffee," she replied.

"We'll get a chance to maybe talk later?" he added quietly, leaning into her. "I was wondering if—"

"You two are just too much, okay?" Sharla admonished. "Enough puppy dog eyes! Honestly. Let's go. Breakfast waits for no man, even if he's a hot shot pro ball player." She dragged them both forward before he could finish.

. . .

The Peppermill was one of the most iconic breakfast places in Vegas. The gaudy disco era décor and a menu longer than some novels meant anyone could get whatever they wanted whenever they wanted. Gretchen hadn't been there in a long time and was thrilled when Josh had suggested it. She was ravenous as well. The muffin and bad hotel coffee had not been enough.

Sharla was buried in the menu and Josh had his arm around her. The waitress brought their coffees, then looked up at Josh with surprise.

"You're Joshua Malvern, aren't you?" she asked.

"Last time I checked, yeah," he replied.

"Oh wow. Can you sign my bill pad?" she said, sliding it out of her apron and onto the table, clicking her pen. "I go to all the Neons games. So much fun this year, especially with you back now."

He signed it, a professional, pasted-on smile on his lips despite his rigid body. He clearly didn't like being intruded upon in private moments. Gretchen wondered if she'd gone with her first idea of getting his autograph if she'd be here right now, on one of the headiest and most unbelievable adventures of her life. She'd clearly shocked him out of his normal response with the abnormal greeting.

"Thanks for your support," he said and handed it back to her, with her pen. "Glad you are enjoying the season."

The waitress gave him a slow, flirty glance, and then took their orders. The aroma of coffee was wafting as steaming cups appeared, and Sharla said some unintelligible words as she cradled the cup in her hands, making Josh laugh. Gretchen felt like she was in some alternate reality. Normally, right now she'd be typing up her notes to send off to various clients, deep into her own analysis, and making a list of wines to taste. Essentially being a boring, simple workaholic while in one of the most hedonistic places in the world. She couldn't care less about that right now. She wanted to sit in this booth, under Josh's arm forever.

She handed the creamer cups to him on instinct, and he chuckled as he took the bowl from her, their fingers brushing and sending thrills through her stomach.

"I never did ask you how you knew what to put in my coffee at the airport."

"I read it somewhere, maybe?" Gretchen answered. "Honestly, I didn't think about it, I just ordered."

Josh hummed at that, and she wondered if he would find that too intrusive. When he didn't respond, she relaxed. He opened one of the tiny cups, pouring it into his coffee, and she watched him, enthralled by the little things. She could watch him do up his shoes, or make his coffee, and she would be a happy woman.

"So. Josh. Did Gretchen here tell you that you're on her *Fuck List*?"

Gretchen looked up at Sharla, confused. Her what? Then it dawned on her. Oh, no . . . that *Fuck List*.

Gretchen turned to her friend, trying to remain as calm as possible. Maybe if she didn't make a big deal out of it, he'd laugh it off. "Oh, that list. Ha-ha. Right. Shar, that was *ages* ago!"

"Her what?" Josh asked, one eyebrow raised. His fingers stroking her shoulder stopped. "A fuck list?"

"Oh yes. When we were in college, we made up lists of famous guys we would like to have our way with," Sharla said, winking. "You were at the top of that list, my friend. She was so obsessed! The year you became a Sixer, man, oh man. I tell you—"

Gretchen sent a pleading look to Sharla, who was ignoring her. She obviously thought it was funny. Would Josh? This was bordering on embarrassing.

Josh looked at her, his eyebrows raised. "Really?"

Gretchen laughed nervously, her face heating. "Well this is

uhhh . . . awkward, but yeah," she muttered. Sharla was stirring more creamer into her coffee, not catching Gretchen's growing discomfort.

"She'd seen you at some game in Boston when she'd gone down with friends. I had no idea who you were, but she said you were ridiculously sexy."

"I am, am I?" he remarked, his eyes sliding to Gretchen. He seemed okay, but he was giving off a wary vibe.

"Yeah. The criteria was it had to be a celebrity—or sports player, in this case—that we were allowed to have a one-night stand with. Kinky, no-holds-barred, monkey-sex kind of thing. Even if we were married or had a steady guy. Like a 'free pass' to be naughty. These are the guys who you'd never in a million years marry but would be good for hot sex in a fancy hotel or something—"

"So, the whole coffee thing was to get in my pants?" Josh asked. He removed his arm and picked up his coffee with the hand that had been around her.

"No, no it wasn't like that—" Gretchen replied quickly.

"Oh, come on, like she'd pass up an opportunity to be with you, Mr. Sunshine. You're hot and her favorite," Sharla interrupted, laughing.

"Sharla. Please," Gretchen whispered, her face so hot she knew her cheeks were likely crimson. This had now passed embarrassing, was bordering on humiliating, and made her sound like she did this all the time.

He stiffened, the grin from not a moment before gone. He cleared his throat uncomfortably. Sharla looked at Gretchen, then at Josh, and her face went white.

"I figured you'd told him," she offered, a worried look stealing over her. "I mean, it wasn't like you'd ever actually do it. It was all in fun, right? You're not the type to roll in the hay on a whim, Gretch."

"She isn't, is she? Couldn't tell," Josh said drily.

"Oh. Shit . . . look—" Sharla stammered.

Gretchen couldn't take it and panicked. The connection they had, the idea that maybe she could see him again after this, it would all be in question now. What would he think of her? That she'd been playing him, that's what. She was going to be sick, the earlier hastily eaten muffin swirling around in her stomach. She shot to her feet and mumbled something about needing to pee, running toward the bathrooms, a hand over her mouth.

*   *   *

Josh watched her leave, his mouth dry. She'd planned all this? Did he just get taken advantage of? Was it all an act?

"Josh. You have to know she'd never intentionally mislead someone. Gretch is—"

He held up a hand, stopping her. "Is what? Let me get this straight. She's known about me since my rookie year, I'm on some sort of 'monkey-sex' list you two cooked up, and she apparently has followed my career closely enough to—"

"Well yes, you're at the top of the list, but—" Sharla spluttered. "Listen, it was stupid, objectifying men we thought were fuckable, you know?"

"No, I don't know," Josh clipped. His mind was desperately trying to pull the pieces together. "So, I'm what, the score she gets to brag about when she gets home?"

105

"I didn't say that, Josh," Sharla replied. "It was a long time ago, and anyone with eyes in their head can see you two are—"

"Are what? Tomorrow's tabloid fodder?" The sick feeling in his stomach pushed the anger he tried so hard to control up into his throat and he ground his molars as he processed. He had to keep his shit together.

He'd been falling for Gretchen. He was going to ask her to stay with him at the end of this to figure out what they meant to each other. Was it all a lie? His chest seized when he thought that. He'd thought she was—he let out an angry groan. He thought there was something serious happening between them.

"Jesus," he ground out, the crazy notion taking over his emotions, "Harv is going to kill me for sleeping with a—"

"Sleeping with a what? Who is Harv, and what do you mean he'll kill you?" Sharla peppered questions at him, holding up a hand. "Calm down, Josh, please—"

"Don't tell me to calm down," Josh snapped. He jerked himself up and levered out a couple of twenty-dollar bills from his wallet, throwing them on the table, making Sharla twitch in surprise.

"Let her explain. You've got something here, don't throw it away because of me—" she pleaded, but then stopped when he let the anger win, and leveled a glare at her that sat her back in her seat.

"I always keep my distance from fans who want to manipulate me. I've seen enough good guys get thrown low by women just out for their status and money, their fifteen minutes of fame. You have no idea."

"Now hold on, asshole, she's not—" Sharla snapped hotly, standing up again, but he turned and walked away, steaming out the door, slamming it as he went. If they started arguing, he wasn't sure what he would do, and everyone in the restaurant was already staring.

He stormed into his car, which was parked nearby, pounding the wheel in frustration. He was so churned up he couldn't go back in, still unable to think clearly, so he started driving. Gritting his teeth, he headed out of Vegas, swerving through traffic toward the desert, not caring where he went.

The entire time he pushed on the accelerator, he was at war in his head. He'd jumped to conclusions and should have waited to let Gretchen explain. But his temper and his worry about being manipulated had won, and now . . .

He pulled into a lookout over Lake Mead and killed the engine. There weren't many people there, and he stalked down one of the paths toward the cliffs. Boats cut through the water, their engines revving from a distance. The wind ruffled his hair and he closed his eyes for a moment in the peaceful surroundings, begging for his heart to stop hammering.

He was an idiot. He should go back. Of course, she could explain. But the paralyzing feeling that he'd screwed up was over-whelming. He needed to call Harv and ask him what to do. He felt out of his depth.

His phone rang. He ignored it. Then a text beeped and he fished it out of his pocket to look at it.

Please let me explain. When you are ready. It isn't what you think.

He squeezed the phone in his fist and lowered his head to it. What was he supposed to think? Do? Gretchen was everything he wanted. She'd fit into his world, and everyone liked her. She'd had him in her hand the moment she'd set eyes on him in the airport, and he'd trusted her. Every part of him still wanted to, but his instinct to protect the one thing that had always mattered had irrationally roared to life the moment Sharla put doubt into his head that they'd really connected. He'd wanted a casual rendezvous. A weekend romance. No strings, right?

He'd gotten so much more. He'd been sure she felt it too. But the creeping feeling that he'd been targeted wouldn't go away.

"Fuck," he said out loud and took a deep breath. For the first time, baseball was coming second to his heart, and it was scary as hell.

chapter 9

The room felt too big. Gretchen looked back at the bed, still completely rumpled from last night, and her heart hurt again.

She'd texted Josh when she'd gotten back to her room, and then lost it—messy crying and hugging his pillow, his scent still everywhere. Ruffling through his bag, irrational guilt plying while she did it, she pulled on the sweatshirt wadded up inside. It definitely smelled like him, which made it worse. Or better—she wasn't entirely sure.

He hadn't replied to her text, even though it showed he'd read it. It was over. Not the way she'd wanted it to end. Holding the collar of his sweatshirt up to her nose, she inhaled. It didn't help; she needed to work and focus on something else.

Finishing up her lists and sending a few emails to clients would maybe do the trick, but the idea of setting up her tasting spreadsheet for later seemed tedious. Closing the laptop, she flopped back on the couch, her eyes flitting to the clock near the bed. Two hours before sampling opened. Sharla was in her hotel room, likely sleeping.

Being alone was probably a better idea right now.

She'd come out of the bathroom at the restaurant, determined to make him understand, her tears dried and her face recovering from being a blotchy, red mess after throwing up, berating herself for panicking. But Josh was gone, Sharla hastily rattling on that he was pretty mad. Their food came not long after, and they bundled it to go, calling a taxi to take them back to the hotel.

The whole way, Gretchen was quietly deflated. Sharla apologized over and over, and she finally hushed her with a hug and told her it was okay. It wasn't Sharla's fault Josh had reacted the way he did. She'd never even thought of that stupid list. It was a long time ago. College. They were silly girls back then, no understanding of how their hearts really worked when it came to men because right now, she'd never felt for a man what she felt for Josh, and it was kicking her ass.

Just like she'd realized, it was going to hurt. What-ifs piled into her head one after another until her phone dinged. It was Sharla asking if she wanted to eat before sampling. She typed back a quick *yes, in half?* Sharla replied with a heart emoji.

It was no use stewing or worrying about what she couldn't change. She wouldn't lose her best friend because of a man, no matter how badly her heart was broken. Sharla—even if she was clueless about other people's feelings unless you bluntly spelled them out—was her person. Gretchen couldn't imagine life without her. She would get over Josh. It would just take time.

A knock at the door pulled her out of her thoughts and she

rubbed her face, padding to the door to open it. An older man stood there, a worn leather laptop bag over one shoulder. He had salt-and-pepper hair and a perfectly trimmed beard and was wearing a simple sports jacket and jeans. She blinked. Who in the heck was this?

"May I help you?" she asked.

"Miss Harper, I'm Harvey, Mr. Malvern's agent."

"How did you get up here without a key card?" she challenged, ready to slam the door.

"Josh gave me the room number yesterday morning to call when I arrived, and I was able to make my way up. May I come in?"

She was going to have words with the front staff about that later, if anything could be done. This kind of thing likely happened all the time in a big hotel like the Luxor. But, despite the obvious security breach, she was curious as to what he had to say, so she stepped aside and gestured in. He moved past Gretchen into the room, taking her in.

"You're her," he said quietly. "I completely understand now."

She thinned her lips, ignoring his observation. He must be here to ask her not to extort Josh or make sure she signed something that would keep him safe. Damage control. Which he'd likely done countless times before. Her frustration bubbled, thinking that Josh couldn't come himself to get his things, that he'd sent someone else to do the dirty task.

"I wanted to—"

"Save it," she interrupted. "I don't want anything. Take his things and go, since he likely asked you to do that too."

She pulled off his sweatshirt and flung it at him, Harvey catching it, surprise on his face. She stomped over to his bag, stuffed everything into it, and slammed it on the floor in front of him.

111

"He doesn't know I'm here."

She stopped short and put her hands on her hips. "Then why are you here?"

"Josh called to inform me of what happened. I decided to come over on my own."

"You clean up his problems, I assume?" she replied, not ready to believe him, wanting to be spiteful. She went on the defensive again. Who did he think he was, coming in here, accusing her of . . . what exactly?

"Never had to. Josh has never gotten himself into a mess before."

A mess? This was a mess? Gretchen's heart hurt, and she rubbed at her chest with her fingers, willing the lump to go away. She'd gone into this with eyes open or so she'd thought. She'd been deluding herself, thinking he would want more. That she could have more.

"For the record, young lady, this isn't a mess. I think this is a misunderstanding."

Her shoulders slumped. Today was already exhausting. She ran her hands through her hair and turned back to the man who had followed her toward the sitting area.

"I see how he hates the attention," she said, sitting. "How he stiffens every time someone approaches him to ask for an autograph or to fawn over him. He worries about getting trapped by superfans. I just . . . how do I explain it? It wasn't anything other than I recognized a good baseball player having a bad day, who needed a coffee, and it went from there—"

Harvey sat beside her and patted her hand, which surprised her. He caught her eye.

"I know, I know. Joshua has a temper, and it gets the best of him sometimes. He tends to leap to conclusions when the stakes are high, and he's protective of his privacy, as you said. Sometimes he shoots himself in the foot. Most times, it's served him well."

"I didn't mean to upset him. I didn't lie," Gretchen murmured. Tears were close again. She did not want to cry in front of this man, and she pinched the bridge of her nose to lock the tears away. She looked up as he handed her a tissue.

"I can see he's had an effect on you," he added. "You aren't the first girl—"

She held up a hand. "Stop. I don't want to hear it."

Harvey lapsed into silence.

Gretchen dabbed at her nose and willed the tears to stay put. "The past two days have been a bit of a roller coaster. We've only just met. We don't know each other. I understand how Josh would assume the worst based on what my friend said."

"Of course. These situations can get out of hand, can't they?" he offered.

She sniffled again, and he cleared his throat, patting her hand again. He seemed like he was attempting to be kind, she thought. It wasn't his fault all this had unraveled, but it was his job to see to his player.

"Thank you," she said. "I hope he can understand I'm not like that. It wasn't my intention."

"I'll let him know when I speak to him. You fly home tomorrow, I assume?" he asked, standing up.

She caught the meaning in that statement and thinly veiled question. Of course, Harvey was here to see her and soften the blow. He was preemptively protecting his player, deflecting him back to his job, and she could derail that. He wanted her to let go and never see him again. It was better for Josh this way.

She nodded curtly. Message received.

"Right. Thank you, Ms. Harper. I'll see myself out."

Harvey picked up Josh's duffel. He hesitated, and they eyed each other. He walked back to her, gently placing the Neons sweatshirt beside her on the couch.

"Chin up, Ms. Harper. Things have a way of working out."

He let himself out of the room as she picked up the sweatshirt and put it in her lap, her fingers tracing the embroidered Neons logo.

That thought lingered as she flopped sideways on the couch, wadding up his sweatshirt under her head as a pillow. *Things.* What things exactly? She assumed he meant she'd go back to her life, Josh would get on with his, and order would return to the universe.

With all the emotions flying through her head, one thought pierced through the fog when the door clicked closed. No matter what, Josh had changed something in her this weekend, and she could never go back to what she was.

She didn't want to.

. . .

Josh drove into his parking spot beside his villa, exhausted and emotionally drained. He was going to call her the moment he got inside; the rental Harv had arranged didn't have hands-free. Hopefully, if she was available, he'd convince her to meet somewhere and just talk. He owed her an explanation and an apology.

He'd already called Harv as he sat on the bluff overlooking the lake, looking for advice. Harv had been curt on the phone, saying he was with another client but would get back to him. He hadn't yet and it had been a couple of hours.

He didn't see Harv sitting on one of the wicker chairs until he was opening his door and jumped when Harv cleared his throat.

"Harv! Jesus, man," Josh wheezed and looked over. His heart stopped.

His duffel from the hotel was at Harv's feet. Which meant he'd been to the Luxor, and he'd seen Gretchen. His temper flared, but he very carefully walked over and sat in the other chair, willing himself not to explode at his agent. Everything inside him was screaming to be angry, to go find her, explain that he hadn't sent Harv. He could only imagine how pissed she must have been.

"You went to see her?" he asked instead, flexing his fingers over the ends of the armrests. White paint flaked off onto his knee.

"I did. She's quite a woman. I understand what drew you to her," Harv said. Josh leveled his eyes at Harv, and the two men stared at one another for a heartbeat.

"She was my responsibility. I know I called you, I needed advice, but that didn't mean you needed to—"

"It's done, son. She understands you need to focus on why you are here, not on some romance that wasn't going to end well," he interrupted, and Josh sat back.

"You didn't say that, did you? Holy shit, Harv, you crossed the line," Josh snapped and stood. "I should call her and explain."

"Sit down."

Josh glared at his agent, his friend of how many years? They'd never had to deal with a misguided fan before, but Josh had heard the stories of some of the disasters Harv had waded into in the past. He slumped and sat back down. Harv was going on the assumptions of a hundred other situations. He didn't know Gretchen or how Josh had felt for her. Harv looked up from his phone as Josh ran his hands through his hair and let out a frustrated growl. *Dammit.*

"Did you offer her money? Did you make her sign anything?" Josh asked as the thought occurred to him. *Please God, I hope not*, he thought. The thought of her having to sign something as distasteful as an NDA made him feel ill. She wasn't that kind of woman, despite his knee-jerk reaction in the diner.

"No, no. I didn't. She was very reasonable. She understood that it was in your best interest, and hers, if she left and let it go," Harv replied. "I am your representative, Josh. I take care of what needs taking care of when you need me. You've been my best-behaved client, but that does not mean I will give you a free pass."

"I didn't need you to handle it," Josh groused.

"But I did, and now you can work on getting yourself better and back up into rotation. I didn't do this to spite you; I did this because if I didn't, you'd never be rid of her and that would be a death blow to what's left of your career. Your head needs to be 100 percent focused."

That was a speech from Harv, and Josh sat back as his agent stood and dropped the duffel at his feet.

"Get your shit figured out, and then you can think about love, son," Harv said as a cab pulled up. "I'll talk to you soon."

Josh kicked the duffel and lay back on the chair as Harv left, exhausted and overwhelmed. Something in him had changed this weekend—Gretchen had pulled him out of the eat, sleep, ball routine he'd chained himself to since his call up. His heart had made decisions for him for the first time in a long, long time.

The wine all tasted flat. It wasn't; Gretchen knew that, and she followed Sharla's notes for each wine they smelled, swirled, and tasted. It would be important for her write-ups later, and she needed something to go by when she recommended a wine other than *it's red*. She trusted Sharla's palate; they'd had very similar notes all through college.

Her heart just wasn't in it. She needed a good night's sleep and wanted to go home.

"Honey, we can go. I think we have what we need," Sharla murmured as Gretchen poured the last of the white she'd tasted into the spit bucket beside the table.

"Okay."

They abandoned their tasting glasses at the door, and Sharla linked their arms as they left, wordlessly tugging Gretchen outside to walk the strip, burning off the buzz of tasting so much wine all at once. The lights and the people talking and laughing were muted. Normally, she loved walking the strip close to dark, taking in the sights and people watching, but now?

"Shar, I think I just need to get some sleep. My flight out is in the morning."

"Can't you stay? I'm meeting His Lordship in L.A. tomorrow, then we're flying to Bordeaux with some investors. Something about a new winery that is doing this wacky thing—transplanting California vines back to Bordeaux to see how they've changed. He wants to see it for himself and maybe invest in the experiment. You could come with us? You'd love it."

Gretchen shook her head. As enticing as that sounded, she just wanted to get back to her apartment, curl up in a ball, and nurse her broken heart. Then she could move on and return to a normal life. The sooner she could do that, the better.

"I'll be busy with meetings. I have to get lists set up with a few of the restaurant groups. Some good picks came out of this."

They walked some more, silent, then Sharla stopped dead. Gretchen looked at her, and she was pursing her lips. "Is it because of me and my stupid big mouth? Are you mad?"

"No!" Gretchen protested loudly, and people turned to see what was going on. She picked up her friend's arm again and they kept walking. "No," she repeated softly. "Never. You're my best friend, and I love you. I am not angry. It's just a misunderstanding."

"You were—" Sharla started, but Gretchen waved her other hand, stopping her.

"Josh was my first weekend fling, and I got in over my head. I stopped thinking with that head, Shar. I have to move on. In the long run, it would have never worked anyway."

Sharla made an irritated noise but didn't respond. She tugged Gretchen over toward the M&M's store and they bought some chocolate to share. They strolled over to the Venetian, and Sharla paid for a gondola ride, parking themselves in the boat, arm in arm. Sharla turned the conversation back to simple things, like upcoming trips and their plans for autumn. Gretchen relaxed and let the tension go. It was time with Sharla, and she would make the most of it.

"Do you want to get together for the Beaujolais nouveau release?" Sharla asked when they had exited the gondola and were headed back up the strip.

"I suppose. What are your plans?"

"His Lordship wants to go to Les Sarmentelles this year. It's in November. Come with us."

France. Les Sarmantelles. Where the new releases were celebrated every November with fresh Gamay wine. Somewhat of a
pilgrimage many sommeliers made at some point in their careers.
Could she afford it? Gretchen thought for a moment, and Sharla
laughed.

"He'll pay for it, you ninny. Please say yes. I want to see more
of you. I miss you. Plus, I need someone to run interference. If I
am alone with the earl somewhere like that, I might murder him."

How could Gretchen say no? If anything had come out of this
absolutely insane weekend, it was her priorities to herself and her
confidence to go with the flow more. Gretchen let out a chuckle,
then it devolved into them both laughing like fools. Her eyes
watering, she hugged Sharla as hard as she could.

"Okay. I'll come."

. . .

The bus seat was uncomfortable and the music was irritating.
They were on their way to Bakersfield. It was late, and Josh
was tired and preoccupied.

Well, not preoccupied, more like mad as hell at himself. He'd
never answered Gretchen's text. He'd been talked out of calling
her by Harv and had listened to his advice. It had been a few days,
and the ache in him about how it had ended had gotten worse,
not faded with concentration on his game and finding a new club
to join.

Now that he was here, on a damned bus, headed toward an
away game, it hit Josh again. She was in his every thought. He
dreamed about her. He replayed their two brief nights together.
He'd been a fool and now it was too late.

Harv had called not fifteen minutes ago telling him there was an offer to trade him to the American League West Texas team for some draft picks or cash, but it wasn't a done deal yet. Maybe that was why he was thinking about her.

Texas. He wouldn't mind living in Dallas, he supposed, but it was farther away from where he wanted to be, which was back in Toronto. Why did he want to go back there? He could play ball anywhere, even if leaving the Sixers sucked because it was the best organization he'd ever played for and had wanted to retire out of.

Gretchen was there. It would be reason enough to find her. That door was closed now, and it was shitty. He'd let his fears and temper get in the way of how he'd felt about her. Instead of trusting her like he had when they'd met, he'd blown it.

Get your shit figured out and then you can think about love, son, echoed in his head over and over. It was the right thing to do. Let her go.

"You okay, Josh?" Neptune asked, sitting beside him. "You're grinding your chiclets good, man."

He sighed and frowned, shaking his head at him. "Yeah, man. Fine. Just fucking tired."

Neptune chuckled and grinned. "Coach says that blond who was with you was the real deal. Said you'd quit ball for her. She coming up to watch you again?"

Josh looked out the window, swallowing the lump that formed in his throat. She was the real deal, and he'd let her slip right through his fingers.

"No, man. She's long gone. Seems she wasn't, I guess, eh?"

Neptune hummed in understanding and then patted Josh's thigh, smiling again.

"She'll be back, man. She'll be back," he said, and then they lapsed into silence, watching the desert slide by.

TWO MONTHS LATER

chapter 10

The Toronto stadium still felt the same, but now Josh was viewing it from the visiting team's bench. He finished lacing his cleats and stepped out onto the turf, hearing the familiar echo of the Sixers already out on the field warming up, making him nostalgic.

He saw Timo and waved. Javier nodded at him. Other players gave their hellos. They couldn't be seen talking to one another before the game, but after, they planned to meet up for drinks. He'd missed their antics. The time he'd been here had given him good friends, even if they were on different teams now.

He grabbed a spot near the rest of his team and began his warm-up stretches. It wasn't long before he was staring up into the stands, wondering if she'd be there to watch.

It had been two months of constant effort, and Josh had focused all his energy on his game. The trade had gone through with Texas after a couple of weeks with the Neons, and he'd taken it reluctantly. He was sorry to leave, if for nothing else than he felt like he contributed to the team; he liked the boys and he enjoyed being a quasi-coach.

"We'd sign you on as a coach in a hot minute, you hear me?" Felicia had murmured in his ear as he'd hugged her goodbye. "Travis won't say it, so I will. You fit here, young man."

It had hit Josh square in the gut as he walked out of the stadium that he really did fit there, but it was time to focus on heading back up to the majors. If he stayed healthy, he'd earn a decent amount of money with the Longhorns. Harv had consulted him about possibly staying another year, then cashing in, or maybe going for more money as a free agent.

For his first game back in the majors, Josh had two hits and an RBI. But instead of celebrating that night, he dragged himself back to the apartment they'd put him in and stared at his phone, looking at her text. He wanted to tell her about the game. He wanted to see her again, and the hollow space that ached whenever he thought about her pulsed as he hovered his fingers over the screen of his phone. He didn't do Facebook or Twitter, but he had lurked on her professional accounts, chickening out every time he thought about pressing the Follow buttons.

Finally, he'd fallen asleep without diving down the rabbit hole and had dreamed about her, remembering her laugh, her hair bouncing and shining, fiery blond and tousled. Her eyes over the rim of her coffee cup, giving him goosebumps. How she'd felt in his arms, surrounding him, letting him in.

He blinked, coming out of his thoughts, as his glove was tossed at him.

"Yo, Malvern, get up. Toss me a few."

He nodded at his teammate, a young guy named Ryder who was a cocky newbie. He'd dived headfirst into the stands at their last game to get a catch. He was lucky he hadn't killed himself.

As Josh tossed the ball, he realized he was getting old. Thirty-two was young in the outside world, but in baseball terms, he was practically elderly. But didn't he do crazy shit like that in his rookie year in Boston?

"What's it like to be back here?" Ryder asked him as they finished up the tosses and headed back toward the dugout. Fifteen minutes to game time.

"It's familiar, but not, you know?" he said noncommittally.

"Got any strategies? You know these guys."

"You know it already, we went over all that this morning, right?" Josh replied testily and sighed. Ryder's enthusiasm shouldn't irritate him so much. "Sorry, a bit on edge."

"All good, my man. We did, so my bad. I'm glad you're here to help us," Ryder replied.

With that, they parted, Ryder parking in his spot on the bench, Josh standing at the fence, craning his neck to look into the stands, feeling the warmth of the sun on his face. With the dome open, there would be a bit of glare. Reaching into his back pocket for his glare patches, his eyes roved the stands once more, and he saw her.

Gretchen was taking a seat at field level, with a really good-looking guy dressed in a Sixers jersey and a brand-new hat with an unbent rim beside her. She was in the front row, just past third. Despite the people around them, he'd know her anywhere, and it was as if the crowd around her was non-existent. They were talking and laughing, Gretchen pointing, obviously explaining something to the guy. Jealousy flashed through Josh as the man put his arm around the back of her seat.

Josh attempted to calm down as he stuffed the emotion back. She wasn't his; he had no right to be jealous.

Standing at the dugout fence, he stared at her, watching her move—the way she gestured, how her eyes squinted as she shaded them to look around. *Dammit.* His stomach turned over the protein shake he'd slammed back after his morning workout. She'd moved on or was at least on some sort of date.

Then Sharla came into view, her arms loaded with popcorn. Maybe this wasn't a date, after all.

Sharla laughed and sorted the food she was balancing, getting popcorn everywhere. Josh sighed, remembering the last moments in the Peppermill. It hadn't been her fault. He wished he could tell her that because he'd upset her with his behavior as well. Not his finest moment.

The past two months had given him time to come to grips with his own stupidity, examining the instinctual reflex of protection roaring to the surface the moment Sharla had mentioned the damned list. So many women had tried—and failed—to get to him because of who he was. He'd steeled his heart from all of them, never connecting on any deeper level. Until her. Maybe that was why it hurt so much two months later. He'd connected with Gretchen, and he should have trusted that connection.

He'd fucked up. Not her.

Sharla sat down, and with the way the man looked at Sharla, Josh's jealousy vanished. He wasn't there with Gretchen. Sharla handed him a popcorn wordlessly, which made the man chuckle, tossing a few kernels into his mouth.

Josh's eyes darted back to Gretchen, drawn to her like a magnet. She was still just as fucking beautiful. She looked happy. She looked—

Fuck. He was going to lose it if he didn't get his head back in the game. He stalked down into the locker room before taking some deep, deep breaths. He had to put her aside and make it fucking work because he was left field tonight. She'd be right there. He could reach out and touch her if a ball went sideways.

"You okay, man?" another of his new teammates, Guy, asked as they passed each other.

"Yeah. Just feeling a bit off, you know? Coming back here. I'll nut up in a minute."

"Whatevs, dude, they're calling for lineups."

Josh shook himself off and cracked his neck, willing calm. He walked back out through to the dugout and took his place on the line, waiting for his name to be called and the game to begin.

.   .   .

Gretchen froze as Josh's name was announced.

"Shit," Sharla swore, and Kevin, beside her, looked at them, confused.

"What's going on?" he asked.

Sharla shook her head and leveled her eyes at her boss. "Move."

Kevin scrambled out of her way, and Sharla put her arm around Gretchen protectively as she sat down. Gretchen was locked on to Josh out on the field, watching him wave, relaxed and nonchalant.

She wanted to cry. She'd read that he had been traded to Texas right before the trade deadline, but it had slipped her mind when she'd booked the last-minute tickets. It hadn't even registered it was his team in the fuss to get good seats and get there in time.

Of course, in the weeks after Vegas, she'd combed the internet for details on him, obsessing, even though she didn't want to. Eventually, she'd had to be quite firm with herself and refrain from looking him up. Move on, put him behind her. The first Sixers home game had been hard, but she'd done well and had only cried after she'd said goodbye to the friends she'd come with. None of them knew about Josh. It was too personal.

Now here he was. Of course, he was positioned at left field today, and she was sitting almost directly across from where he would be standing. Her heart was in her mouth and she clutched her best friend to keep from shaking. Thank goodness she was here and in town with her boss. Kevin and Sharla were headed to a winery in Niagara he had a share in, and they'd made sure to see her when they flew in. It had been Gretchen who had offered to take them to a game, thinking Sharla's British boss might like to go.

"Do we need to leave?" Sharla whispered in her ear. "I am sure His Lordship here will understand."

"No. No. Just give me a minute," she said weakly. "Does he know?"

Sharla shook her head, and Gretchen sighed in relief. The fewer people who knew about her botched love life, the better. They stood for the anthems, and she barely heard them, watching him look studiously anywhere but over her way.

"Can I borrow your hat, Kevin?" she asked. "The glare is hitting my eyes and I forgot mine today."

"Of course," he clipped in his perfect British accent and handed it over. "Here you go. The crowd is quite wonderful, the energy!"

It was Kevin's first time at an American baseball game. Despite the fact that Gretchen wanted to panic and run away, she was enjoying his reaction to one of her favorite places. He was a happy, playful, and gorgeous man, and she wondered why Sharla was cross with him all the time. She jammed the hat over her head, tucking up her hair, and Sharla traded over her Audrey Hepburn-esque sunglasses for Gretchen's more subtle shades to complete the look. Hoping it was enough—unless Josh had already seen her—Gretchen shrank down even farther in her seat.

"Hopefully those will help," Sharla whispered in an understanding tone.

The Longhorns were first to bat, and when the bottom of the first inning arrived, Gretchen's mouth went dry as Josh jogged out to his spot on the field. He looked good. Too good. He'd gotten into better shape, if that were possible, and she noticed he was wearing his pant cuffs low tonight, instead of high socks, an outline of a knee brace visible on his left leg. The Texas flag-colored uniform suited his darker hair that was cropped short, instead of a little mussed up, lightened from the sun and curling at his collar. He caught a couple of balls to warm up, his jaw flexing as he chewed on his gum, laughing at something a teammate said.

And so it went. Josh, standing fewer than twenty feet from her when he was in the outfield. Achingly close. She watched his every move, torturing herself as he slid to catch the odd ball, making a double play, throwing hard. He was playing better. His shoulder wasn't locking and the way he could jump meant the brace was helping.

At one point he lifted his hand to acknowledge the two-out sign, and Gretchen let out a little breath, seeing his arm muscles bunch up, reminding her what those arms felt like wrapped around her. Kevin, completely absorbed in the game, hadn't noticed that Sharla was practically holding her up in her seat.

"Three more innings, honey," she said. "We can go early."

Gretchen shook her head. She didn't want to deprive Kevin of his first baseball game. He had offered to buy box seats, but she was the one who had insisted a better experience was at the front, right in the action. *Dammit.*

The very next pitch went foul and hit the low wall right in front of them, bouncing back onto the field. Kevin whooped in surprise, making everyone laugh. They were still giggling when Sharla went abruptly quiet.

A hand was holding out the foul ball right in front of Gretchen, and when she looked up, there he was. His face was serious, but there was that sparkle in his eye and a knowing look. He'd seen her, all right, and now she couldn't breathe or think or even move.

Sharla saved her by picking up the ball from Josh's outstretched hand. Gretchen would have dropped it anyway. Her hands were shaking, and the jumbotron had the camera trained on them. The whole stadium was watching.

"Thanks, Mr. Sunshine," Sharla heckled, palming the ball and handing it to Gretchen without looking.

"Enjoy the game," Josh drawled, his eyes never leaving Gretchen, tipping his hat. He then walked back to his place as if it were an everyday thing—handing a ball to a once-in-a-lifetime fling that had gone horribly wrong.

Gretchen held it to her chest, willing herself to breathe. It was warm and hard. It had just been in his hand, and that made her unable to think. The tears started, and Kevin looked on, confused.

"Shar, why did you call that player Mr. Sunshine? Do you know him? Why is Gretchen crying?"

"It's a long story. Sort of. *Reader's Digest* version, okay? That is her favorite player, he used to play for the Sixers. I think she's just starstruck."

Starstruck, pfft. How about bleeding anew from the massive wound in her heart? She needed to be anywhere but there. The inning was over at that point, and Josh jogged in. She let out a breath.

"Shar? I think I'm going to go use the bathroom," she managed, and handed the ball to Kevin. "Here. A souvenir of your first baseball game. You should have it."

Kevin took it and looked at it, thumbing over the scuff from where the ball and bat had connected. "Lovely—thank you, Gretchen!"

Leaning against a pillar once she was in the concourse, she caught her breath, shaking. In the bathroom, she locked herself into a stall and let out the tears she'd held in since the beginning of the game.

She was not over him. She was nowhere close to being able to put it behind her.

After a few minutes of messy crying and deciding that sitting in a bathroom stall was ridiculous, she got up, washed her face, and touched up her makeup. Pushing through the bathroom door back out into the stadium, she heard the stands erupt as if on cue. Assuming the Sixers had just stopped a runner, Gretchen rushed back to the top of the stands to catch the action. Josh was up to bat. Lord, she had timing.

Her body wanted to turn and run, the visceral reaction to protect her heart rearing up. *Get yourself together, Gretchen!* she thought. It would do no good to fall apart every time she saw him, and she was done with crying and hiding. He wasn't going anywhere, so neither would she. She could handle the last few innings.

"You good?" Sharla asked as she sat back down.

"I'll be all right."

Josh hit a double, and, without thinking, she clapped and cheered when he did. A few people around her looked at her like she was a traitor.

"What? He gave us a game ball!" Sharla snapped, glaring at the people who were booing her. "He used to be a Sixer. Back off," she added for good measure.

A few people muttered but left Gretchen alone after that. Kevin tilted his head.

"Shar, I have a question. That night in Vegas when you were texting me those horrid pictures of you with some baseball team, was your Mr. Sunshine there as well? I think he might have been in the background of one of them."

Gretchen put her head in her hands and groaned. Kevin was an observant man. It made no sense that Sharla had been sending him drunken selfies, but then, Sharla sometimes made no sense, so she hadn't really worried about it then.

"Yes," Sharla said in a clipped tone, then sighed. "We met him with the team he was playing for then, that night. Now butt out."

Kevin raised his hands and sat back but caught Gretchen's eye and she frowned.

"Yes, we met him," she mumbled. "He's . . . he's very nice."

"Ah," was the simple response. Gretchen appreciated his tact right at that moment.

Josh was on second and taking a huge lead off the bag. The

next batter was swinging wild and she figured he wouldn't get much farther, but as soon as the pitcher set up to throw, Josh made his move. He launched forward, the muscles in his legs bunching through the fabric. The batter swung and missed, and the catcher stood and fired it at third the moment the ball was in his glove. As Josh was sliding, the third baseman reached high for the ball. Gretchen held her breath as both Josh and the fielder met in a cloud of red dust toward the bag. Both of them were sprawled, the third baseman stretched out from where he'd had to meet the ball.

"Is he safe?" Kevin asked excitedly. "Good show if so!"

Josh stood and dusted himself off as they waited for the call. The ump signaled him safe and he fist-bumped the third-base coach. The play was instantly replayed on the jumbotron in slow motion. Josh had been mere seconds to the base before the base-man's glove had tapped the bag. Gretchen let out her breath, and as she sat up, clapping politely along with some others in the crowd, he turned and pierced her with a very direct, fierce look that pinned her to the seat.

"Define *safe*," she muttered to herself, because her heart was anything but, thumping wildly the moment their eyes met.

chapter 11

"Good steal tonight, man. You still got it."

Josh waved tiredly at the passing compliment and slumped over, braced on his thighs. He was bone-tired and mentally wiped.

"Thanks, man," he said, not sure who had said it.

He was beating himself up—walking the ball over to her like a magnet pulling him in, letting her know he knew she was there. What was he thinking? She was wearing ridiculous sunglasses and her friend's hat jammed over her head, her gorgeous fire-cracker hair all tucked up under it. She'd sat immobile, her mouth open in surprise as he'd handed her the ball. It was obvious she did not want him to see her there. She'd been hiding, for Christ's sake.

He'd wanted her to take off her glasses so he could see her eyes, but the words stuck in his throat when she'd made a small sound of terror. He would have stood there like an idiot, and thankfully Sharla had diffused the situation as only she could. It had been the cue to get his ass back into the game.

He was not over her yet. Maybe he never would be.

When he'd stolen third, he'd looked back at her without even a thought, and she'd been sitting up in her seat, cheering for him, her sunglasses in her hand, and their eyes met. The heat that had risen in him almost caused him to walk straight off the field and pull her to him, to connect that heat back to its source. But he couldn't, of course, and now she was long gone. He had no idea where she lived in the city, or if she would even want to see him. Her reaction to him when he'd come over with the ball had spoken volumes anyway.

"Dammit," he swore to himself. He had drinks to go to with friends, and he'd likely be on the list to interview based on his steal, considering it had made the game reel on ESPN.

There wasn't time for her.

. . .

"Drinks and food," Sharla said. "Where should we go? You need something like a stiff scotch, at the very least."

"The One Eighty is really nice and has great views of the city. It's one of the restaurants I consult for. I'm sure we can get in and have a late dinner."

"Sounds perfect," Sharla said and hailed a cab. "Kevin, we're going for supper. Coming?"

Kevin leveled a possessive gaze at Sharla and strode over to her, putting his hand on the small of her back as they hopped into the minivan that had pulled up. Gretchen remembered, as she stepped in, how Josh had put his hand there when they were boarding the plane.

Tonight was going to be hard. She was the third wheel, and in a weird way, it was dredging up memories of Josh.

"Where to, folks?" the cab driver asked cheerily.

"Bloor Street West. Um . . . fifty-five," she stuttered as she sat, caught in a memory of Josh holding her as they banked into Vegas. It felt like just yesterday. Her hand went to her stomach, the sensation tingling her nerves.

They zoomed off, the lights and cacophony of downtown Toronto jumbling together. Kevin chatted about the game and Gretchen relaxed, zoning out, half-hearing the conversation. It would be okay. Josh would be long gone by now, back to his hotel. They were playing again tomorrow, but she wasn't going. No way.

"Earth to Gretchen," Sharla said, snapping her fingers in front of Gretchen's face.

"Sorry," Gretchen said, turning from the window. "What was that?"

"We're talking about November and how we're all getting to Beaujeu," Kevin offered. "I'm very glad you decided to come."

"Oh! I'm excited about it!" Gretchen replied, meaning it. It would be her first trip to Europe in years, and she planned to spend a few days touring some of France before she went home after the festival. A solo trip seemed decadent, but she was energized by the prospect of it.

"Good. I'll send you the ticket information soon, and we'll look after the hotel. Sharla will, of course, keep you posted."

Sharla grinned like the Cheshire cat. "We are going to have so much damned fun!"

The cab made it to their stop, and Kevin graciously paid the fare. It wasn't a short trip up to Yorkville, and normally Gretchen would have taken the TTC, but people like the Earl of Rathwell didn't do public transit, even if he eschewed personal cars and such when he traveled.

They took the elevator up, and Sharla sounded like she was being strangled when they took in the view and held on to the wall, her eyes squeezed shut. Gretchen had forgotten Sharla hated heights and took her hand, but it made Kevin laugh and carefully edge her over, his arms around her. Her hair was blowing in the breeze, and he gently tucked it back behind her ear as he cajoled her into opening her eyes. It was sweet, and it finally made sense as she watched them.

"Oh Sharla," she sighed to herself. A good guy was in love with Sharla, and she was scared of what that might mean. Thus, she was doing everything she could to push him away. Classic Sharla.

Gretchen arranged a table near the back, well away from the edge, and waved them over after she was settled. They joined her, Sharla admonishing Kevin for trying to kill her, and they bantered back and forth, the mood lifting.

"This place is very nice," Sharla complimented. "I'm loving your list here. Bravo."

Kevin looked up. "You're the sommelier here? Don't they have one on staff?"

"They do not. I consult and do a lot of the legwork for the owner. I do the same for quite a few of the restaurants in Toronto, a few chains. It's steady work."

"How lovely. What do you recommend to go with beef?" Kevin asked. His very own sommelier was sitting right beside him, but he looked at Gretchen in his entrancing way of talking to someone directly. He was rugged and handsome, like a movie star. That he loved wine as much as he did was not apparent, since he was as fit as any athlete. She immediately thought of Josh and the way his stomach flexed, the way the muscles on his shoulders shifted when he—

Gretchen bit her lip to clear the vision. Josh was invading her every thought. She was going to lose her mind. She had to put him out of it so she wouldn't.

"Well, obviously a red. If you go with the ragout stew they have here, I suggest a deep red, like a zin, or a cab. With the rib steak you could get away with something a little bit lighter, like that merlot, three down," she said, focusing on the page, clearing her mind to remember the list.

Kevin skimmed the list with his finger. "I do believe I will try the merlot. A good steak seems in order after baseball."

Sharla looked at her boss with surprise. "Merlot, Kevin?"

"I am game to try what Gretchen suggests, Shar. She's as good as you. What would you have suggested?"

Sharla sighed and pointed to the exact same two wines, throwing an exasperated look at Gretchen. "I think he winds me up on purpose."

The two of them wound each other up all the time, and normally it was humorous to watch them interact. This felt different. She was going to have to corner Sharla later to ask what exactly was going on between her and Kevin.

More conversation flowed as they drank their selections, the food arriving not long after. Gretchen wasn't particularly hungry and nibbled at her beet salad, knowing she needed to put something in her stomach.

Jumbled conversation and deep, male laughter burst onto the restaurant floor. She froze, a beet halfway to her mouth, dripping red onto her plate.

Of all the gin joints. Josh was with a bunch of the Sixer and Longhorn players, and they were taking a table out on the overlook patio. All of them in dress shirts and designer jeans, expensive watches flashing, looking like the millions of bucks they earned. Gretchen could hear drawls and Spanish accents, but then she heard Josh's laugh above it and put her fork down. She couldn't take this again. Not tonight, when everything was still emotionally raw. She was an idiot for still feeling this way about a silly, spontaneous hookup. She was broken in some way, still pining for him, wasn't she?

"What is it?" Kevin asked. "You look white. Are you ill? Shar, Gretchen looks ill."

Sharla looked over at Gretchen and peered into her face. Gretchen pointed discreetly from her lap over to their table, not trusting her voice not to crack or tears to start if she spoke aloud.

"Oh shit," Sharla swore, and swung into action, signaling the waiter for their bill. "I'm taking her into the bathroom. Can you settle up? We'll get her home after that, okay?"

"Of course," Kevin said, and rose to go with the waiter to the bar to speed the process along.

The problem was that they had to walk past the door to the outer dining area, where the players were seated. Josh was lounging on the end, his tall frame relaxed, which pinged at her abdomen despite how awful she felt. He ran a hand through his shorter hair, and Gretchen groaned inwardly, the memory of it wet and slicked back in the shower as he—

"Fuck," she swore under her breath. He was devastating and she wasn't supposed to care.

He looked up, sensing them, and their eyes met, his surprise evident. Gretchen quickly looked away and they hurried down the hallway toward the bathrooms. Sharla shoved her inside and stayed in the hall. Gretchen leaned against the door frame as it closed, wiping at the tears that had fallen as soon as their eyes had connected. She was such a marshmallow and needed to figure this out because she couldn't go around being ridiculously sensitive all the time. Hadn't she just resolved not to do this anymore, at the ball game?

She listened as Sharla greeted someone, muffled through the thick wood, her bitch tone on in full spades. The person answered back.

"No."

Who was Sharla talking to? Then she got louder. "You've done enough, don't you think? You ghosted her. Never called; never texted. You made it clear what was more important."

"Just let me talk to her, Sharla. Please. We left it—"

She put her hand to her mouth. *Josh.* She rattled the doorknob, pulling, and it was snapped closed quickly. Sharla must have a firm hold on the handle. She stopped yanking as Sharla launched into a tirade.

"Not tonight, big guy. She's had enough, that stunt you pulled giving her a game ball was hard enough."

"Wasn't a stunt. I want to see her. I—"

"Really, asshole? Because it felt like one. Your memory might be foggy, but you left that restaurant, not letting either of us explain. You just stormed out. What gives you the right to act like nothing happened and just saunter over? Did you expect her to fawn over you like . . . like . . ." Sharla countered, her voice snapping with anger.

Gretchen put her forehead on the cool, smooth surface of the door. She wanted to see him, interrupt whatever it was that Sharla was, in her own way, trying to fix. But she also knew that the moment their eyes met, she would not be able to resist touching him and that would not be a good idea.

"I—" he replied and she cut him off, launching into another tirade.

"Since you don't know her well enough, let me fill you in, Mister. She's been an emotional wreck since Vegas. You broke her heart, dammit! She was so into you, and any idiot could see that both of you were like lovesick puppies! But ultimately you didn't trust her, and you fucking lost the best thing you could've ever had. I won't let you fuck around with her head again. Nuh-uh."

"I—" Josh started again, then stopped. She could picture him with his fingers through his hair in frustration. "Tell her if she wants to talk to text me if she still has my number. Tell her—"

"What, Josh? Tell her what?" Sharla snapped back.

"Tell her I'm sorry. For all of it."

At that moment, Gretchen was sorry too. For not trying harder to explain, for running away when she should have defended herself and made him understand. She tried the door again, but it wouldn't budge, and she put her hand out flat on the cold metal, wishing she could see him, tears dripping down her face.

A few more beats of silence and a knock at the door. "Gretch, you okay? He's gone now."

She opened the door and peered at her friend. Kevin was standing just behind her, a concerned look on his face. That was when she let out a sob and launched into her best friend's arms.

"I think Mr. Sunshine is more than just a favorite baseball player," Kevin offered.

"We—" Gretchen started and then let out another sob. "I don't want to talk about it."

"No need. I'm sorry you've had such a trying day. Let's get you home." he replied. They turned the corner, and the elevator mercifully opened, letting some people out.

"After you," Kevin offered, gesturing, holding open the doors for them.

As they turned, she saw Josh pacing quickly toward them, and his eyes met hers, pleading with her to hold the door. She stepped forward, reaching to stop the doors from closing, but Sharla blocked her.

"Stop. Wait to talk to him when you aren't about to faint, Gretch. Bad idea, honey," she rattled off and stabbed the Close button repeatedly.

"Wait. Gretchen, please—" was all Josh got out as he reached the elevator and the doors closed. Gretchen sagged against the wall as they descended.

"Maybe I should talk to him. He looked really upset."

"I agree with Sharla," Kevin piped in. "You are in no shape to deal with the big emotions I see radiating from both of you. Cooling off first is likely a good idea. What on earth did he do?"

"He fucked up," Sharla snapped, and for good measure, glared at Kevin.

The elevator was silent for the rest of the journey to the ground floor and they stepped out into the warm Toronto night, the hubbub of Yorkville all around them. Kevin hailed the taxi this time, and they piled in, one on either side of her.

"Thank you," Gretchen muttered quietly. "I'm sorry I ruined your night."

Kevin looked down at her, kindness echoing as his eyes swiveled up and shared a look with Sharla. She rested her head on her friend's shoulder, exhausted.

"Not ruined, my dear," was all she heard in a crisp British accent before she focused on the city passing by outside the window, lost in thoughts of Josh.

chapter 12

Josh wanted to hit something. Badly.

He paced his hotel room, then stood, looking out at the dome view. The lights were on; the maintenance crew still hard at work. He'd watched them before from the rooms along the open side of the stadium, but tonight, it just made him restless instead of passing time.

He'd left the restaurant after he'd sparred with Sharla. He couldn't be around friends right now and had feigned tiredness. He got the usual ribbing about being an old man, but Timo, who had obviously been paying attention, asked him if it was about the blond. He hadn't answered him, and Timo told him to call later, patting his shoulder knowingly.

When he saw Gretchen at the restaurant, it had shocked him, not trusting his own eyes. But when she had looked his way, the ache to reach out and pull her to him—to beg for forgiveness—was a gut punch. But Sharla was one protective friend, making that impossible. She had every right to be. Gretchen had looked, well, not her usual self, that was for sure.

What Sharla had said hit him hard. He'd hurt her. Badly. And now, he couldn't make it up to her. The damage, based on how she had looked at him, was done. *Fuck.*

He kicked a pillow across the room, swiping another, sending it flying. He contemplated kicking the coffee table over, and stopped, Harv's voice shouting at him in his head to calm down and think. He let out a big breath and sat on the couch, his head in his hands, unsure of himself and the anger he was trying hard to control.

He looked at his laptop and opened it, clicking around on it aimlessly. Noting he had three new media requests, he fired them off to Harv.

Josh kept looking over at his phone, anxious to talk to her, wanting to explain it all. But he held back because maybe it wasn't a good idea, just like back in Vegas, when he'd caved to Harv's pressure to let it go.

A text was not the right way to talk to her. It felt impersonal. Or was it?

He picked up his phone and thumbed over to her last text. He stared at it, his fingers hovering over the keyboard. What would he say at this point? His doubts gave way and he tossed it down beside him, then picked it up again like an idiot, repeating the process. This pacing and hesitating was not going to help. He needed to get out of his own head for a bit or do something to at least calm down. He gathered up his key and his wallet and blew out of the hotel room, not really aiming for anywhere. Just not wanting to be cooped up. Walking was one of his anger-management tools anyway, right?

It was getting late, and the downtown core was teeming with people, the summer night beckoning them outdoors. He headed toward Dundas Square, where he could get lost in the sea of anonymous faces and it wouldn't matter who the hell he was. A walk—maybe a drink and a sports game in a bar—could be what he needed.

The lights and people were background noise, distracting him only slightly as he threaded through the late-summer crowds. Thoughts of what he should have done followed him. He should have been more insistent with Sharla. Or maybe he should've just walked away without trying to see her. Or maybe he should've said something to Gretchen at the game.

He arrived at the Imperial and stepped in, heading straight for the polished wood bar, the din of conversation washing over him. He slumped into his seat and the moment he threw his phone on the counter, it vibrated.

Hi, it's Gretchen. I hope I still have the right number.

Gretchen. His stomach flipped and he grabbed his phone like it would walk away from him if he didn't. He quickly typed back *Yes, you do. Hi back* and held his breath.

I'm sorry about tonight. Sharla is overprotective.

That was an understatement. He stood up, nervous energy pinging through him. Maybe he could see her tonight and set all this shit straight. Even if it meant they parted with the damage meter at zero, he had to try.

Before he could reply to her, she added, *We should talk.* "Sir, do you want anything?" the bartender asked as he stood there, his heart beating in his ears.

"No, no, I have to go. Sorry," he mumbled and strode out the door like a bull in a china shop. The night air hit him as he scanned for an empty cab, and he took some big, cleansing breaths. He could picture her wild blond hair around her face, the phone lighting up her skin, her teeth sunk into her lower lip. Finally an empty cab pulled up beside him. He needed to be where she was. Now.

"Where to?" the cabbie said as he ducked into the back.

"Shit. Don't know. Hang on."

I will come to you. Where are you? In a cab now, he typed, hit Send, and then held his breath again as he waited for her to respond.

"I don't got all night buddy," the cabbie said, irritated. "Tell me where or get out."

His phone dinged, he let out another breath and looked up from his phone. "Yonge and Sheppard, please."

. . .

Gretchen sat at her table, waiting for the call up that he had arrived, nervously drumming her fingers. The twenty-four-hour concierge downstairs was an excellent perk of her building, one she relied on when she was working. The guys usually got a first look at most of the cases she had delivered. Thankfully, the night guy was a wine drinker, and she often gave him a bottle or two to try to get his opinion.

This delivery was not wine. Far from it.

Her stomach fluttered. She had reached out, unsure of herself, but determined to make this right. It had been an emotional day, and with that scene in the restaurant, it was high time to put the misunderstanding to rest. Seeing him had been exhausting, but also a reminder of how she had felt about him, the emotions bubbling up like a geyser of need. Two days they'd had together, and it was as if the months after had been nothing.

So, after she was alone in her own apartment, she realized she had to see him. If she wanted to move on from him at all, she had to try. He'd already tried, hadn't he?

She'd fended off Sharla staying with her for the night, and the moment she was alone, she'd picked up her phone, stared at it for ten minutes, and then texted Josh before she wimped out and went to bed. It was late, and she half-expected him to already be asleep.

But he was on his way here. Now. She had changed into fresh jeans and a tank top since the clothes she'd been wearing felt rumpled and disorganized, much like her emotions. She straightened her bedroom, fussed with her hair, then simply let it be, the layers cascading around her face, uncontrollable.

This wasn't anything other than perhaps a chance to set the record straight with him, send him on his way, and close the door. Nothing more, right? But her stomach fluttered with nervous energy, and she passed a hand over her lips. To kiss him again, to hold him. It was a memory that was branded on her skin. His touch, his caress.

Her phone buzzed and she jumped, surprised.

"Hello?"

"Gretchen, my dear, your guest has arrived. Shall I send him up?" George's kind, deep voice echoed in her ear. He was also chuckling.

"Yes, please, George."

"I must say, you can pick them. My, my. Can I get his autograph, do you think, as the price of entry?" he added.

"You can ask, George, but he's likely not in the best frame of mind for fans right now."

"I should say not. Land sake's, he looks ready to eat something alive. You sure, honey?"

"Yes please, George. I'll be fine."

With that, the call ended and Gretchen stood, smoothing her palms down her thighs, feeling as nervous as she had the first time she'd seen Josh in the airport. Only this time the stakes were higher. He finally knocked and she blew out a big breath, shook her hair back, and went to answer the door.

"Two cream, no sugar," she whispered to herself. No backing out now.

She opened the door and he was there, his hands in his back pockets. He was still dressed in his after-game dress clothes. His shorter hair was still a new sight, but she didn't mind it at all. It showed off his cut jaw and high cheekbones, giving him a honed and tough presence. But no matter what, he looked as he always did.

Gorgeous and dangerous to her heart.

"Hi," he said, clearly unsure of himself, his shoulders raised, his eyes asking if this was okay.

She gestured inside and he stepped through. His soap-and-aftershave scent caught her and she stumbled slightly, her knees weak as she closed the door behind them, setting the lock.

"Can I get you a drink?" she asked and walked past him toward the kitchen area, not trusting herself to look at him, her head down. A hand came out and caught her arm before she could get far, and she turned back.

"Gretchen," he rasped out. The regret was plain on his face, and the heat from his hand drove all other thoughts out of her head. The tension from today, seeing him, the worry—all of it melted away the moment their eyes met.

"Josh," she breathed and stepped to him, meeting him halfway, their arms around one another. The shock of him against her made her quake and she held him tighter, soaking him in, his strong arms holding her up in the face of emotion she was desperately trying to shove back inside.

"You feel good," he whispered to her. "I'm sorry. So damned sorry."

"Me too," was all she got out before he lifted her, his lips claiming her hard, his hands on her, big and strong just like she remembered. She held on to him as he backed her up against the edge of the kitchen island and pulled back to look at her.

Just like that, she forgave him and let the hurt go. Where it went from here, she had no idea, but that morning in Vegas was turned to dust with his kiss.

He was intoxicating and every fiber in her was screaming out to absorb him, their closeness not nearly enough. One of his hands slipped under her, cupping her bottom, and Gretchen wrapped her legs around his waist, making him groan softly and push his hardness in between her legs, showing her how aroused he was. It was like they'd thrown gasoline on a fire, the way they had jumped one another.

"We need to—" Josh started, but she shook her head. He let out a groan of defeat and set her gently on the floor, letting her go. Taking his hand, she led him toward the couch in her living room. The lights were off, but the cityscape was sparkling and her curtains were open, the room dimly lit enough they didn't need lamps right now.

"Gretch," he started, but then stopped as she pushed his chest and he flopped to the couch, his eyes questioning her hungrily, hit by the awareness of what she was doing.

Gretchen straddled him, her hands on his shoulders, her knees digging into the leather cushions underneath them. She looked down into his eyes, making the decision to just go with it and damn the consequences.

"We can talk later," she whispered and ran her palm over his jaw, thumbing his cheekbone, the skin feeling rough from where his glare patches had been this afternoon. She leaned forward and kissed each of the spots, then sat back and stripped off her tank.

*   *   *

Gretchen was warm and soft and smelled so goddamned good Josh nearly lost his mind right there on her couch as she straddled him, her hair tickling his cheeks, her hand on his jaw.

When she stripped off her shirt and challenged him with those stunning eyes, all the blood in his head went south. He wrapped his hands up around her waist, then onto her back, caressing, touching, remembering her as the months they had been apart melted in a moment.

"My firecracker," he murmured and pulled her hands to thread his fingers with hers. Could she really be here, with him, right now? The need to talk, to get her to hear him evaporated as they touched and reconnected.

A small, impatient mewling noise from her made him press into her, kissing her gently. Then with more force, her tongue dancing with his as she moved on him, tightening into him. He was pulsing with the need to be inside her, the feeling of her all around him almost unbearable. She gasped as he moved to her neck, biting, and gently kissing the spots he bit as he moved down her collarbone. As he sucked a nipple into his mouth, she arched into him, her gasp of breath filling her ribs out under his hands.

She felt so fucking perfect in his arms he forgot about why he was there and what had happened. It was just her, half naked, on his lap.

He nuzzled her some more, then came back up to her lips while her hands pulled open his jeans and shoved them off to land on the floor. As they lowered to the couch, a flurry of their hands stripped her bare as well. His shirt went flying next; he wanted to be close to her, to feel her skin on his. As she ran her hands up over his shoulders, her lips connected with his neck, like completing an electric circuit.

Heaven.

"Josh," she murmured when skin met skin. Her eyes opened, languid and hot, her hips moving out and up, asking him to be inside her. She didn't need to speak . . . he knew that look. He'd memorized it and had dreamed about it.

He groaned and slid inside her, the tightness and warmth sparking his nerves immediately, her eyes popping, biting her lip as she spread her hips wider to let him in. She uttered out an earth-cracking moan and clung to him when he thrust forward, pulling him over onto her, her fingers digging into his back, raking. *More of that*, he thought. He'd missed how that felt.

Burying his head into her shoulder, he rolled his hips, slowly at first, feeling her out. His hand threaded into her hair, the other holding her thigh as he moved, her muscles bunching around him with each thrust, having her writhe under him while he held her fast. Then, she bucked under and found his thumb close to her mouth, sucking it in, her eyes sharpening to that piercing, wicked quality that always forced him to open the valve, forgetting restraint and control.

"Josh. I want—" she whispered and moaned as he stroked in again, her wetness velvet against him.

He abandoned the thought of control and let her have it, her gasps in time with his deep thrusts. They rolled, and he lifted her to sit on him as he balanced on his knees in the soft couch cushions. It had been too damn long. It hadn't been enough, and he wanted to see her, feel her, plaster himself to her. Holding her, one hand on her lower spine as she undulated over him, he shook with the effort not to explode, her erotic movements more intense than he could have imagined.

"Josh," she breathed again, and he groaned, dragging his mouth to hers and muffling her moans as she came, shaking like a leaf around him. He thrust one more time, cried out into her mouth, and came, shooting into her, joining her orgasm with his, the sheer pleasure of it obliterating the world around him.

They collapsed on the couch, both out of breath, and he looked into Gretchen's eyes, now heavy-lidded and soft. How could he have been so stupid? She was it; she was the one. He kissed her, smoothing her hair back off her face.

"You want that drink now?" she asked when they both returned to normal breathing, and he wheezed with laughter, propping his forehead on the couch beside her.

.   .   .

He leaned on the counter as they each sipped a quickly made coffee, his dress shirt the only thing she was wearing. Gretchen couldn't help but notice how his jeans rode low on his hips, the ridge of muscle through his pelvis on either side like a big, shiny arrow pointing down.

They hadn't said much as she'd made coffee, him watching her with a feral, possessive look, his hair a mess, his chest bare, the marks from their lovemaking clear across his skin. Perhaps the sex had been words enough, or they were still getting their bearings, but she was nervous again.

He put an arm out to her and she stepped into it, snuggling herself against his side. She looked up, and he looked down, thinning his lips.

"I really am sorry, Gretch. I was wrong to think what I did about all that stuff Sharla said," he started, and then let out a big breath, looking up and away from her, clearing his throat.

She took another sip of coffee, and then set it down behind her on the counter, her hand automatically going to his chest, gently smoothing over his neck to feel his Adam's apple bobbing. She wasn't sure why she felt the need to touch him, but it was compulsive, and she had been giving into that particular feeling since the moment they had met.

"I'm sorry too. I felt terrible, and that whole list thing was so embarrassing. I don't handle conflict well, and I panicked," Gretchen offered, lowering her hand again. "I'm glad we can put this behind us. Sharla was right. I did know you way back from Boston, and you have been my favorite player, but I totally forgot about that—"

"List, shmist. I should have trusted you like I did the day we met at the airport," Josh interrupted, kissing the top of her head and squeezing her. "I also think we both got spooked by Harv. He told me to let you go and that I had to nut up and focus on baseball."

"He was very kind. He didn't scare me," she replied.

"I didn't ask him to talk to you, I hope you know that."

She was fully aware that Harvey would say and do what was needed to get results out of his players that he needed, and the more she had thought about it in the days after, the more she realized that Josh didn't operate that way.

"I do. I feel terrible about how we parted. I mean, it was only supposed to be the weekend, but I felt like I tainted it by—"

"I wanted you to stay," Josh blurted out, interrupting her again.

"Yeah?"

"Yeah," he repeated and set his own coffee down to hold her with both arms. "I wanted to . . . hell, I didn't know, but I wanted it to be more."

"Me too," she said quietly, thinking of the reality of what he'd just said. Her chest constricted, and she moved away from him, needing the space to think clearly. Doubt and fear crept up her spine. Fast. They'd combusted when they touched, and part of her was regretting her abandon of restraint, because it was making this harder.

"It still can be, Gretchen," he said quickly. Her breath hitched. She was not emotionally ready for this, and she bit the inside of her cheek to keep it together.

"Texas, though," she replied as casually as possible, picking up her cup, pacing toward the couch, where their clothes were strewn. The cushions were completely dented and sideways. She set one up properly and sat, pulling her legs up defensively.

Josh had stayed put, leaning against the countertop. He was deadly silent. After a beat of them just looking at each other, he pushed off, stalking toward her with intent. The stress was pulling across his face, but his walk was sexy and her abdomen loosened as he leaned over her, hands balled into the couch, sinking her into the leather.

"I want you, Gretch. For more than tonight," he gritted through his teeth. "I know it isn't perfect, I know we're far apart but—"

"It isn't so easy," she replied, not meeting his gaze. He took the coffee cup from her hands and forced her chin up, looking into her eyes. *It's time for honesty*, she thought, studying him, knowing full well he was about to smash her objections to bits. She wanted to let him, the tears pricking at the backs of her eyes.

"It's as easy as we want it to be. I'm not going to force an answer from you tonight. It's a lot. But I want you to know—" he ground out, and swallowed, levering off her, turning.

"Josh?" she asked quietly. He was facing away from her now, looking out the window, his shoulders bunched. "You want me to know what?"

"The past two months have been shitty for me too," he replied, his voice rough. "I should have answered your text or picked up the fucking phone or just figured out how to get to you somehow. We barely know each other—"

"You had to focus on your career. I get it."

"I was scared because of how I felt for you. It was the first time in my life a woman made me second-guess my priorities. So I tucked my damned tail and ran," he said.

Whoa. She understood that. She'd run as well, sort of. "Me too," she replied quietly.

"Then let's stop running," he said and turned to her.

"I need time, Josh," Gretchen murmured. "I don't know if I can."

It was silent as they looked at each other. Disappointment crossed over his face, his sharp intake of breath at her words slicing through her.

She burst into tears that tracked down her face. She wanted to leap into his arms and tell him the fairy tale could be real. But she wasn't ready to do that. Thinking clearly, balancing her life here and now with the way it would change was her priority. Her practical side told her more heartache would be coming if they tried to be together, a country apart—he was playing in Texas, and she was here, in Toronto. How would that work? How often would he truly get time to see her with the way they played year-round—in spring training, then regular season, likely postseason. It was a huge commitment on top of their already ridiculously busy lives. Gretchen had already endured two months of up-and-down emotions that were affecting her life in ways she didn't want.

He sat down beside her, his hand on her leg, and she put her hand on his. "What we have is special," he murmured. "I need to know that what just happened here isn't goodbye. Not yet."

Goodbye. The word cut into her. It couldn't be that black and white. They'd found each other again, and she had hoped to make it through tonight without getting messy. Well, it was messy, and she was confusing herself as much as she was likely confusing him. She had to steel herself and let him go, and the idea of that was ripping her in two.

Her lack of response to his open question spurred him off the couch with a frustrated growl in his throat. He picked up his T-shirt, stuffed himself into it, then found his socks, pulling them on with a jerk. She watched him, brushing her wet cheeks, wishing she could just let herself have this.

"I'm sorry. I don't know what to say," she sniffled. "I don't want it to be goodbye either. I—"

Josh knelt down in front of her, his thumb tracing a tear, his touch making her ache to just let him hold her all night and throw away the reasons holding her back. He looked right into her eyes, the intensity searing her, begging her to listen to him.

"You have my damned heart. You have to know that."

"Josh. I want to answer. I need to think," she said through her tears. She needed to process the emotions currently flinging themselves at her faster than she could process them. He stood, backing away from her.

"I have a game tomorrow, and we fly out right after. But you know where I am. You have my number if—"

Before she could ask him to stop, or tell him to stay, he picked up his shoes and strode out, the front door clicking quietly in the expanse of the condo.

Gretchen let out a sob, covering her eyes, and flopped over on the couch, the emotions too much.

He'd all but told her he loved her, she'd pushed him away, and now he was gone.

chapter 13

Gretchen was making her morning coffee when Sharla called her, checking in after last night's debacle. Gretchen told Sharla about inviting Josh over and what he'd said. She left out the incredible sex. That part was hers alone.

"So that was it, he poured out his heart and left?"

"Yeah."

Sharla hummed irritably into the phone. "He's friggin' messing with you again. Telling you all that bullshit and then—"

"I don't think it's bullshit, Shar," she replied. "But it doesn't matter. It wouldn't work."

"Says who?" Sharla bit in, then sighed. "Sorry, hun, I know this sucks. Have you talked to him since?"

"I texted him to tell him that I wanted to answer him but to give me a few days. He's due to get on a plane this afternoon after the game, headed to Milwaukee for his next series, I think."

"Ah," came the reply, then the phone got muffled, and Gretchen could hear her talking to someone before the phone was uncovered. "Kevin wants to know how you are."

"Tell him I am a lovesick fool but otherwise recovered."

"She's fine," Sharla said shortly, and then sighed again.

"So. About His Lordship." Gretchen poked. "I have to know what in the hell is going on, Shar. You guys are—"

"I can't talk about it right now," came Sharla's soft but serious reply. "It's really, really fucking complicated."

"Understood. But we will, right? I'm here for you, too, you know."

Sharla went quiet on the other end of the line, then let out a sad breath that Gretchen could read clear as a bell.

"I know. I love you, Gretch."

"Love you, too, Shar. We'll get together soon," she said, meaning it. If nothing else, this whole crazy thing had solidified their friendship. Gretchen couldn't have gotten through it without her, even if Sharla was meddlesome and overprotective. She loved her best friend now more than ever.

"Yes. Listen, our breakfast is here, I have to go. If you so much as even think about flying to see him, you tell me so I know and can be there to pick up the pieces."

"Okay," was all Gretchen could say, the tears threatening to spill again.

Sharla made kissing noises into the phone, and then the call ended. Gretchen pulled herself out of bed and looked at the clock. It was early, and she had three meetings this afternoon. Sundays were normally not a day for client visits, but a couple had insisted because they wanted to update their fall wine lists early, and these days she'd just wanted to stay as busy as possible.

The cooler weather was prompting more people to order heftier dishes; more harvest table items were in vogue in late August as well. So, it worked.

Gretchen showered, then made another coffee, yawning from the late night catching up with her. She ran her hands over the couch. It was still dented from the night before, her jeans still on the floor. His shirt, which he'd left behind, had been crumpled up beside her pillow, and she'd put it back on when she'd got up, trying to keep him close in some way. She'd have to mail it to him eventually since it was a Burberry, and it wasn't right to keep such an expensive shirt.

"Fuck," she muttered as she looked out the window to the morning light, Toronto already well awake below her. She felt different, but everything else was the same. Because he loved her; he wanted her.

Why couldn't she just admit her own feelings to him last night? He had her heart too. The last two months of angst had shattered the moment they touched. But no matter how many times she played out every scenario in her head, being with Josh would mean upheaval for both of them, and that fact had halted her words last night.

"I love him," she said into the air around her, testing the words out. She didn't break out into a cold sweat. "I love him!" she yelled.

Well, there it is.

Admitting it meant she had to think about compromise on a level she'd never had to face before. She'd never been in a long-distance relationship before; the farthest apart a boyfriend had ever been from her was Oshawa, less than an hour away, and that hadn't lasted long because he was a shift worker at the GM plant, and their schedules never synced.

This was on a whole other level, and it sobered her once more. They were in different *countries*. Love might not be enough.

As Gretchen sat down in front of her laptop to get her day started, the thought flitted through her head that the distance wasn't the problem. Falling in love with someone the way she had with Josh?

It would change her life irrevocably, and that was the scariest thing of all.

, , ,

Josh set his suitcase down on the bed in his apartment back in Dallas with a thump, and he landed beside it, exhausted. They had hoofed it back from Milwaukee, and tomorrow was a rare no-game day before starting a stint at home. The Sixers were coming to them for the following series, and he was looking forward to seeing Timo and Javier and maybe taking them for brisket.

Thinking about Toronto made his chest hurt because he'd had no word from Gretchen other than her message telling him she needed time. He'd spent the entire series in Milwaukee distracted. He was mid-lineup and his at-bats hadn't been stellar, but he was at least pulling his weight in the outfield. He needed to sort things out before his batting average slumped too far again.

He flopped onto his back, closing his eyes, Gretchen invading his mind the moment he did. How devastated she had looked when he'd told her she had his heart. How hard it was for her to respond. Obviously he'd pushed too hard, or they would be figuring this out now, together.

But he didn't regret what he'd said, and he knew it was true. How could he not love her? The way she made him feel, how he reacted to her touch, the idea of her making him whole, the energy that would jolt out of him when she touched him. It all made sense.

He was fucked. She was there and he was here, but worst of all, they weren't on the same page. He was a mess all because of a coffee and an impulsive night in Vegas with a stranger who'd become a woman he could see spending the rest of his life with.

He'd thought about where they'd live, how they'd handle her business. How long he'd stay in the Show if they were together. He daydreamed about a home, a real one, where he could unpack his things without the anxiety that he'd have to pack them up again at a moment's notice.

All the way home from Milwaukee on the plane, Josh had run the hypotheticals like he would plays on the diamond. How could he make it work for both of them? What could he do to blow away the fear he'd seen in her eyes? It was up to him to bridge the gulf, at least it felt that way. He chastised himself for jumping the gun with all the bullshit of settling down with her. They weren't even dating and he was already thinking of white picket fences and a dog. Those were strange thoughts for him to have.

He had no clue what to do, even after all that. How long was he supposed to wait, he wondered, before he let her go again? His heart wanted him to stand and fight, because the way she'd reacted told him that she felt their connection. He was certain she loved him as well but couldn't make that leap the way he had. What was holding her back?

The questions hung in the air as Josh unpacked, and he threw a load of laundry into his machine. The swish of water echoed as he padded to the kitchen, looking out the window down to the pool. A lone swimmer sent ripples out that wavered in the soft lighting. A swim would be great, but he was so tired he wasn't sure it was worth the effort.

He took out his phone and looked at the texts, finding hers. He quickly typed out *just got in, wanted to see how you were*, erased it, typed it out again, and hit Send before he could talk himself out of it a second time. Communication with her kept the lifeline open.

His phone vibrated, but it wasn't her responding, it was Harv. *In Dallas. Breakfast tomorrow?*

He called Harv instead, wanting to hear a familiar voice, his thoughts too jumbled in his head.

"Harvey."

"Harv, it's Josh. Just got your text. Everything okay?"

"Josh. How are ya?"

"I'm okay. Could be better, long flight. How are you?" he replied, realizing he'd just launched into it, not asking Harv how he was specifically, worried this was a preemptive call. His nerves over his job performance were paper-thin right now.

"Doing fine, son. Listen, I need to talk to you about Neptune. We've got a bit of a situation."

Josh sat up, his tiredness gone. Neptune had come to the Longhorns batting practice two weeks ago at Josh's invitation. It had been a blast, watching Neptune hammer some balls into the stands, and good press for him, Harv sending out the word for scouts to come see the kid in action. Josh was pleased he'd helped get Nep signed with his agent. Harv seemed to think he had big talent lurking in those lanky bones.

This late in the season, he would likely get invited for spring training, and then seed himself in somewhere if Harv worked his magic well enough. But you never knew. If a team wasn't going to postseason, they could call him up to get some experience that was less pressure. The Sixers often gave their youngsters a chance to stretch their legs late in the season.

"Is he okay?"

"No, he isn't. He was pulled over two nights ago outside Vegas. He wasn't drinking, but they found a very, and I mean *very* small amount of coke in his glove box. The cops searched the car even though he was doing nothing wrong, and they found it. Wrong color skin in the wrong part of town is my best guess. But the damage is done."

Shit. Josh let out a big breath, the disappointment hitting him in the gut. This could be a career-ender. Cocaine. *Fuck.* That boy knew better.

"That doesn't sound like Neptune, Harv. He's a good kid, he knows the stakes."

"I wanted to tap you for some support for the kid. I know he looks up to you, and you're a damn fine example to him."

Josh bowed his head, humbled. "Of course. What happens now?"

"It gets murky. It wasn't Neptune's car; he was borrowing it from a friend and had only been driving it for fifteen minutes when he got tagged."

"Obviously not enough for intent to sell?" Josh asked.

"Exactly, and he tested clean," Harv replied. "Team management is meeting tomorrow to figure out what's needed. Lawyers, all that crap."

Josh could hear the frustration in his voice. This was no easy task. Harv had been down this road before with other players, and it sucked every single time. You wanted the best for your prospects. You worked hard for them. There was a payday, but also a sense of satisfaction that you helped get a boy to where he needed to be as a man, not just a baseball machine. Harv had once explained it to him that way, and it stuck with Josh.

He thought about it a moment. He'd write a character testimony or even fly to any hearing he needed to. That was a given. But as for Neptune himself, he needed a plan.

"Can I call him?"

"He's in lockup, son," Harv said. "He's waiting to be arraigned. He wasn't released on bail at his hearing because—"

"He's Dominican," Josh finished for Harv. It was frustrating. Neptune wouldn't have run.

"I'll call Travis in the morning and find out what I can do to support the team, at least," Josh added. "Still want to meet for breakfast? I'm off tomorrow."

"Sounds good, son. I'll pick you up around nine?"

They ended the call and Josh checked his phone. No answer from Gretchen. He sighed, set the phone down, and sat heavily in one of his kitchen chairs. Exhaustion washed over him, and he leaned against the table. The clock on the wall ticked a few times and he wearily dragged himself toward his bed, suddenly too tired to think about anything other than sleep.

. . .

Gretchen's phone buzzed and she automatically looked over. A bunch of notifications had come in, one labeled #*Neons*. She hadn't had one of those for a while. She tapped it, and Neptune's smiling face came up, surprising her.

After Vegas, she'd set up an alert for news items about the Neons, more for her own torture than anything else. It was silly, but she wanted to immerse herself in that world to remind her of her life-changing weekend and reading up on the team was part of that. She was already subscribed to several Sixer newsfeeds, and now Longhorn news, plus an alert simply labeled #*Malvern*, which she berated herself for. But here was a news blip about Neptune Gilbert, and his arrest for possession of cocaine.

"Damn," Gretchen uttered. She thought of Josh and wondered if he knew. Likely. It was a shame since he had high praise for the young player. It didn't seem like something that Neptune would do, but she didn't know him, and life could be crazy.

She thumbed over to her messages. There was one waiting for her, a text from Josh that she had somehow missed. She hesitated. She couldn't string him along, but she was still at war with herself over what to do. She read over the text and smiled despite herself. He'd sent it last night, likely when he'd landed back home.

Doing okay. Saw news about Neptune. So sorry.

It immediately pinged back a response. *At breakfast with Harv, talking about Nep now.*

Ok. Talk later? she typed back, then added. *He's a good kid, I'm sure it will be fine.*

She set the phone down and turned back to her laptop, reviewing some of her invoicing. She hated accounts receivable work, but it was a necessity when you were your own boss, and she hadn't contracted it out to a firm since it was manageable between her and her accountant. The sun was shining through the windows; it looked like a perfect day to be outside. She thought of calling friends, but put it off, inexplicably wanting to spend time with Josh, missing his touch and craving the way he felt near her.

She looked at her calendar. She had no client meetings for three days. Usually she'd catch up on paperwork and business planning, but suddenly, she didn't want to. It was all infuriatingly tedious. She needed a break.

It hit her when she saved her Excel sheet and closed it. She'd just given herself the answer to at least a few of the questions that had poked at her the past couple of days, since she and Josh had last seen each other.

The weight lifted off Gretchen's shoulders, and she did a turn in her swivel chair, hands on her head, letting the idea of flying to see him sink into her piece by piece. She could channel some of the abandon she'd experienced in Vegas, and see how she felt afterward, maybe? It would certainly be preferable to waffling back and forth about playing safe with her priorities. She was avoiding one of the best things to ever happen to her because she was afraid of the what-ifs.

The idea of trying long distance, or if she could uproot her business, flew in and out of her head as she thought it over. Restless, she blew out an unsteady breath and paced to the kitchen, opening and closing the fridge absently, putting away dishes from the drying rack, realigning the tea towels on the stove handle three times. *Just do it, Gretchen.* Pacing back to her office, she plunked into her chair, then got back up and paced around it. She sat back down, swiveling in circles as it all tumbled in her head.

Her heart and her brain were wrestling with each other. All the damned whys and hows could take a flying leap. She was getting nowhere if she didn't just woman up and answer them.

"Should I?" she asked herself, and when no one answered with any objections, she opened a browser window and typed *flight to Dallas.*

She had to find out.

chapter 14

Josh arrived at the stadium for a late-morning workout, the Texas sun already baking the asphalt, radiating heat. He ignored it, Neptune's predicament still weighing heavily on his mind after Josh and Harv had chatted over breakfast.

He was mulling over all that Harv was planning to do the next few days when he got stopped in the parking lot by a fan hovering near the souvenir and ticket office, clutching a rolled-up poster. Josh didn't see him until he practically bumped into him.

"You're Joshua Malvern! Can you sign my stuff, man?"

Without his normal standoffishness, Josh signed a ball cap, and then a Longhorns poster, continuing on, preoccupied. He waved as the fan said "Thanks!" and took off toward the visitor parking lot.

Normally that would have made him moody and tense, but

today, not so much. It was different now. He knew he was a lucky SOB to be here. One wrong move and he wouldn't have been. All the hesitation and protective barriers he'd put up over the years had paid off. But there had been times he'd been foolish and had simply never gotten caught. Neptune wasn't as lucky.

The gate security guard let him through with a wave, and as he walked down the concrete underground corridor toward the Longhorn locker room, someone stuck their head out a door.

"Malvern," he barked.

Josh steered himself around and went back toward the coaching pit, approaching the junior coaching staff. Their manager, Coach Davidson, was there, as well as their fitness manager. This didn't look good, and he swallowed the tension that immediately hit his throat.

"We want to give you a few days off."

Well, at least there was no beating around the bush. Josh dropped his duffel and looked at the coaches. None of them looked at him, clearing their throats. Were they expecting a fight? The story of his temper was no secret, so he assumed his reputation had preceded him. It had been stupidity on his part not to be more in control when the Sixers had optioned him out. It felt like a lifetime ago already.

"Can I ask why?" he replied, settling one hip on a desk. He would not get angry. He would stay calm. This was not a demotion, but it was still stinging. He folded his arms across his chest and took a silent, deep breath through his nose as discreetly as possible. "I'm not sure I understand."

"Your shoulders are locking again, son. We need you for the series with the Sixers; you're getting a pass on this one," Davidson replied.

Josh nodded, swallowing nervously. "Okay then. Am I IL-ed? Do you need me in the dugout for the games?"

"Nope. Go take some time off, see a girl, go home to your mom and dad." Davidson grunted and stood.

Obviously they had no idea what his life was like. Go see his mom and dad? Christmas and Thanksgiving were about the only times he saw them. That wasn't happening.

A woman, on the other hand. . . . He thought about going to see Gretchen, but then shelved it. It was too soon, and she needed more time.

"I know what you're thinking. We just want you to rest, get some diagnosis on that shoulder, and be back in time to hit against Carlos. He's the starter for the 3ixers series Game 1 and you know him. We're hoping to put you in fifth. If your shoulder proves to be a stuck pig, then we may IL you, but we aren't cutting you."

"Okay," Josh answered. He shook hands with everyone, picked up his duffel, and left the pit. No temper tantrums and no animosity. How about that? He was exceedingly calm.

He now had four days off instead of one. Last year, that would have felt like a death sentence, but now? He was free and clear to do what he wanted.

He stopped in at the gym and did some mobility on his shoulders, not wanting to waste the reason he was here. They were stiff and he grunted in pain as he stretched them out. The thought that this was not how he wanted to end his season badgered him as he went through the motions. What if this was it? That the wear and tear was finally too much?

He thought about it as he spent some time on the treadmill, slowly jogging, the sweat pouring off him from his big breakfast at a local greasy spoon. It was Harv's favorite, and he'd indulged him. He had eaten far too much protein, which was now haunting him.

His thoughts went from breakfast to the Longhorns. Dallas was a good club. He enjoyed it, but he didn't really feel like he fit. He hadn't made many friends in the short time he'd been here, but he was respected for his longevity in the majors. Teammates often asked his opinion before disregarding it, gave him space to do his thing, and did not engage him on a level that meant anything.

But that wasn't what he wanted anymore. He wanted to be on a team that wanted him there for the good he could do, not just to fill in the roster with experience points. He thought back on how validated he'd felt playing in Vegas while he was there and how the contributions he made to the Sixers team were valued.

Harv had said Josh could be a free agent next season. He could look around to see where he'd like to finish out his career— either stay put or maybe find a more lucrative club. New York or maybe Boston again. The Longhorns hadn't indicated if they were re-upping him, but it was a consideration that he could jump ship.

Then he thought back to Travis and his offer to stay in Vegas.

Was he done with the Show? Was he changing his mind about where he wanted to be, what he wanted to do? His entire life was in a bit of an upheaval. Now was not the time to make these decisions, but here they were, butting in.

He zoned out for a few moments, the rhythm of his steps on the treadmill relaxing him, the simple effort of running evaporating the stress. He racked up a few more miles at a slow pace, his mind wandering to Gretchen, wondering again if he could fly to Toronto and surprise her. If she would want that.

He desperately wanted to see her. He could talk to her about all this shit. She'd understand.

His phone pinged in his earbuds and he touched the screen. A text from Harv.

Headed to Vegas. Got the notice of your days off. Want to join?

Then another ping, and Gretchen's name popped up. He stopped the treadmill and picked up his phone, her name forcing goosebumps through the sweat. Speak of the devil.

Flying into Dallas tonight.

"Well, okay then," he said and pulled his earbud out. He knew exactly what to do. Maybe this was what he needed to figure it all out.

Meet me in Vegas instead. Flying there with Harv. I'll send you the ticket, he typed, then flipped over to his message from Harv and agreed.

.   .   .

Gretchen stepped out of the cab, her small carry-on behind her, and looked up at the floodlights inside the Neons stadium. They were playing tonight; the game was already well along.

She had canceled her ticket in the nick of time, and with very few details from Josh except for a quickly emailed direct flight from Toronto, she flew into Vegas instead. This time, flying in, she didn't feel the excitement. This time she had no idea what she was doing.

She walked toward the west gate, where he'd texted to pick up the pass he'd left for her. The ticket agent looked bored, and Gretchen had to clear her throat twice and say excuse me before the woman looked up from her screen.

"I have some tickets here for me? Under Gretchen?"

The woman handed her a pass with a lanyard. "Over there, honey, that small gate. Show it to the guard."

She looked down at it. A temporary staff pass? What? She slung it over her neck and strode over toward what was obviously a service entrance. The guard there took one look at her, his eyebrows rising, and he let her in the door, no questions asked.

As she tapped down the hall, dragging her suitcase, she could hear the crowd and smell the hot dogs cooking. This stadium was magical in a way. It was what baseball was supposed to be: the roar of the people cheering on their favorite team under the floodlights at dusk, stale popcorn, greasy food—

"Over here, Ms. Harper," called a female voice.

She turned and saw an older woman dressed head to toe in a black-and-red velour jumpsuit with the Neons logo. She was curvy and spunky-looking, with pom-pom socks peeking out of her sneakers and her fingernails painted bright red to match.

"You must be Felicia," Gretchen guessed, remembering Travis's story. Who else could it be? Josh had mentioned the woman a few times, saying how much fun she was, how she kept the team on the straight and narrow, like a den mother.

"I am." Felicia opened her arms. "Now you come here. I'm a hugger."

She pulled Gretchen in, giving her a squeeze before letting her go, studying her from head to toe. She made a sound in her throat that Gretchen couldn't quite translate. Was it good or bad? She tucked some of her hair behind her ear and looked back at the woman.

"That boy," Felicia said, not elaborating. "Follow me. We'll go up to the box."

Gretchen lugged her suitcase up the wooden stairs, narrow and curving, until they reached a door. From the look of memorabilia and plaques on the walls, the upholstered seating, and the prime view, they were in the owner's box. It was empty except for Josh and Harvey, both leaning on the bar, each with half-finished beers. Felicia went to the back of the box and let herself through another door, and Josh looked up and saw her. He was a thirst-quenching relief, her entire body thrumming with warmth as his eyes met hers.

Mischief promised, she thought, her body tingling everywhere. Josh quickly bridged the distance between them. She tilted her head up and he broke into that smile that always made her lose all her thoughts.

"You're here," he murmured and took her bag from her, setting it aside, his other hand hovering and hesitant to touch her. She reached out to him, giving him permission to do the same. He was clearly as nervous as she was. Well, of course he would be, after what they'd said to each other.

He put an arm around her, pulling her close with a groan that came from his toes, and kissed her with a roughness that felt possessive, sending her senses whirling. She clenched his jacket lapels in her hands, not only signaling to him that she liked what he was doing, but holding herself up, which was difficult because he was turning her to jelly. Josh slid his hand down her back and then up to the nape of her neck, burying it in her hair as he deepened his hold on her. If they had been alone, she would have already been working on getting him naked. They were ridiculously combustible when they touched, apparently.

"All right now, you two, no hanky-panky in the box," Felicia said as she came back in. She held a cardboard tray with a slice of pizza, some popcorn, and what looked to be beer. She set it on the counter. Gretchen detached herself from Josh, who immediately pulled her into his side, not ready to let her go yet.

"Eat. You must be starving," Felicia ordered, and then winked at Josh.

Gretchen's phone buzzed. Sharla. She opened it, typed that she was fine, on the ground, and to butt out. Then she put it away.

She still hadn't spoken to Josh directly, and he was completely quiet, watching her. She eyed the pizza, the smell of it making her stomach rumble. Lunch had been on the plane. A long time ago.

He pulled her over beside him, and she touched Harvey on the shoulder as she sat, dragging the pizza over in front of her.

"Harvey. How lovely to see you again," she said softly. He was half engrossed in the game, his phone in front of him, his email open.

"Ms. Harper. Josh didn't tell me you were flying in," Harvey said, flicking a glance at Josh, who had a hand on her back, the other on his beer. She could see him grinning out of the corner of her eye. He hadn't told Harvey she was coming? Sneaky. And worrisome. Josh was here for Neptune, not her, and she suddenly hoped that she wouldn't be in the way.

"I'm sorry to hear about Neptune," she offered. "I hope you can sort it all out. It seems like he was set up, or maybe it was just bad luck."

Harvey grunted, his eyes on the game. "We'll figure it out."

"Harvey thinks that Nep telling the cops whose car it was will help," Josh added, his own eyes back to the game. "We think this friend might have some information they can use to bring in someone bigger." He muttered under his breath as a player walked.

Gretchen folded the slice and took a bite, washing it down with possibly the best beer ever. She was hungry.

The two men on either side of her were bristling tension now that she was there. Silence enveloped them as they watched the game, both Harvey and Josh muttering or letting out random swear words. It seemed the Neons were not having a good night. She left off conversing, feeling intrusive.

"When is the arraignment?" Gretchen finally asked once she had finished her food.

"Tomorrow afternoon. The club lawyer is on vacation, so they're trying to secure someone else," Josh replied, his hand sliding up and down her back. "He deserves more than a county-assigned dimwit because the club's regular lawyer isn't here."

"We'll find someone," Harvey said with grunt as Gretchen's phone buzzed and she picked it up. It was Sharla.

"My protector," she murmured, and Josh chuckled.

"Oh my God, Gretchen, are you insane?" Sharla spat into the phone the moment she took the call.

"Hi, Shar," Gretchen laughed, flicking a glance at Josh who was still chuckling. "I'm fine. Say hi to Josh."

Sharla huffed on the other end. "If he fucks with you, I will personally end him. No good, hot-shot assh—"

Josh, who could obviously hear both sides of the conversation, leaned over to Gretchen's phone and interrupted her.

"I certainly hope to, Sharla. You have my word," he said playfully.

Gretchen blushed as Josh moved his hand all the way down to pat her ass, and Sharla growled on the other side.

"Fine. It is a lucky thing he is ridiculously good-looking. I trust my girl here."

Gretchen heard Kevin ask Sharla who she was talking to, she muffled some words to him, and suddenly Gretchen was on speaker.

"Gretchen, darling. How are you? I hear you are back in Las Vegas with your Mr. Sunshine?"

Gretchen laughed at Kevin's use of the nickname Sharla had inadvertently given Josh. It had stuck. He'd never live that down now.

"I am," she replied. "He's here to support a friend. I was flying to see him anyway, and, well . . . here I am."

"Well, keep us posted," he said, and then Sharla took the phone off speaker.

"I need to go. Love you, Gretch. Be careful, okay?" Sharla said quickly and hung up.

Josh was absorbed in the game, standing at the edge of the box, his beer in one hand and the other in his pocket. He looked relaxed except for how square and high his shoulders were. Gretchen was looking forward to maybe running her hands over them later. The thought made her stomach flip.

Cheers came up from the stadium, and they turned back to the game. It looked like the Neons had loaded the bases, and the opposing team manager was walking out to the mound, the fielders converging on the pitcher. From where Gretchen was, she could see gloves covering mouths as they discussed what to do, bobbing heads with ball caps and gesturing coaches.

"They'll pull him and put in a fresh closer now," Josh remarked. "I really hope they can convert this. Will do good for the morale on the team."

The phone on the wall rang, and Josh reached to grab it. A few *uh-huhs* and then a *No, you have it right, I think that is a good call.*

"Who was that?" Harvey asked when Josh hung the phone back on the cradle.

"Coach. He wanted my opinion on switching out a player to face the closer they're bringing out from the bullpen. I batted against him a few times last year, and the guy they have up next in the rotation won't do well against him. He's a leftie."

"Have you thought about moving to coaching when your playing days are done?" Gretchen asked carefully. She didn't want to poke the bear, but she was curious. The look on his face and the change in energy around him was evident. He had a head for the game; he was able to see things that maybe others couldn't.

"It was a path I had contemplated," Josh replied. He thinned his lips.

"You'd be good at it, son," Harvey remarked. "You'd be a good agent too. But not yet. You got play in you left."

"Thanks, Harv," Josh said quietly and moved to the railing to watch the play.

The batter moved into position, and even from where they were standing, they could see how nervous he was. This was a huge play. If he could convert, they would win the game. Gretchen put her hand on Josh's arm, and his forearm muscles corded.

Two pitches went wide. Another fouled off. Then the batter swung for the stands and the ball went up and hit the back decking, bouncing back on to the infield warning track. The crowd was thundering, and the Neons on base were booting it as an infield grand slam was a distinct possibility if they moved their asses.

"Jesus," Josh said, gripping the railing. "Now this is baseball."

They added three runs while the batter was tagged at second, enough to tie the game with two outs. Josh turned to Gretchen.

"We don't have to stay if you're tired. I'm booked in at the Delano, near the Mandalay Bay," he whispered and covered her hand with his. His touch felt so good she almost dragged him out of there with his offer. But she didn't. He wouldn't want to miss this. It was good ball, and she was enjoying it too.

"We can stay until the end. They could win!" she replied and stepped into him as he lifted his arm, breaking their touch, to surround her shoulders. He let out a big, contented sigh and slouched against the rail as they watched the next batter step up.

"Okay, we'll stay," he said and kissed the top of her head.

chapter 15

The Neons had won, and Felicia told them that Ric was driving the bus the next day to Neptune's arraignment so the whole team could go. Josh had stepped in, shown his support, and chatted with Coach. Harvey left before Josh had gotten a chance to talk to him. Now, there was nothing else to do but go back to their hotel room and wait for tomorrow.

Josh looked over at the woman sitting next to him in the car and his heart stuttered at the sight. She was here. This meant something. She was maybe willing to try. She was his—for now, at least.

She was leaning on her hand against the door, quiet, taking in the scenery. She looked over at him and cocked her head.

"What?"

"Just looking at you. Happy you're here," he replied.

She looked down, biting her lip. "I hope I don't get in the way. I mean, you're here for Neptune."

"I am here for him, yes, but you came. This means a lot to me, Gretchen," he said. When he'd left her apartment that night, he'd walked to the subway and rode it back to the stadium, thinking he might never see her again, which meant he'd been a mess afterward. Tears weren't a normal thing for him, but he had cried when he'd made it back to his room.

They pulled into the parking lot for the Delano, both of them quiet. Josh sat, hands on the wheel, debating whether to bring it up now or later. Gretchen was fiddling with the strap on her purse. She looked both worried and exhausted.

"Come on," he muttered. "You look ready to collapse."

He leaped out, picked her small suitcase out of the back seat, and handed it to her. As she extended the handle, he stepped in front of her. He had to know what she was thinking and needed to touch her.

"Gretchen?" he asked quietly. "What's wrong?"

"What if—" she sputtered and stopped, then lifted her eyes to him. She was scared. His breath caught.

"I know," he said and lifted her hand to his mouth, kissing her knuckles, holding it tightly. How could he convince her? Or could he? It had to be her decision. He'd told her his. He studied her face. This was torture.

"Let's just enjoy tonight, and tomorrow, and go from there?" he finally suggested, remembering what she'd said before, the last time they were in Vegas. "No what-ifs."

"Okay," she said, letting him lead the way into the hotel.

The big rocks embedded haphazardly into the floor of the lobby and the artwork studded throughout distracted her as they made their way to the elevators. The warmth from her hand, her little noises as she stopped each time to look at something, the simplicity in how they felt together—Josh was storing all of it in his memory. This was all part of the Gretchen he loved.

"I would have never thought to stay here," she remarked, as they passed a hanging sculpture. "The lobby is amazing!"

He had never stayed here either. He wanted to find a place that wasn't much of a casino hotel but more intimate, where they could have some downtime. He'd Googled the most romantic hotels in Vegas and this one had been at the top of the list.

When they got to his room, Gretchen walked straight to the bed and flopped down face first, groaning. Josh stashed her suitcase and used the restroom. When he came back out, she was lying on her back, and she turned her head to him.

It was different tonight. There was less urgency, less need to strip and go at it like bunnies the moment they touched, despite the welcoming kiss he'd given her asking for just that. He felt like he needed to take his time, just be with her and focus on her, not move straight to the stellar sex that they could have together, which was, of course, on his mind as well. If they were going to get on the same page, he had to be patient. With her and himself.

He watched her shift on the bed, twitching as she let out a soft, happy sigh, stretching as far as she could along the length of the bed.

"Damn," he whispered as he leaned down over her, unable to stay away. She lifted her fingers and traced his nose, down his lips, crooking them in his shirt collar, pulling him forward. She kissed him gently, probing, asking him to open up to her.

"Gretchen," he whispered as she moved her lips along his jaw-line, her hands working up and down his arms. "Honey—"

She stopped and he took a breath, closing his eyes, willing calm. His jeans were about to burst; he wanted her that badly. They sat up as his eyes opened and she put both hands on his face, cupping his jaw. She looked him in the eye.

It shocked his heart and took all his breath because the way she was looking at him was going to kill him right there. She kissed him gently again.

"I want this. Us," she whispered with a nervous waver in her voice. "I don't know how to do this, but I want to at least try. I'm scared it won't work and my heart won't be able to take it."

He pulled her in, wrapping his arms around her, his breath shaking at her admission. She was crying. He kissed her cheeks, stroked her hair, anything to calm her down. He decided he hated it when she cried. Happy, sad, or otherwise.

"I'm a huge mess," she laughed and shifted into his shoulder as he settled her in further. "I'm sorry."

"You Canadians apologize too much," he replied lightly. "You aren't a mess. But if you were, you'd be my mess."

She snorted another laugh through her tears, and he held her closer, rubbing her back as her hand fisted his shirt. They lapsed into silence, and he let himself relax, the comfort of her touch soothing him as she dried her eyes.

He was dozing off when he heard her breathing deepen and he opened his eyes. She was calm and completely relaxed and he brushed the hair off her face, just to look at her like that was spinning his senses.

"Goddammit, Gretchen," he whispered, swallowing the emotional lump in his throat. "I want us too. So fucking much."

She was asleep and likely hadn't heard him, but he wanted to say it anyway. He needed to say it. He'd never felt like this for a woman and he wanted to tell her, and the world, just what she meant to him. Shifting, she mumbled something, reaching out for him as he slid down to get comfortable.

"I didn't catch that," he prompted in her ear. She let out a little sigh that nearly undid him right there. How could she be so emotionally heavy and still turn him on? Was this the difference between sex and intimacy? He had no clue but assumed maybe this was it, and he was okay with it.

"I love you," she murmured back, making his world utterly complete.

. . .

At some point, Gretchen had gotten out of her travel clothes and was now asleep under the covers naked. She had a hazy memory of getting up to pee, and then stripping as she walked back to the bed, her clothes a trail from the washroom to the bed. Josh was beside her, still snoring. He'd done the same, but she didn't remember him doing it. They had both been exhausted.

They had fallen asleep after she had told him she wanted to try. She'd also told him she loved him. It hadn't felt forced, or weird, and as she lay there, the room still dark, it still felt okay. Like a piece of the puzzle was locked into place.

She looked at the clock on the nightstand. It was three in the morning.

She turned her head to Josh and studied his sleeping face. The fashionably sexy stubble, the eyelashes that should be illegal on a man, his chiseled jawline. She reached out and ran a hand over it, up into his hair, and shimmied toward him, feeling the heat from his body as she curled up against his side.

He let out a deep sigh and suddenly his hands were on her, pulling her under him, his lips on her neck. "Want you," he murmured.

In his half asleep stupor, he ran kisses over her neck and shoulder, her hands in his hair, the shocks of heat roving outward, the pleasure in his touch loosening her abdomen. She trailed a hand down his back and as she did, his muscles twitched wherever she touched. He moved to her breasts, down her waist, and onto her hip, pulling one leg out and up.

"Touch me," she purred, guiding his hand to her center. He slid down her body, pushing the comforter back, his hands holding her hips steady as he nudged her thighs apart with his head. Looking up, his eyes were full of heat and desire as she spread herself before him. She shivered in anticipation as his breath slid over her skin.

He wasted no time and plunged his mouth over her, sucking and kissing her, his fingers joining to thrust into her. Rubbing and caressing as she spiraled into a haze of pleasure. He sucked her nub into his mouth, his tongue plunged with his fingers, and Gretchen knew she was going to come fast if he kept that up.

"Like that. Let go," he murmured as her legs began to shake from the intensity.

Josh rose up, kissing her, fingers still plunging into her fast and hard. Tasting herself on him, erotic and hot, she exploded, her hands holding fistfuls of the sheets as he held her down on the bed with his mouth and fingers alone.

Before she could catch her breath, he pulled her flush to him, and stroked into her slowly, his body hard against her. The muscles in his arms and chest flexed and she stretched herself to let him in fully.

"Open your eyes."

She did, meeting his; the fierce need in him evident. She ran her hands over his face, up into his hair, seeing the emotion clearly for what it was. Love. Possession. She was his and he was hers.

She hooked her heel, digging into his hamstring, asking him for more. The power that was in him to lose control in her, to abandon his restraint and give all to her in that moment.

"I love you so damn much," he gasped as she squeezed her inner muscles around him, begging him for more.

With that, he devoured her mouth, and she clung to him as he went deeper and faster. She arched into him with the force of the emotion they shared and he let out a guttural moan and came, gasping her name as she held him tightly, tears bursting out at the intensity. She bit into his shoulder, urging him on, her pleasure building once more around him as he buried himself into her to the hilt, shaking.

When he let go, there was nothing else in the world—just him and her, shattering together. Always together.

He slumped against her and they stayed entwined, her throbbing with the knowledge that it could not be any more perfect than that.

chapter 16

The entire Neons club had shown up to the courthouse in their home uniforms. Travis was sitting up with Neptune's billet family, and Harv was on the other side, both with squared, tense shoulders and locked jaws. Beside Harv was another man, in a dark tailored suit, much more relaxed.

"That must be the lawyer," Gretchen whispered, reading his mind.

Josh and Gretchen stood near the back, taking the scene in once they had made it through security and been briefed on the rules. It had taken a full fifteen minutes to get through the detectors and wands. Apparently Gretchen had metal in her bra, and the wand had shrieked loudly. She had to let the female guard frisk her. Her face had made Josh laugh. Then he got frisked by a very large, very sweaty male guard and he stopped laughing.

It was a frigging circus.

Part of it was the activity around them. The craziness of a court in Las Vegas was not lost on him: women in skimpy clothing, people obviously coming down from a high, the sheer number of young men. The smell of cigarettes and sweat permeated the room, and he could not see Neptune in the defendant's holding area. A few harried lawyers and officials were sorting papers at the front of the room, the judge looking as if he'd just swallowed a lemon.

"Lots of support," she whispered. "Where do you want to sit?"

He ran a thumb over their joined hands, wishing he were anywhere else but there. Ric waved at him, gesturing to an empty spot. They made their way through the crowded room to the polished wood benches. Josh felt like he was on some sort of crime drama set, the way the dark wood and white plastered walls echoed the noise from the activity around them.

"Ric! How is your new baby!" Gretchen asked.

"She's wonderful. We named her Evangeline. She's almost a month old now," he said, beaming. He pulled out his phone, and as Josh waved to Harv and Travis, Gretchen oohed over pictures of Ric's newborn.

"Congrats, man," Josh said and punched Ric's shoulder.

"You next, bro," Ric teased and wiggled his eyebrows at Gretchen.

Josh pretended to look shocked, but in reality, the statement had not made him silently freak out like it would have before. Babies. Marriage. No longer an impossible thought for him as he looked at the woman beside him. She was a touchstone to a life he wanted. He cleared his throat as Gretchen laughed.

Several of the players waved and said hello to her as they settled to await Neptune's turn. Everyone was on edge. Josh was hopeful that things would go well for Neptune and that they could take him out of here today.

They sat through a few arraignments—some of them quick and to the point, some more drawn out. Most were guilty pleas and repeat offenders, while some were fines and releases. Groups of defendants were led out and the next group shuffled in. It was a conveyor belt of desperation and hardship. People brought low, people who hadn't been able to figure life out.

Not what anyone here would have envisioned for Neptune.

Josh felt the intake of breath around him and knew Neptune was in the room. Everyone on the Neons bench was rigid as he sat with a bunch of other men, these ones chained in a line by their hands. He was wearing a gray jumpsuit, had a swollen black eye, and looked utterly exhausted.

"Shit," Josh swore under his breath. Harv and the lawyer were deep in conversation, and he watched Neptune's billet mother stand up, then get pulled down by her husband, her hands on her mouth. Felicia, who had been hiding with the team, let out a *Lord Jesus, help* in her unmistakable midwestern accent and stood as well. She spied Gretchen and scooted over to sit beside her, shooing Ric out of the way. Ric chuckled and moved over beside Josh.

"Honey, it is good to see you here," Felicia said and squeezed Josh's arm for good measure as she took Gretchen's hand. "Neptune seeing all y'all will lift him. Lord knows."

Josh kept his eyes on Neptune, hoping the boy would look up and see everyone who was here for him. He looked utterly defeated, and Josh worried.

"Look up, dude. See us," he breathed to himself. Harv, Travis, and the lawyer couldn't see the defendant box easily from their spot at the front of the court.

When Neptune finally did look up, Josh got his attention. Neptune's eyes widened and he craned his neck, taking in the team. Then he looked back at Josh and tears started falling. His hands were restrained, but he lifted them in thanks. Josh swallowed, a lump in his throat. Some of the boys were quietly saying "Hey, Nep," and saluting him. *No talking to the people brought in for arraignment*—that had been one of the rules barked at them, but they did it anyway.

"It's okay," Gretchen murmured in his ear. "He'll be okay, Josh."

Josh was gripping the back of the bench in front of him so hard his knuckles were white. He relaxed, and she put her hands on his, pulling one into her lap, her touch soothing.

Travis had finally come back toward the team, his face a thundercloud. He saw Josh, then spied Gretchen, and a small smile lit his face, cutting through the scowl. Josh put his arm around her again, and they all moved over to let him sit beside his wife.

"Well. I knew you'd be back," he said simply.

"Tra-vis!" Felicia hissed and then giggled.

"Docket number 84754—Neptune Gilbert. Possession of a Schedule 2 drug without intent to sell," droned the court bailiff, and Neptune was led to the front of the court. The lawyer wove his way out beside him.

"All right, let's hear the plea," the judge said.

"Not guilty, Your Honor," the lawyer said.

"On what grounds?" the judge intoned, and tilted his head, as if studying Neptune.

"Your Honor, I would like to move that my client's Fourth Amendment rights were breached and that law enforcement performed an illegal search. My client was not driving his own vehicle; it was borrowed from a friend. He was not speeding, and the officers would not tell him why he was pulled over. Furthermore, he was not aware of the drugs in the vehicle. This also shows a lack of intent," the lawyer rattled off, placing papers on the desk in front of him.

"Let me see those papers," the judge said, beckoning to the bailiff to bring them up. He flipped through them quickly, and then he sighed and rubbed his eyes.

"Son, this wasn't your car?"

"No, sir," Neptune replied, his voice all but a hoarse whisper.

"Do we know whose car it was?" the judge asked.

"We do, Your Honor, and are working with law enforcement to find him. He has not been seen since my client's arrest."

The judge grunted and looked straight down at Neptune, who raised his head and looked back. Josh was proud of him for that. He had nothing to be ashamed of. What this would do to his confidence long-term, he didn't know.

You could hear a pin drop in the room.

"Son, you have a promising future ahead of you. May I suggest, in the future, you make better choices in who you associate with? I'm sure this experience has given you a good eyeful of what will happen if you do go down the road the officers thought you were already on."

The judge was a condescending asshole, but he was also, from the sounds of it, giving Neptune the benefit of the doubt. Every single person in that room was holding their breath now.

"Charges dropped. See the front office for your personal effects, and you are free to go, young man," he said and whacked the gavel once. The court bailiff handed a release package to the lawyer, and Neptune was deluged by his billet mom, her husband behind her, patting his shoulder once his restraints were removed.

The courtroom erupted in cheers, and Josh sagged in his seat, the stress evaporating. Gretchen was being hugged fiercely by Felicia. The noise forced the judge to bang his gavel.

"Out of here with that noise! I hate banging my damned gavel."

They exited quickly, and stood at the front of the courthouse, talking quietly in groups. No one was leaving until they saw Neptune walk out those doors. The team bus was parked illegally alongside the curb, so Ric drove around the block a few times waiting for everyone to come outside.

Felicia and Travis joined them not long after, and finally, Neptune bounced down the steps with his billet mom and dad.

Josh put his arms around his friend and hugged him for all he was worth. The relief at seeing him was the best thing. They thumped each other on the back for good measure.

"You're here for me," Neptune said into his shoulder.

"Of course," Josh replied and let him go. Neptune saw Gretchen and his eyes lit up. He reached down and hugged her, too, and she patted his back when he picked her up.

"I told you, man. She'd be back," he said as he set her down. "She's the one you're gonna leave baseball for. I know it."

"I'd never ask him to do that," Gretchen said and took Josh's hand. His chest swelled. It was a simple thing for her to say, but the meaning behind it was huge. It meant she wanted to make it work, even if it meant he was on the road and not where she was. For now.

"I see it. He loves you. Has since he met you. You're the one." A big toothy grin spread across Neptune's face, then he ambushed Josh for another hug.

"Means a lot, you being here," he said, muffled.

The team surrounded him, and Josh stepped back to let them. They saw Harv and made their way over to him.

"All good? Where's the lawyer?"

"Gone already. Had to catch a plane, he said," Harv replied.

Neptune looked exhausted, but his spirit had returned, the toothy grin a mile wide, his hands gesturing as he talked. Josh butted in and shook Neptune's hand.

"Listen. I'm in town until tomorrow morning, and you need to get your shit together after all this. So, end of season, come see me in Dallas again, okay?" he said, and Neptune grinned widely and agreed. The rest of the team shook Josh's hand, saying goodbye. It was all a blur, but it felt good.

"Joshua Malvern. You are bringing this young lady for dinner, you hear?" Felicia called over. He would prefer to spend the next twenty-four hours in bed with Gretchen, but you didn't say no to Felicia.

"Do I have a choice?" he called back.

"Seven tonight," she added, wagging a finger.

Harv put his hand on Neptune's back. "Let's get you home, son. A good meal and a good bed."

Neptune waved as Harv and his billet family pulled him away. The team left for the bus, and suddenly, the noise and crowd disappeared. They were alone in front of the courthouse. He pulled Gretchen in for a hug.

"Whatcha wanna do now?" he drawled. "My plane to Dallas doesn't leave until eleven tomorrow. Other than dinner—"

Gretchen laughed and kissed him, wrapping her arms around his neck as she did. "Anything," she said breathlessly as they started walking toward the parking lot.

chapter 17

Gretchen stood in the middle of a wine shop, trying to decide what to bring for dinner. She didn't want to be too upper-crust but felt she should share a good bottle. Something from California would be best, but she also wondered if she could branch out into Old World and have it not be too much. Travis and Felicia were down-to-earth folks. Likely a good roast or casserole dinner—good, homemade food. She was looking forward to it.

"Do you think they would like white or red?" she asked as she picked up a bottle of oaked Chardonnay and frowned, setting it down again. No, that wasn't right.

"Felicia likes her wine sparkly. She puts ice cubes in it. Whatever you pick is going to knock their socks off. Travis prefers beer."

Gretchen decided to gift two bottles. A Prosecco and a red.

One for Felicia, one for dinner if they so chose. A red went with most meats unless they did seafood, but sometimes a red would go well with something like paella or a rich bisque.

She was overthinking it again. She turned to look for the sales staff. They were alone in the wine shop, which was attached to a French bistro, and it was charmingly set out with the wine in wood baskets, paper packing spilling out. People came in and browsed, most walking back out. The prices were a bit high for her liking, but she knew she could get vintages here she likely could not get at one of the liquor stores on the strip.

"Excuse me? I am looking for a specific prosecco," she said as she finally spotted a store clerk.

The young man who was unpacking a crate looked up and walked over. "What is it? We don't carry a lot of prosecco."

"Casa Vinicola Morando, the Ferrina, either 2015 or 2016," she said, thinking back on what she had tasted last year. It had been the lightest and fruitiest of the proseccos she had tried. It would suit perfectly, even if you put ice cubes in it, which was a horrible thought. Then she checked herself. No judging. To each their own, right?

The clerk thought on it as they walked over to the lookup kiosk in the center of the store. He typed it in and two bottles came up, one of them a 2015. He looked back at her expectantly.

"Yes, that one, please."

"Anything else, Miss?" he asked.

"Do you have any Blackstone Merlot? Any vintage is fine."

He held up a finger and scooted off, bringing her back a bottle of just that. "Excellent choice. My go-to bottle for every day. Reminds me of a ripasso. Pairs with anything, honestly."

She hefted the bottle. "This is one of my favorite California merlots. I love the texture as well as the bright flavor. It doesn't taste young, and you don't have to set it down."

He looked at her, seemingly impressed. "You know your wine."

"I'm a sommelier," Gretchen offered, shrugging. She didn't want to be snobbish or demean his own expertise. It felt nice to be perusing and thinking about wine without teaching or advising. After a hectic day, the stress of the courthouse fraying her nerves, it was a welcome change of pace.

"I'm studying to do that too. This job created a monster," he added, winking. She wished he would quit flirting with her, his eyes shifting to her chest.

Josh came up behind her and took the merlot from her hand, kissing her on the cheek as if on cue. The store clerk looked at him, and then stepped away, coming back with the prosecco bottle, less excitement on his face.

"Fancy," Josh said, eyeing the bottles, running a finger over the gold label. "Do you want to pick anything else up? We can ship it back to your place?"

She bit her lip as she shifted the prosecco into her arms. A zinfandel would be nice to take home, one she couldn't get easily in Canada. "Do you have any Gary Farrell zin?"

"The Grist or Maffei?"

"One of each, please. I want to try them before I attempt to order a case from somewhere."

The clerk tapped his screen and then took off, and Josh put his arm around her while she waited. "He likes you," he murmured in her ear. His arm was tightly possessive, his hand secure on her shoulder.

"He likes that a girl can talk wine with him," she replied. "I'm sure there's nothing more."

"Oh, no, darling. Your top button is undone. He likes you."

She looked down and indeed, she was showing a bit of cleavage. She grimaced and did the button up quickly, as Josh laughed behind her, his chest shaking.

She gave him a stern look over her shoulder and moved toward the cash register. The clerk brought her two zin bottles to the counter, and Josh gave him a credit card.

"Let me," he said and shook his head as Gretchen opened her mouth to protest. "No, really—let me."

"Okay but keep the receipt; I can write off part of the cost of the zin as research," she said as Josh picked up the bagged wine.

"You can do that?" he asked, surprised.

"Uh-huh."

"I think we need to do more research then," he quipped, plastering a cheesy grin across his face. She laughed and swatted at him.

"Thank you," she said to the clerk and he stepped away from the register again, his attention diverted by someone else looking through a bin of bottles.

"Off to the McGoverns," Josh said cheerily, his mood bright and playful. She looked at him and saw how relaxed he was, the change in him. He was already gorgeous, but when he was relaxed, he was something else, and it took her breath away. Had since the day he looked up at her in the airport.

"This place is good for you, you know that?" she blurted.

He turned as he reached the car and tilted his head. "You think so?" he replied, giving her a kiss that was relaxed and gentle, yet promising more later.

"You are good for me, Firecracker," he said when he let her go, breathless and rumpled. "Now, let's go."

Josh swirled the last of his beer and chugged it, standing on the back deck. It was just dark, the tiny tiki patio lights glowing multicolored against the pergola they were strung from. There was traffic noise and laughter from next door. There was a slight breeze. He was enjoying every second of it.

He and Travis had talked baseball all evening—discussing the team, some of the division stats, and the Longhorns' chances in the postseason. It was completely comfortable. On a back deck in the suburbs, drinking beer, and talking baseball. A quiet, normal evening.

Felicia laughed at something Gretchen said, and he turned to see the coach's wife flipping the ribs on the barbecue, Gretchen wielding a basting brush as she did. They had been talking non-stop as they flitted to and from the kitchen. Gretchen reached out to peck his cheek, and he pinched her butt as she passed by him. He turned back to Travis, who was silently turning his beer glass in his hand, watching his wife and Gretchen as well.

"Son, I gotta say, she's a good influence on you. Harv is wrong about her."

"Harv? What'd he say?" Josh asked. "I know he talked to her when she was here last, kind of gave her the shove to get me back on focus, but—"

"He thinks you're gonna leave baseball because of her. He relies on you as a star on his athlete roster. You're one of his biggest paydays," Travis said quietly. "He's pushing you to find another contract, but he's mentioned free agency as well, yeah? He's looking to make sure you top your salary out."

"He's a good man, Coach. He's helped me get where I am,"

201

Josh replied, interrupting him. "I understand where you're coming from, but—"

"He was agitated about her being at the courthouse today. Said something about her butting into business not meant for her, even though having her there was a good thing."

Josh didn't know what to make of that. He refused to believe Harv wouldn't be happy for him finding Gretchen, falling in love.

"Do you love her?" Travis asked, reading his mind.

"I do," Josh said quietly, admitting it to another person for the first time. He shifted a bit on his feet. It was truly real now.

Travis grunted at that and turned to him, shaking the top of his glass at Josh. "Marry her, then. Don't wait. Figure out the travel after. If she's the one, don't waste time, son."

He blinked at the direct advice. "Coach? You okay?"

Travis twisted his lips, and then cleared his throat, clearly uncomfortable. Gretchen came back out and placed a bowl of corn cobs down on the table, winking at him, and the moment was over. Travis stood straight up, taking Josh's glass out of his hand. "Get more beer," he muttered and paced away. He was moving slowly, a hitch in one hip, and Josh frowned. When did he get old? Josh got up and poked his head in the back screen door.

"Can I help?" he called to Felicia.

"You just stand there and look gorgeous," Felicia said back, laughing. Gretchen was pulling the ribs off the barbecue, so he took a moment, slipped in, and stood beside Felicia, who was cutting some fresh baguette to go with what looked to be bruschetta.

"What's up with Coach?" he asked quietly. "He's not himself, Felicia. Something's wrong."

Felicia's hand tightened on the bread knife, and then she put it down. Josh put a hand on her back, sensing he had asked the absolute wrong question. She was quiet, clearly debating whether to tell him something. She took a big breath in and out, her face grim.

"He isn't, Josh. He's sick," she blurted. "It's his prostate."

Shit. Josh hung his head, the news hitting him square in the chest. Cancer. She didn't have to say it. There was usually only one thing an older man had go wrong with that body part.

"How long?" he asked.

"We don't know. We only found out a couple of months ago," she said, then looked him square in the eye. "The staff and team do not know, honey. He doesn't want them to."

"Shit," Josh swore. "I'm sorry."

He encircled Felicia with his arms, needing the hug more than wanting to comfort her. The weight of the news on him, the idea that Coach would be sidelined by this—let alone have to leave the Neons—sunk in and he cleared his throat, trying to lock the emotion away so he wouldn't lose it. Travis had been the manager there for years, even before Josh had found his rookie feet in Boston. It would be a huge blow to the organization as a whole.

"What can I do?" he murmured, finally gaining some control. "I want to help."

"You are helping, honey. He's always had a soft spot for you, coming into the league by your own bootstraps, working your little tush off to make it big. You're practically family, considering the number of times you've stayed with us. That you're here, now? It raised his spirits a bunch."

"But—"

"No buts, honey. He's a grown man. He'll fight it. Just be his friend," Felicia said firmly, let him go, and then picked up the knife, continuing to cut slices off the bread. She added as he turned to go back outside, "The offer still stands, Josh. You fit here. When you're tired of the glam up there in the big leagues, think about us and the good you could do."

Josh stood for a moment inside the kitchen. Was nothing ever easy? Despite the stress of Neptune's arrest, it had been easily handled, and he'd had Gretchen by his side. But now, here was a new stress to weigh him down, on top of his potential IL if his checkups weren't good. It felt like he was riding a roller coaster.

"Fuck," he swore softly and squared his shoulders. Well, he'd deal with this too. Coach was too damned important to him.

He caught Travis's eye as they sat for dinner on the deck, and Travis looked at Felicia, then back at him and thinned his lips. Gretchen was uncorking her red wine and filling glasses. The candle flames were dancing in the breeze. The normal, comfortable feeling was gone, and he took a deep breath. He had to say something but now was not the right time.

"You told him, didn't you, woman," Travis snapped abruptly.

"He's not stupid. He practically guessed, Travis. Yes, I did. Now do you want a full or half rack to start?" Felicia said matter-of-factly, leveling her gaze at him.

Gretchen looked between the two of them, confused. Josh picked up her hand, folding it into his, thankful for the anchor. He looked at Travis, studying the man, seeing the stress from him, understanding it for the first time.

"I have cancer," Travis said.

Gretchen's mouth formed an *O*, and she squeezed Josh's hand. As Felicia filled their plates, she continued squeezing. He lifted his glass, the scent of the wine appealing. He needed a drink to steady his nerves. He held his glass up farther, and the other three joined him.

"To kicking cancer's ass, Coach. If you can whip a bunch of green-eared punks into a good team, you can beat this bullshit."

Travis was silent, then shook his head, a smile ghosting across his lips as he took a sip, his eyebrows rising as he tasted the wine.

The rest of the dinner went well. Felicia exclaimed three times how nice the wine tasted and wrote down the name on her grocery list after her second glass. Travis finished his glass, which made Felicia stare at her husband in shock.

They stayed outside after Felicia had forced apple pie on them. Travis had gone into the house to grab playing cards, and it was just Josh and Gretchen looking out into the night sky. The cicadas slowly appeared, weaving through the rosebushes and grass in the garden, making their noise as the light completely left the sky. Gretchen leaned her head on his shoulder. The peaceful feeling had returned, thankfully.

"Can we capture this moment forever?" she sighed. "I know the news you got tonight sucks, but this is really, really relaxing."

Josh hummed a response and squeezed her. It was. There was more to them than just sex, and the roller coaster of emotions the day had given him was making him think thoughts he shouldn't right now.

They played Euchre out on the back deck, Felicia draining the bottle of Prosecco that Gretchen had bought, much to Gretchen's delight. As they were leaving, Josh shook Travis's hand, then pulled him into an uncharacteristic hug. The older man stiffened but then relaxed, welcoming the gesture.

"I won't say anything, but think about it. You should. Look how that team rallied around Nep today. Let people help, Coach. You aren't done yet," he said in Travis's ear.

It felt like the world to him when Travis squeezed him harder, then let him go. "You've become a good man, son. Thank you."

"If you need me, you call, right?" he said to both Travis and Felicia, winking. "You always ask me to stay. Maybe next time I will. You've got a good thing here."

Laughs all around at that statement, more hugs, and then they were walking out toward the car, parked on the street.

"Hotel?" Josh asked.

"Can we go see the fountains? It's a hot night, and I'd love to walk the strip for a bit," Gretchen replied.

"Sounds perfect."

chapter 18

They stopped for Italian sodas and walked up the strip, heading toward the fountains. Gretchen learned that Josh hated blueberries when he tried her blueberry-flavored soda. He'd been game to see if it tasted fake enough for him to maybe like it, and the face he'd made had doubled her over with laughter.

"Okay, blueberry is off the list," she giggled when he'd finally cleared the taste from his mouth, and they continued on, onlookers smiling at them knowingly as they walked hand in hand.

The quiet they shared as they walked was wonderful, the crowds surging around them. Gretchen was turning over Travis's news. It had to be painful for Josh. His playful and happy mood from earlier was gone, replaced by worry lines in his forehead as he tried to keep it locked inside.

The fountains were blasting away, the music trumpeting in the background, and she leaned along the wall to watch. Josh pulled her into his arms, resting his chin on her head, and they just breathed together as the lights and water played up and down.

"I don't want today to be over," she said.

"No. Me neither. You have to go home tomorrow?" he replied.

"Yeah. I took an impromptu vacation, but the paperwork is still there waiting for me," she sighed and turned to face him. Looking up, Josh's face was turned away from her, unreadable in the semi-dark as the lights of the fountains played across the angles of his jaw and cheekbones. She watched that for a moment, the sight of him setting off tiny flutters in her stomach. She wondered if it would always be like that when she looked at him. She hoped so.

"Well, we can merge calendars, see when the next sync-up is," he offered. "I know it isn't ideal, Gretch. But I want this to work."

He looked down at her then, and she couldn't help it; she reached up and touched his face, smoothing her thumb over his cheekbone. Josh closed his eyes.

"Whatever it takes," she said.

"You feel so damned good," he whispered and leaned down to kiss her, the stress of the evening bleeding through.

She rose to him, and they locked into each other—the crowd, the fountains, and the noise disappearing. Everything but his touch and his breath and his lips parting hers went away. She didn't care who saw, and if anyone dared interrupt them, she would raise holy hell. No autographs tonight, folks.

He was hers.

She broke the kiss to look at him again, sensing him tense. "I—" he started, but stopped, swallowing.

"What?"

"I can't ask you to leave your life. I can't leave mine. I hate the idea of being so damned far away from you," he stuttered and hung his head. "I know what I want, but I don't know how to do it."

"I feel the same. It was overwhelming at first. My best friend jet-sets everywhere, I never see her, but I make it work with her," Gretchen said, feeling it was a poor comparison. "I mean, it isn't the same, but is, in a way, right? We work hard to make sure we talk almost every day. We can start there, Josh. You don't have to figure it out alone."

"You said it wasn't so easy, that night at your place. I said it is as easy as we want it to be. It's not right, but it's not wrong. I'm feeling really overwhelmed right now," he confessed.

"You don't have to make any decisions tonight," she added, hoping to calm him some. "We have time. You need to process everything that was thrown at you today, and you need to focus on your shoulder when you get home."

Josh took her hand and started walking. Gretchen followed, being pulled along, and when she caught up to his long stride, he put his arm around her to walk in step, slowing himself down.

"Let's go back to the hotel," he said quietly. "I want to curl up and just hold you, let everything else go away."

"I like that idea," she said, determined to be what he needed.

.   .   .

Harv had left him three messages to call him back, and he ignored them all as he sat on the bed and packed his bag. Someone had seen them last night on the strip, and because of that, Harv was in a stew. He'd mentioned Gretchen in his third exasperated message.

Josh already knew about that, had seen the photographer out of the corner of his eye. It was the first time that he hadn't cared.

Josh wasn't sure what to say to the man. Harv was still his agent, and their relationship was important to him, but what Travis had said nagged at him. He didn't want to be dubious of Harv's intentions. He'd told Gretchen what he'd said, and she'd actually defended Harv, saying it was important to clear the air. He had to think about his own job and his bottom line, she said. She agreed that it was kind of a dick thing to talk to Travis about it before him, but she encouraged Josh to bring it up with Harv and to set it right.

"We avoided each other for two months and look what happened," she offered as he had grudgingly agreed to her advice. "If we'd been more truthful, we'd have had a lot more sex."

That got him laughing and less upset, and she had pushed him over. He discovered not long after that that she was very ticklish when they had started tousling across the bed.

So yes, he would talk to Harv. But right now, he didn't want to. He had more important things to get through. His flight was leaving an hour after Gretchen's, so they were going to the airport together. She was answering some emails on her phone, her small suitcase already packed as soon as she had gotten up and dressed. She was efficient, he had to give her that.

She looked like perfection, her wild hair falling around her face, her jeans molded perfectly to her sexy-as-hell hips and ass, a black blouse clinging to her in all the right places, and a turquoise necklace that hung perfectly down her cleavage. His firecracker.

He could watch her forever and not get tired of her.

She looked up, sensing his eyes on her, he hoped. Their connection was deeper than ever after all they had done and said in the past two days. Josh felt like she was a part of him, which was making it hard to know they were going to be separated soon.

They had come back to the room last night and made love for hours, slowly learning each other again, making the most of their time together. She'd let him explore her completely. There wasn't one inch of her he hadn't kissed or stroked. He knew her by heart now.

The memory of them intertwined while he slowly rocked in and out of her, her soft sighs as she moved, loose and hot, would be etched in his brain forever. How he'd lost his mind when she looked into his eyes and told him she loved him, breathless as her entire body shook with an orgasm he was teasing out, buried deep inside her.

The comfort and intimacy of just taking their time and drawing it out had blown him away. The softness erasing the stress that had built inside him, from the courthouse to learning about Coach's cancer.

Gretchen stood and walked to him, placing a hand on his shoulder.

"You are thinking too hard again," she murmured and leaned in to kiss his cheek. He swerved and caught her lips, wanting to taste her, the thought of the sex they'd had making him hard as a rock in an instant. She relaxed and sank into him, crawling up onto his lap.

"I am hard, thinking about you," he half joked, and she looked down, quirking an eyebrow at his erection bulging through his jeans.

"Josh," Gretchen admonished. "Seriously?"

He patted her bum and stood her up. "Yeah. What can I say? I'm—"

"Don't say it!" she laughed, holding a hand up. "Good grief."

He chuckled and they did a final room check before leaving, the time upon them to make the break from their sanctuary into the real world and their obligations. He didn't want to leave, and took a long, last kiss from her as they stood at the door to the room. She hadn't minded; she was dreading it too.

At the airport, they stood hand in hand. She was going to the international terminal, so they had to say goodbye before going through security. It was tearing his heart apart as they stood, arms wrapped, tears falling from her eyes.

"I love you, Gretch. I'll see you soon," he promised, wiping her tears with the palms of his hands. "This hurts way too fucking much, but—"

She finally wrenched herself away from him and headed toward the door. He followed her, grabbed her, and kissed her soundly one more time.

"I love you," she mumbled through his kiss. "So much. Be safe. I'll call you tonight."

With that, Josh let her go, his hands in his pockets as she waved once more and disappeared through the swinging doors.

He turned and headed for his terminal gate, the weight of the world on his shoulders, big decisions hanging over his head, and a long day to stew on them.

*　*　*

Gretchen dropped her bag at the foot of her bed and immediately dialed Josh. He answered on the first ring.

"Hey," he drawled. "How was your flight?"

She flopped onto the bed. "Good. I was thinking about you the whole way."

"Yeah? Dirty thoughts, I hope," he said, his voice husky as she laughed.

"You are the worst, Joshua Malvern," she said, then sighed. "Okay, maybe a few dirty thoughts."

That made him laugh, and she did too. Phone sex was not out of the question, but she was tired. It hit her that he was all the way in Dallas, when all she wanted was to have his arms around her.

"Dammit, Josh, I wish you were here," she blurted, frustrated by their distance.

"I wish I was there too. Listen. I am wiped, and I have to be at the stadium tomorrow morning early, then to the clinic to get my shoulders assessed. I really, really need to sleep."

"Okay."

"Before you hang up, go into your suitcase," he said. "I left you something. I know you haven't opened it yet."

She bounced up from the bed, lifted her case up, and opened it quickly, putting the phone on speaker beside her. Sitting on top of her clothing was the dress shirt he'd worn the night he'd come to her place—the night he'd told her he loved her. She'd brought it for him, and he'd put it right back in when she wasn't looking. She picked it up, inhaling his scent, and an envelope fell back onto the suitcase.

"You keep the shirt. It looks better on you. In fact, if I get up to see you, I expect you to answer the door wearing nothing but that, you hear?"

Gretchen laughed and held the shirt closer, picking up the envelope. "What is this?" she asked, flipping it. "When did you do this?"

"Before you got out of bed, when I went down to the lobby to grab coffee. I snuck it into your suitcase after you packed," he chuckled. "Open the envelope, Gretchen."

She did and pulled out a glossy five-by-seven of the two of them kissing at the fountains. It was a good photo of them, lit very nicely with the fountains in the background. The photographer had a good eye.

Josh had one arm around her, bending her back a bit, the other hand buried in the hair at the nape of her neck. Her hands were on his face. She ran a finger down the image, recalling how deep that kiss had felt, into her toes. She had pictures of him on her phone, funny selfies they had taken, but none of the two of them like this, that was for sure.

"Who took this?" she asked, worried. "Were we being followed last night?"

"It was on the front page of a sports fan gossip website. Timo sent me a note with the link. I think this is why Harv was trying to get in touch with me. He's miffed I didn't give him a heads-up to manage the press around it because of my days off. It also seems I have a female fan base that's very upset that Joshua Malvern might be off the market, given the comments on the news article."

"Well, you *are* off the market," she quipped.

"I had the hotel staff print them from Timo's link. The other one I brought home," he replied, his voice thick with emotion. "And yes, I am."

"It's a good picture. I know this likely makes you a bit frustrated, being followed during a private moment," she murmured. "Thank you."

"Nope. I couldn't care less, believe it or not," he said and sighed. "Okay, now I have to go. I am falling asleep here, gorgeous. Give me something to help me dream."

She sighed, and tilted her head, looking at the image in her hand. "I love you, Josh," she said. "And I'm going to wear your shirt to bed. Unbuttoned."

"Oh my God," he groaned. "I like that idea."

"I'll bet you do," she replied.

"Good night, Gretchen," Josh said with a yawn. She pushed the End button before they devolved into a no-you-hang-up-first teenage romance phone game. She looked at the image in her hands more and carefully placed it on her dresser.

It was getting a nice frame tomorrow.

She climbed into bed, wearing his shirt, the scent of Josh helping her feel a little closer to him as she drifted off.

chapter 19

Josh was sitting in the doctor's office when someone knocked and a middle-aged man in a sweater vest peeked in.

"Mr. Malvern," he said and offered his hand, which Josh shook. "I'm Dr. Kilborne. I've had a look at the images from your file."

Josh stiffened. He hadn't wasted time, just launched into it. Most of the doctors on retention by the league were quite busy and to the point, so this wasn't unusual. But Josh was on edge. The ultrasound technician had made some odd noises at his appointment and sent him for X-rays. The X-ray technician sent him for an MRI, and all of that had been sent to the organization doctor on retainer. Josh had been shuttled from one lab to another in quick succession.

"Okay, so what's going on in there?" Josh asked.

The doctor sat and pursed his lips, crossing his legs. He looked Josh in the eye. That was never a good sign.

"You have degeneration in both shoulder joints, as well as what looks to be bursitis in the right one. Not severe, but it is stiffening your joint. Both shoulders have mild calcification, more so in the right."

"I know they've been stiff, and there's the usual soreness from working out, but I'm not in a lot of pain," Josh countered, rolling his right shoulder. It was as stiff as it normally was, but maybe that was why they were locking. The bursitis would lead to swelling, which would lead to less range of motion. Which meant a shitty swing with a bat in his hand.

"Do you have a history of arthritis in your family?"

Josh shook his head. "Nope. But it explains why my swing has been weak as shit lately."

The doctor chuckled, and then held out his hands, sobering. "I'll level with you. The degeneration is early signs of osteoarthritis. I won't lie and tell you we can fix it, because we can't. The bursitis is inflammation that we can reduce with anti-inflammatories, but you can't cheat time and it will come back if you stress the joint. Thankfully, your rotator cuff is in pristine shape, which, if you keep to a good fitness routine, will help immensely from losing basic mobility. We can do cortisone shots, but those are just a Band-aid solution and not a road you want to go down if you can help it."

"But will it improve performance?" Josh asked. Anything at this point was under consideration.

"Given your track record and fitness, yes. Six weeks to six months of relief per injection, but we don't like injecting more often than three or four times a year."

"So, I would be getting a few good games then—"

"A slow decline until your next injection," the doctor finished for him. "Your bursitis would be helped by this, too, since you have a fairly normal impingement. But I would be cautious because any irritation can lead to further impingements down the road."

"What are you saying?" Josh asked quietly, lacing his fingers together, leaning on his thighs. "Am I done?"

"No, not necessarily. But this will affect your performance more and more over time. You might want to think about negotiating less time in the lineup or your plans for retirement."

Retirement. There it was. The *R* word. He looked down at his hands. He could keep going, take the pills and injections, push his body, but then where would he be? He didn't want to be the guy who was forced to retire with the words *Mendoza Line* attached to his profile. He wanted to be remembered as a good all-round player. One who could do his job well.

"Okay. What's the plan for right now?" he finally said. "I assume I am going to be IL-ed with this?"

"I will recommend that, yes. The bursitis will get progressively worse if you don't treat it now. I'll put in the rec for physio, and we'll get you started on some NSAIDs. Think about the injections and discuss them with the coaching team. Have you taken any prescription anti-inflammatories before?"

"I'd rather take the time off and use ibuprofen. I've seen what that shit can do to a stomach," Josh replied testily. He'd only been on the strong pills once, and it was awful.

"Fair enough," the doctor said crisply. "I also have a note here to look at your knee if you wanted?"

"No need. Straight up twisted it in spring training, and it's been a bit weak since," Josh replied, wanting to be out of there, his stomach turning and his nerves jumping. "It's well on its way to being mended. Physio helped."

The doctor stood and offered his hand again. "I'm sorry, Mr. Malvern. I know this wasn't the best news."

Josh shook his hand quickly, and then let out a big breath, attempting to stay calm and friendly "No, but it's better to know now, not when I'm forced out and looking like I crashed and burned, right?"

The doctor handed him the paper prescription, agreed good-naturedly, and opened the door for him. Josh stalked out, rode the elevator down from the offices, and stepped out into the Dallas afternoon sun, more at a loss than ever before.

His mind was whirling as he drove over to the ballpark. If he retired, what did that mean for him? The idea of not being beholden to baseball and the hustle to keep playing was a huge, scary black hole. It was all he'd done for the last ten years. Longer if you counted his play in college.

His thoughts wandered to what it would look like, not playing baseball. He could go live anywhere. Do anything. Have a house that was his, not just a rented condo. Coach's spiel about seeing the sunrise while he could poked in too. Coach would need him in the future if he had to take time off. If he wasn't playing, maybe he could take the Neons up on an offer to coach, if a position was open.

Retirement meant he could spend more time with Gretchen; potentially forever.

He parked and sat, hands on the wheel, his stomach tight as a clammy sweat stole over him. He knew what he had to do; what he wanted to do. Could he do it? Could he really retire from being a baseball player?

Josh needed some advice, and the first person he knew he should call was Harv. He pulled out his phone.

"Josh. Been trying to get a hold of you," Harv answered gruffly. "What did the doctor say?"

Josh looked down at the prescription on the passenger seat, and on cue, his shoulder twitched in pain. He hissed, rolling it forward. "I have early-onset bursitis in both shoulders. Throwing arm is worse. Permanent damage."

Harv swore, knowing exactly what that meant. "You going to take some injections?"

"I don't think so. I need to talk with you about plans for the future," Josh said and held his breath. This wasn't going to be easy with Harv. What Coach had said still stung, and the voice messages he'd left hadn't indicated he would be happy about what Josh was about to say.

"Is there another treatment plan then? Are you on the list until you get this shit sorted out?" Harv asked.

"Yes, on the IL." Josh hesitated, unsure of how to broach the subject. "Harv, listen, I think it's time."

Harv grunted. "Time for what, son? A second opinion?"

"Retirement."

"Are you out of your mind? Take a few days and think about this. That is not a hasty decision to make," Harv snapped. "I didn't teach you to lie down after the first punch, boy. You get back up and keep fighting."

"I've thought about it. I'm ready. I want to go while I'm still in the game, not struggling to keep my ass above the cut. You have to understand that," Josh replied, hoping he could make him understand. This was his decision, not Harv's. He needed his support to make this decision, not try and talk him out of it.

"What I understand is that you are giving up. You've got a chance at another year as a free agent, sign somewhere lucrative. I was working on a deal with you to end up in New York, for God's sake. You want to throw away a multimillion-dollar contract?"

Josh's anger bubbled at that statement. He let out a breath to temper his response. "It isn't about the money. I've made enough. It is about my life, my body. I want to still be able to throw a baseball when I'm in my forties, Harv. Be a coach at little league for my kids."

"This is about Gretchen. I knew it," Harv said, the anger in his voice crackling out over the phone. *Shit.* He was still mad about that damned picture and the article.

"It has nothing to do with her."

"Bullshit. It has everything to do with her. Since you met her, your head's been up your ass, son. A woman isn't worth your career," Harv said.

"She's worth every damned bit as much as my career, Harv. But she isn't why. Why are you against this? It isn't like I'm twenty and need you to steer me around all the bullshit," Josh snapped back.

"She is a phase. She got her hooks into you in Vegas and now—"

"I'm in love with her, and that is not changing. She is in my life, likely for good. I'd appreciate it if you didn't insult my girlfriend, Harv," he interrupted.

"She's not your girlfriend, She's a passing fancy."

Wow. Josh pinched the bridge of his nose. Was that what Harv really thought of him? After all this time, he didn't trust him to know himself? He was arguing not only about his career, but his personal life too. Had he let Harv run his life, with an influence beyond what he should have? His parents had never been there for him to advise on what he should do, and Harv had picked up that slack when he was fresh into the farm system and needed that guiding hand.

He looked up at the stadium at the other end of the parking lot, looming large and steady, and his determination solidified. He was his own man now. This was his call, and he was going to make it.

"Enough. I need your support to do this, Harv," he said in a clipped tone. "You've never steered me wrong, but this time, I am making the decision."

Harv grunted again. "I'm in Philly right now. I can't get to Dallas until tomorrow. Hold off until then, at least? Let's talk before you make a huge mistake."

Mistake. It would be a mistake right now to waffle on this, and the timing was good. They could set out the notice of his IL, and then he could gracefully exit with a retirement notice postseason, still on a major-league roster, not filtering out to the farm system and fading into obscurity. If he waited, he risked changing his mind. If he changed his mind, he was in for the remainder of a career that was slowly tanking.

As he absorbed Harv's words, Josh realized it wasn't just because of his shoulders. He was tired of the hustle. He wanted to settle down. Try something new.

"I'm at the stadium to meet with the management team. They'll have the doctor's report already. I'll conference you in."

Harv sighed loudly into the phone. "You sure, son?"

"Yes," Josh stated.

"Fine. Call me when you are in with the team," Harv said, then hung up.

Josh stared at the phone a moment, understanding that the conversation he'd just had with Harv had severed their friendship. Maybe not permanently, but it still felt as if everything had changed. Maybe he had? Had the past few months given him that push to truly look beyond the focus of the day-to-day of his job?

He looked at his watch. He didn't have time to call Gretchen; they needed him in there as soon as he arrived, and he'd delayed it by talking to Harv.

He pulled the key out of the ignition and made his way in to talk to his team.

*   *   *

Gretchen heard the news alert beep on her phone and stopped what she was doing. Her heart leaped into her mouth as she read the tag from the app notification and tapped the #*Malvern* tag.

Josh was officially on the injured list. They were citing an upper body persistent injury that would keep him out for at least the rest of the regular season. It had just been released, and she let out a bleat of surprise.

"Oh no," she said and bolted to her feet in surprise. She dialed his number, but it went straight to voice mail.

"Josh. I just saw the news. Call me when you can. I'm sorry. I love you."

She paced around the condo, picking things up and putting them back down, rearranging the throw pillows and lap blanket. She wandered into her kitchen, forgetting why she went in, and then walked out.

Eventually she settled back to work, and when evening fell, she looked at her phone. No texts, nothing.

"He must be tied up with things," she muttered to herself, restlessness nudging at her to pace around her condo. Her stomach grumbled in response to walking from her office into the kitchen. She opened the fridge in the darkened room, noticing that once again, she had neglected to get groceries, catching up on her work.

"Frig," she muttered.

Her phone buzzed as she was sifting through the takeout menus magnetized to the side of the fridge. She leaped and answered it without looking, hoping it was Josh.

"Hello?"

"Hey, girlie! How's it going?"

Sharla's voice was not the one Gretchen had wanted to hear, but she'd take it. It would be good to talk to someone.

"Hi!" she replied, trying to sound cheerful and carefree. "It's late where you are. What's up?"

"What's up is that I saw the news on Josh. He okay?"

"I don't know. I haven't heard from him yet. I left him a message but—" she let out a sigh. "I'm pretty sure he's dealing with a lot."

Sharla made a noise on the other end of the phone that sounded like irritation.

"I know, I know. I'm sure he'll call," Gretchen added lamely.

"Oh honey, it isn't that. I just realized I forgot to invoice someone. Look. I'm in England right now, at headquarters. Kevin forwarded the news on Josh, and I wanted to make sure you're okay."

Gretchen pictured her friend sifting through paperwork, in some wood-paneled office at Kevin's estate, likely in her flannel Looney Tunes pajamas, completely out-of-place in a stately home, air-quoting *headquarters* with an annoyed look on her face.

"Seriously, it's like, middle of the night there. What are you doing up still?"

"Can't sleep," Sharla replied wearily. "Jet lag."

"Sweetie, you need sleep."

Sharla snorted a laugh. "I need a lot of things, Gretch."

"What's up, Sharla? Something's not right," Gretchen countered. Maybe if Sharla wasn't face to face with her, it would help her unload what was bugging her, which she had an inkling was about Kevin.

Sharla sniffled and let out a sigh.

"I don't know." Sharla let out another sniffle, obviously holding in tears. "I mean—"

"You love him, but you're afraid of what that might mean?" Gretchen guessed, getting right to the point.

"Something like that."

"Tell me, then," Gretchen said.

"It's not like we'd work long term, and I love what we've built here, you know? I'd have to leave if we—oh hell, Gretch. It's not like I'm more than a passing fancy for him, I'm not what he needs."

"I doubt that. Why wouldn't it work, honey?" Gretchen prodded quietly. "Why don't you let yourself have this? He's pretty friggin' awesome, and he obviously cares. I've seen it."

"He's an *earl*, Gretchen. I'm a nobody from Hicksville, Ontario. His mother hates me, and—"

"And what?"

"If we were together, I'd have to be this polite and perfect society wife who goes to balls and functions and royal things. I'm not cut out for that. I might even have to meet the Queen, and could you just picture that disaster?"

Gretchen wanted to reach through her phone and hug her friend, who clearly didn't think she was worthy of the guy she loved. Which was, of course, completely wrong. If anything, Kevin saw Sharla's worth and how amazing she was. Intelligent, beautiful, and even though she wasn't a typical classy society snob, she could hold her own when she put the effort in and the chips were down. She would be a force to reckon with, and Gretchen had a mental image of her friend ringside at a polo match, downing mint juleps and heckling the riders out on the field with her big, brassy voice, like the scene from *Pretty Woman*. Gretchen held in a laugh.

"Oh sweetie," she said instead. "I could tell you to just do it, and it's what I'm supposed to say. But I understand."

More sniffles. "I don't know how to get from where we are to what he wants. I just don't."

"Do you need me to come over there?" Gretchen asked.

"No, no. I'll be fine. I need to fucking sleep, is what I need. Sleep and figure my own shit out, right? Be the big, tough, redheaded girl everyone thinks I am."

"I don't have any advice for you, Shar. I wish I did, but I'm not exactly the poster girl for relationships," Gretchen replied, getting up and pacing to the window.

Sharla yawned. "Maybe talking to you about it has helped. I'm fucking drained now."

They said good night and Gretchen ended the call, holding her phone to her chest, thinking about Sharla and her predicament. A pang of loneliness hit her. All of the people she loved were far away from her and hurting. One was facing a big career-ending decision and the other was in love with her boss and couldn't reconcile it.

Her stomach growled again, reminding her she had yet to eat. She stuffed her feet into shoes, grabbed her purse, and left. Some fresh air and a walk to the local bagel place might help. A late-night lox and cream cheese would be the perfect antidote to the frustrating feeling bubbling up inside her.

She checked her phone as she rode down the elevator. Still no news. She didn't want to be that girl and message her man incessantly until he answered, but she was worried about him all the same. She toyed with sending him another text, but then let it go. They had to come from a place of trust if it was going to work. It had been tested already, and she did not want to go there again.

She pushed through the revolving door, the cool night air refreshing. She took a big lungful, grateful to be out of her condo, cooped up all day catching up on work. Tomorrow she was running everywhere, which would be a nice change of pace. She emptied her negative thoughts as she walked, trying her best to think of positive things. She had a France wardrobe to buy before November for her trip, she had clients to secure before she did that, and she had to think about flying to Dallas soon, especially if Josh was not playing.

Before she knew it, she was at the bagel shop. The lights were blazing inside, the late-dinner crowd gathering, the talk and laughter surrounding her as she entered the shop a happy sound. The owner waved at her, and she happily waved back. She sometimes advised him on wines, and he loved debating with her over how Italian wines were better than anything Canada could produce. It was so much fun to listen to him talk about the beautiful wines he would drink as a young man in Italy. His wife would roll her eyes and add an extra bagel into Gretchen's bag, winking. She had promised Josh to bring him here next time he was in Toronto, as he'd never been in the years he played with the Sixers.

Gretchen wished he were with her now as she perused the flavors of cream cheese, wondering which one he would like. Did he even like cream cheese? They still needed to get to know each other, learn all their little oddities and quirks. As she thought about trying new things, she passed over the plain cream cheese in favor of herb and garlic and grabbed some packaged lox beside it. Rounding the corner to the counter to order her usual dozen sesame-seed bagels, she looked up at the line in front of her, and her heart stopped.

Josh.

He was reaching to grab a paper bag of bagels from the clerk, his overnight duffel on his shoulder, his beat-up carry-on under that.

She rubbed her eyes, not believing them. She knew that back anywhere, even with the hoodie he was wearing. It was further cemented by his favorite Sixers cap, on backward, the corner of the brim rough from where he would adjust it on the field. It was unmistakably his. His jeans were well-worn, the outline of his wallet on the right pocket.

He turned, saw her, did a double-take, and when he smiled widely, it shocked her back to life. He was here. She looked around, and then back at him, wondering if she was hallucinating.

"What—" she spluttered, the crowd in the store turning at the sound of the laugh he let out. People were looking, a couple of them figuring out who he was, and she caught the flash of phones come out as he reached her.

"For breakfast tomorrow," he said and put his arm around her. "Surprised?"

She just laughed and let him kiss her, his arms full of bags and bagels.

"Definitely," she replied.

chapter 20

He brushed a crumb off her breast, and then licked at the glob of cream cheese that had landed near it. She tasted deliciously salty, sweat from the amazing sex they'd had as soon as they got home evaporating into the air. Only afterward did both of them realize they were ravenous, and they quickly toasted some bagels and brought them back to bed.

She let out a giggle, his heart jumping at the sound. She was the exact thing he needed. There was no other choice.

When Gretchen had appeared in front of him at the bagel shop, Josh thought he was going to drop the damned bag. The look on her face had been priceless, the surprise much better than the one he had planned, which was to bribe the concierge of her building and make his way up to her door, bagels in hand.

He had caught a last-minute flight from Dallas to Toronto and was already taxiing down the runway when he remembered he hadn't called her. As he'd sat on the flight, he'd figured it might be fun to completely surprise her.

Her voice mail that morning had been all he'd needed to book the flight. It had been a tense couple of hours after that. Lots of calls and emails and a courier delivering the legal documents, back-and-forth calls with the club figuring it all out.

"So, you're really going to do it?" she asked, nibbling on the end of her bagel.

"Yeah."

She ran a hand up his arm, onto his shoulder, and held it there. "I can't imagine how tense today was, I mean, this is—"

"Baseball. My life. I know. Moving from city to city, never getting too settled anywhere. Analyzing everything I do, careful about the goal. I love being a baseball player, but I want to go out when I'm still, you know—" he finished as she stuffed the last bit of bagel into her mouth, her eyebrow quirking.

"Good," she mumbled as she finished chewing and leaned in, kissing his cheek. "I get it."

"So, the Longhorns are going to pay out your contract, and then you retire with a pension at the end of the season?" Gretchen asked, scooting out of bed, brushing sesame seeds off her body. He wanted her back in bed with him, the sight of her naked riling him up in an instant. She had a birthmark just beside her bellybutton that was always begging to be kissed. She turned and walked toward the bathroom, and her butt cheeks jiggled.

Goddammit, she was perfect. Josh cleared his throat. She'd asked him a question, what was it? Oh right. Pension.

"Yep. I have a monthly pension that builds, and because I was in the club for ten years, it's significant. I don't need it, but if I access it later, it's a bigger payout. There are health care benefits, that kind of thing too."

She was in the washroom now, door open, the square of light punching through the darkness of her bedroom. He shifted onto his back, hands under his head, and stared at the ceiling, trying not to think of her naked, and leaned over. He heard her rummaging, muttering to herself.

"So, really, a cushy retirement package all around. You poor baby," she joked.

He turned his head as she came back through the door, a pot of something in her hands. She gestured for him to sit up, and then wiggled her way in behind him on the bed.

"What are you up to?" he asked, trying to look behind him.

"Sit still. Are you allergic to anything?"

He shook his head, her thighs on either side of his hips making his hands itch to hold her, and he twitched as she leaned into him.

"I used this stuff when I pulled my calf muscle—it's really nice. It's all natural, with arnica and calendula in it. It might help with the stiffness. Can't hurt, anyway," she added, the top of the jar popping as she opened it.

Gretchen smoothed something cold across his shoulders and down his back, and he winced, then relaxed as her warm hands immediately melted it. The citrus smell and her touch sent shots of pleasure across his skin, and he was hard in an instant, her breasts pressing into him as she worked over his traps, which honestly, were still tense, even now. She massaged his lat muscles with smooth, sensual strokes, and Josh groaned.

He wanted her. Again, which was ridiculous, given how tired he was. As she finished spreading the cream, he grabbed her and dragged her around into his lap where he could see her. Her hands, warm and slick, ran up his chest and over his neck.

"Thank you," he murmured as he leaned in and kissed her.

She glanced down between them. "Oh my."

He raised one eyebrow at her, daring her to make fun of him. "You have your hands all over me, for all I know that stuff is an aphrodisiac, and you just want to have your way with me again. You're insatiable, woman."

"Maybe," she replied suggestively, and reached down under the sheet, running her slicked hands up and down his now fully hard length. "But I doubt I needed a cream to do that."

Her hand moved faster, sliding up and over, her thumb rubbing the tip the way she knew he liked it. He groaned and leaned back as she yanked the sheets down, scattering sesame seeds everywhere.

"Mmm. I need to snack in bed with you more often," she said and leaned over to brush more crumbs off his stomach.

"I need to surprise you more often, maybe?" he countered, and she stopped, sitting back over his legs. Dammit. Maybe it hadn't been the best idea to say that.

"Well, maybe not so often," she replied. "But I'm glad you're here, though."

"I'm sorry I didn't call you," he offered, reaching out to pull her chin up, looking into her eyes. "I should have."

Gretchen waved her hands. "I understand, Josh. It sucked, I was worried, but I had to trust you were doing what you needed to do. It isn't like we're married."

"No," he said, and pulled her closer, sex forgotten in the need to reassure her of how he felt for her. "But we're together. You deserve to be part of my decisions. If I'm not playing ball—"

"Josh," she intoned.

"What?"

"I'm not going anywhere. You're a good baseball player, but that isn't all you are, and you know it."

"What I do now will be a huge decision, it impacts on what happens here," he added, gesturing between them. "I don't want to be away from you anymore, but I need to figure out where I'll land. What I'm going to do with my life."

"Well, if you decide to become a beekeeper in Nebraska, I'd be down for that. I like bees. Think grapes grow there?"

He absorbed the ridiculousness of that statement for a moment, and then let out a huge laugh, falling back to the bed. She laughed right along with him.

"Beekeeping, huh?"

"The point is, it doesn't matter," Gretchen replied. "Remember when you told me you'd go anywhere with me?"

He studied her face, which had gone serious. He did. He'd meant it then, too, even though he'd been an idiot and forgotten not even a day later. He'd always regret that. He tucked her hair behind an ear, smoothing it.

"I do," he replied. "I still will."

"Then same goes, Mr. Sunshine," she drawled and slid up the length of him, her hand sliding down at the same time, sheathing him in her palm once again.

"Nebraska it is," Josh said as he instantly hardened. The emotional ups and downs with this woman were wild, but with her statement, need slammed back through his body, drowning out the worry.

Their lips met as he rolled her on the bed until she was half underneath him. She was his, no matter what happened. They would work it out. But right now? The scent of the citrus cream and her was enough to put his mind back to where it was when she had her hand wrapped around his cock the first time.

"Where were we?" he murmured.

"You were about to make love to me again, I think," Gretchen replied and wiggled suggestively under him. "We need to practice. I hear winters in Nebraska get cold. We'll have to be good at staying warm."

He laughed with her as she kissed him and caressed down her leg, pushing them apart as he slowly stroked his fingers into her wet, hot center.

She stopped laughing, her breath catching. "Oh Josh."

"You are so wet and so ready. So perfect," he said, his thumb on her clit, two fingers sliding in and out of her. He wanted to make her feel incredible. He'd said what he'd needed to, and now he wanted to show her.

She pressed into him, her arms around him, her free leg hooked over his hip. They were skin to skin, his hand between them. He moved his fingers down, spreading them between her center and her butt, and she whimpered.

"Yes?" he questioned, and she nodded and moaned again as he penetrated everywhere at once.

"Fuck yes, Josh . . . I love that. Fill me—all of me," she stuttered out between breaths.

It was intense, as if he was already inside her with his cock, joined and complete as she pushed into his touch, giving him permission. He plunged in deeper, the pink of her cheeks darkening, her breath coming in gasps. He loved watching her orgasm, the way she would tremble and completely let go of any tension in her body as it took hold. He would never get enough of the way he could make her feel. He hoped it would always be like this between them. Easy, honest, and open.

"I want to watch you come again," he murmured, leaning in to kiss her shoulder, her resulting hiss of pleasure making his cock jump. It was hard to hold back when she was like this, but he was determined to give this to her first.

"I'm going to come, don't stop," she gasped, her eyes opening wide to his. "I'm—"

She let go with an intensity that floored him, her lips crashing to his, her nails digging into his back. He held her tightly, fingers pumping in and out of her as wetness covered his hand, their bodies fused.

"Oh my God, Josh, oh my God—" she chanted as her entire body went slack. He grinned against her lips.

"Good?" he asked, pulling his hand carefully away, her scent everywhere around them. She nodded and stroked her hand down his body until she found his length again.

"Now," she demanded, breathless. "Your turn."

"Yes, please," he said. She guided him into her, slowly sinking back, his eyes glued to hers as their bodies merged again.

"Every damned time. So perfect," he growled as she opened to him, stretching as he filled her.

He slid in and out of her gently, and she wrapped her arms around him, encouraging him, letting out gasps every time he did. He wasn't going to last long, the way she was moving with him, pressed to him.

"I love you," she breathed into his ear. "No matter what."

She trailed kisses along his shoulder, teeth grazing, and she let out a cry as he shifted and angled upward with his stroke, her words filling him with an indescribable strength.

"Yes, like that!" she cried as she began to shake again. With one last thrust, he groaned loudly and emptied himself into her.

No matter what. Her words echoed in his head as he slumped to the bed and pulled her into him. He believed her. No going back, no more doubt.

"I love you, too, Gretchen. No matter what," Josh said, and his world was complete.

Epilogue

"What time do you have to be at the airport?"

Gretchen looked up as she was closing her suitcase. She frowned, wishing she had a luggage scale because her bag was obviously overweight. Maybe she should rethink all the shoes?

"Nine," she replied.

Josh peeked around the corner, a toothbrush in his hand. "Okay. I can drive you then."

He winked and tucked himself back behind the door of the bathroom to finish. She listened to the water swish, the tap of his brush on the edge of the sink. All sounds that were now routine and comforting.

She hefted her bag off the edge of the bed and set it on the floor with a pang of sadness that Josh wasn't coming with her. She was headed to Beaujeu for Les Sarmantelles, and she was excited beyond belief. A trip to France, time with her best friend, and wine? Perfect, except that she wanted Josh with her.

He had moved in with her the moment the ink on his retirement papers was dry. She had offered since it seemed natural to her. He was traveling back and forth to Texas to finish out his contract obligations and needed a place to stay anyway. A few times he'd been in New York, and Gretchen had tagged along for one of the commercial shoots he had done, curiosity about his world outside of actually playing ball getting the better of her.

He had said, on the ride to the airport when they were headed back to Toronto, that he was very glad to be done with "this shit" and kissed her senseless in the Uber, raising the eyebrows of the driver.

He said he hated photo shoots and "acting," as he called it. She had laughed when he'd said it, prompting the kiss, because when he had been in front of the camera, he had soaked up every minute. He was a good actor if he could pull off that he loved it.

"Do you think you'll miss me?" Josh's voice rumbled in her ear, his hand traveling down her spine, pulling her back to the present. Goosebumps followed where he touched, and she wished for more time to strip him out of the clothes he'd just put on. He was reading her mind again.

"Maybe," she teased as his fingers brushed aside her hair and he kissed the back of her neck.

"No running off with some fancy French winemaker who is named Jacques and has a twirly mustache, okay?"

She let out a snort of laughter and turned as he folded his arms around her, looking down into her eyes. She was going to be gone for two weeks, but with their closeness now, it would be a long time.

"No promises," she replied as he burrowed into her, playfully grazing his teeth along her shoulder and buried his face into the crook of her neck, holding her, letting out a tense breath.

"Okay, out with it. What's up?" she asked.

He released her, and she grabbed his hand to stop him. How could she reassure him? She felt his absence already. Miss him? Yes, she would.

"You know I will miss you," she offered, and as his eyes met hers, studying and serious, she added. "There's still time to come with me."

"I have to be in New York tomorrow, and then Boston for the World Series start," he replied.

"I know. But it's France," she wheedled, trying her best to show him how much she wanted him there with her. She leaned away from him, feigning drama. "*Très romantique, n'est-ce pas?*"

Josh chuckled and shook his head, wrapping her up in his arms once more, his forehead pressed to hers.

"I love you," was all he replied.

.   .   .

"Jesus, get in here, girl!"

Sharla enfolded Gretchen in a hug that squeezed the life out of her, and she closed her eyes, feeling the weight of the embrace beyond just a happy-to-see-you energy. Sharla had dark circles under her eyes, her hair was feeling the humid climate in spades, and she was drooping ever so slightly from her normal, fiery-redheaded posture.

"That bad?" she said quietly, and Sharla laughed, but flicked a glance around her before slinging an arm over Gretchen's shoulders and letting out a big breath.

"Yeah. He's . . . I don't know Gretch. He kissed me last night. We got into a bottle, and I was talking out my ass, saying I needed to find a purpose, and he leaned in, and—" Sharla said, then stopped, her hand rubbing her forehead in frustration.

Gretchen picked up the handle on her carry-on suitcase, Sharla hefted the other one, and they strode toward the front doors of the small airport to their waiting car.

"Oof. What did you do?"

"I let him, dammit," she snapped, and then let out another huff. "I shouldn't have."

Gretchen let out a whistle that made her friend roll her eyes. "Okay, enough."

"You want to talk about it?"

"No," Sharla shot back as they slipped into the car. As the door closed, cocooning them in leather and muffled silence, Sharla leaned back on the headrest and closed her eyes. "He told me he loves me."

They each looked out the window for a moment, the airport concrete giving way to the countryside. The sun dappled the trees along the side of the road, and the colors came to life outside Gretchen's window, the shimmer of the leaves flying across the glass. It was absolutely beautiful here.

"Do you love him?" Gretchen asked, grabbing for Sharla's hand again, holding it on the seat between them. Sharla bowed her head and then looked at her.

"Yeah. Dammit," she murmured. "I do. But—"

Sharla didn't finish her thought, just swallowed and looked out the window again, and Gretchen didn't press. That *but* was a biggie. As much as she wanted to have all the answers for Sharla, she didn't. This was a decision her friend would have to make for herself.

After an hour gliding along, they turned onto a dirt road, and the villa came into view, surrounded by vines stretching beyond the little courtyard on three sides. A small lake sparkled on the fourth and she sat up.

"This is where we're staying?" she asked. "Holy shit, Shar!"

Sharla laughed then, the moment of seriousness gone, and she shook their joined hands.

"Wait until you see the pool!"

.   .   .

The crickets were in full evening song as Gretchen adjusted the shoulders of her dress, the balcony doors open, bringing the crisp scent of the autumn breeze in. It was almost dusk, and in the courtyard below, strung lights gave the villa a festive, almost movie-set vibe.

She'd been here three days, and it was already heady beyond words. The heat had been high for the time of year, giving them a welcome break to just relax, gossip, nap, and read.

Pure bliss.

The local winemaker association dinner they were going to this evening was apparently semiformal. Gretchen had pulled out a soft, dark-blue midthigh dress that had a wide boat neck and was comfortable but also form-fitting. A nip in the evening air meant the velvetlike fabric would keep her warm. Sharla walked in, adjusting an earring, let out a muffled *rawr,* and then they both giggled.

"Love this dress! I've never seen it before!" Sharla complimented as she fluffed Gretchen's hair, which did as it always did in humidity: poof wildly. Sharla reached for her frizz-tamer spray and scrunched some through Gretchen's hair, then her own, as Gretchen patted her lips with a bit of gloss.

"I bought it for the trip," Gretchen said. "I thought sophisticated might be a requirement, given Kevin's circles."

"Has Josh seen this?"

"Nope," she replied, grinning. "I'll wear it for him sometime, I suppose."

"He'll love it," she replied saucily. "And then he'll remove it."

They both laughed. It was true. He would probably do just that. She wondered if she could get away with wearing it in winter in Toronto. It got very cold, and the dress was short. Maybe she'd pack it the next time they visited Travis and Felicia in Vegas.

Giggling, they caught each other's eyes in the mirror, and Sharla put her head beside Gretchen's. They stood in the mirror, Sharla's wild red hair and flashing gold hoop earrings next to Gretchen's blond mane and more sedate sapphire drops.

"I'm glad you're here," Sharla said and squeezed her before letting her go.

"Me too," Gretchen replied as she picked up her phone. No recent messages. She missed Josh like mad, more than she ever expected to. The romance of the landscape was intoxicating, and she was loving time with Sharla. But there was just this empty spot beside her that he needed to fill. Her friends had asked her when the wedding was after they'd met Josh.

She was giving him time, but part of her was hoping he would be ready soon. She loved him, she wanted him in her life, for life. To start their family. She never voiced it, not wanting to pressure him.

"He's fine, Gretch. Seriously," Sharla chided as Gretchen frowned and sighed. "You two are inseparable! Do we have to give you a stupid couple name like JoGretch or Greshua?"

They both laughed at the silliness of that. The fan pages had not been kind to her at first, but no one had given them a moniker yet, thank God.

She had texted Josh that morning that she was headed to a fancy dinner tonight, and he'd responded with *Great, have fun!* but nothing since. He was likely neck-deep in World Series stuff in Boston by now.

"I don't know what—" It felt silly to pine for him; they were in one of the most beautiful wine regions in the world, dressed like movie stars, in a villa out of her dreams. She shook herself mentally. Obsessing was not something she did anymore. Josh had helped her throw off "boring Gretchen" forever, seemingly that first night in Vegas, and ever since.

Seize the moment, right?

"Let's go drink some wine and pretend we're rich society mistresses, shall we?" Sharla joked as Gretchen picked up her clutch and dropped her phone into it.

"Indeed," Gretchen teased back.

Sharla stuck her tongue out at her, then rolled her eyes, obviously seeing the irony in her own joke. They quickly descended downstairs to meet Kevin, who was in a lovely red velvet dinner jacket, pacing the floor in front of the staircase.

"Gretchen! You look splendid!" he said, beaming, and kissed her on both cheeks before offering his arm to Sharla, his eyes glued to her, the ache in him evident. Gretchen followed along behind them, Sharla fussing with her silky, ankle-length dress in a striking green, her strappy gold sandals flashing as she did.

"I love this dress on you. Always have," she overheard Kevin say as they descended the steps, and Sharla furrowed her brow at him.

"It is your color," Gretchen added.

"Pipe down, peanut gallery," Sharla said as she flipped her hair over her shoulder.

They reached the bottom steps of the front doors, but the driveway was empty. Kevin grumbled something under his breath and looked at his watch. "Where is the bloody car?" he snapped, irritated, and bounded back up the steps, likely to find someone. Kevin wasn't normally irritated by much, and it took Gretchen by surprise. She looked at Sharla, who just shrugged.

"I'm sure they just got held up," Gretchen said and linked her arm with her friend's. "There isn't a hurry, is there?"

"None. Not tonight," Sharla said and wiggled her eyebrows at Gretchen. "Dinner arrival times are just suggestions here in France."

Just as she said that, the flash of chrome caught their eyes and a Bentley limousine crested the small rise to pull around front, stopping directly in front of them. It was silver, and Gretchen could see her face in the tinted windows.

"Wow. This is our ride?" she asked, and Sharla stepped away from her as Kevin came back down the steps, stopping beside Sharla, the two of them now practically beaming. Sharla forgot herself and leaned into Kevin, who put an arm around her immediately.

Gretchen looked at them, sensing something was afoot. Sharla was suddenly much, much too happy. "What is going on?" she asked. The soft thud of a car door made her turn back toward the driveway.

"No. This is your ride, this evening," Sharla said. "All yours."

There, in a suit and tie, was Josh.

It took Gretchen a moment to register that once again, he had completely surprised her by being where she had never expected him to be. She stepped down to him as he reached her, and she took in his suit and the slight nervousness in him as he said a quick hello under his breath.

"What are you doing here?" she asked, incredulous.

Josh raised his hand to Sharla and Kevin and took her arm without another word, leading her toward the car. Gretchen looked back at her friend. Sharla wiggled her fingers at her conspiratorially.

"You and I are having words later!" she called out just before Josh opened the door and ushered her inside the soft, dark interior of the car.

Sharla's laughter echoed after them as they drove away, Josh beside her, his arm around her shoulders, his nose buried into her hair.

"Surprise!" he murmured.

"You are making this a habit! What are you doing here? I mean, I'm glad to see you, but—"

She didn't get to finish her sentence, because Josh kissed her, effectively shushing her, possessively taking her mouth, and she responded, her entire body thrumming at his touch. He ran his thumb along her jaw, fingers threading in her hair, and she let him pull her in, the sensation of him obliterating everything.

"Your lip gloss tastes like vanilla," he murmured when he finally let her go, breathless and rumpled. He ran a thumb along her lower lip, his eyes meeting hers, dark and intense. "Nice."

She grabbed him by the lapels of his suit and shook him slightly.

"You are a troublemaker, Joshua Malvern."

He laughed and gently covered her hands with his, the warmth from them echoing up her arms.

"I am, am I?" he replied, his voice rumbling in her ear as she leaned into him. "What kind of trouble do you want to get into? We have the whole limo to ourselves."

She swatted at him and he chuckled, but his hands left hers, roaming her body, making appreciative noises as he did.

"I was thinking of how nice it would be to have you here while I was getting ready for dinner, which, by the way, we are currently missing. And here you are! I don't know how you do it," she stammered. He felt so good touching her; she wanted him. Now. Hard and fast.

"I like this dress, by the way," he said after a few more kisses. She wiggled a bit.

"Yeah?"

"Oh yes. You're beautiful, Gretch," he replied.

The car stopped as she reached up and palmed his jaw, and he leaned in and kissed her hard, both of them aroused. His hand slid down her back, over her butt, and down her leg, pulling her up onto his lap, her skirt riding up, effectively pinning him to the seat. He was hard, her thighs rubbing along his crotch, and he groaned in frustration as there was a tap on the window near them.

"Mr. Malvern, we're all set,"

Josh knocked back, and the driver opened the door. He stepped out of the car and reached back a hand to her in the blink of an eye. Gretchen stepped out, straightening her dress, and as her eyes adjusted to the change in light, she noticed they were along a cliffside, with some benches and a small lookout. A bottle of wine and two big cabernet glasses were on the stone retaining wall, a pretty metal lantern glowing beside them, the driver holding a lighter as he gestured forward.

"Pour vous," he said, and smiled at them.

Their feet crunched on the gravel as they walked over, and she took in the view of the valley below, lights from homes dotting the landscape. It was beautiful.

Obviously, this had been well orchestrated, with help from Sharla and Kevin, and Gretchen shook her head. Of all things, Josh would surprise her here, in France, for a simple romantic gesture. He popped the cork on the bottle, filling their glasses with deep red wine, and set them back down, turning to her.

He smiled, the smile she loved, that went all the way to his eyes, and turned away from her for a moment, reaching behind the lantern. He turned back and handed her an empty to-go coffee cup.

Not just any cup. The logo on it was from the Toronto airport, with "two cream, no sugar" scrawled boldly across the paper sleeve. She shifted her gaze back up to him. What was he up to?

"Open the cup, Gretchen," Josh said, his voice thick, gravelly, full of emotion.

, , ,

Josh was sweating through his best suit. He'd been hiding out in the wine cellar of the villa for hours, worried Gretchen would see him, praying this would go well. Then he'd practically stripped her in the car, that dress hugging her in all the right places, temporarily rendering him useless.

She was all his, and in that dress, he couldn't take his eyes or his hands off her. She hadn't minded. He couldn't wait to slowly pull it off her later.

"Josh?" she said, his name a question, pulling his eyes back to hers and the moment in front of them.

"Go on," he replied. "It isn't coffee, obviously."

If there was ever a time and a place to do this, it was now. He'd had a couple of months to think about it, being with her, feeling her confidence as he flailed in the face of what to do with himself now that he wasn't in the MLB. The doubts he'd had about them being able to make it work were long gone.

Gretchen gave him that look she always did when she was humoring him. The one where she tilted her head slightly and pursed her lips, trying desperately not to laugh and losing. Then she popped the plastic lid off the cup.

He opened his mouth to say what he'd rehearsed over and over and over.

He couldn't speak.

This was where he needed to tell her everything. To tell her he loved her, how much he needed her, and how a chance meeting in an airport meant the greatest gift in his life was now standing in front of him on a hilltop in France. Not a grand slam or a Gold Glove or a World Series. No ball diamond triumph could compare to what Gretchen meant to him. She had walked into his life, turned him upside down, and then showed him that life was more than baseball. It could be so, so much more.

But his throat wasn't working and he swallowed nervously as they simply looked into each other's eyes, hers wet with tears. How was he going to put into words what he wanted?

"Josh?" she asked again and picked the ring out of the cup, holding it between them. He'd chosen it carefully, having it made the first week he'd flown back to Toronto, Travis's story about Felicia echoing in his mind. Travis had said it again when they had visited. *Don't wait. If it feels right, then do it, figure out the future later. Go watch the sunrise.*

The ring had sat buried in his ball gear ever since, the one place Gretchen wouldn't ever think to rummage, taunting him to just ask her, and Josh had waited too long already. The carefully chosen chocolate solitaire diamond in an offset square just like the infield winked out in the dusky light. Well, it wasn't a sunrise but a sunset. Did that count?

"Gretchen," he managed and cleared his throat, letting her go to pluck it from her outstretched fingers, then slowly went down on one knee in front of her. *Screw it*, he thought. The only words that mattered were simple. "Marry me?"

She looked down at him, tears slipping down her cheeks, her hands over her mouth, and she nodded.

At that point, he pulled her hand away and slipped the ring on while she wiped at her tears with the other one. She still hadn't said anything, and he stood, pulling her into his arms again.

"My firecracker, for once, is speechless. Say something, Gretch," he said quietly, brushing the last of her tears away. She let out a small laugh at that and put her hands on his chest, looking at her ring, he supposed, but then she tilted her head back to him. Her eyes were glittering with more tears, her perfectly tousled hair floating in the breeze that had sprung up around them.

"Best damned coffee I ever bought," she replied.

"It sure was," Josh whispered before he lowered his lips to hers, kissing her, sealing the deal.

Acknowledgments

So many people have encouraged me as this book went from concept to where it is today. Truly, it would not be possible without them.

First, my family. My children—who aren't allowed to read my books yet—for giving me the quiet time to write when I ask and thinking Mom is already famous. The many extended family and friends who have celebrated each success, and especially my in-laws, who have been our rock as we keep reaching for our goals. This book is one of those goals.

Secondly, the team at Wattpad. From obscurity to Featured to joining the Stars program, winning a Watty, and then onto Paid Stories—it has been a wild ride! Both the Stars and Paid teams have been rockstars. Special acknowledgment must be made to Emma Szalai, Deanna McFadden, and Jen Hale. You have believed in me as I navigated the wondrous world of what happens *after* you write the book. Your guidance and patience with this rookie author have made all the difference.

I must also acknowledge the readers on Wattpad. Their enthusiasm for this book has humbled me, and I am grateful for all of it.

Most important out of all the thank-yous is to Royce, my husband. He tolerated my late nights, writing marathons, frustrations, and moments of woe. Through it all, he pushed me when I doubted whether I could do this. Thank you for believing I could and your support while I did.

About the Author

Caroline Richardson has played competitive paintball in the Skydome, galloped million-dollar racehorses for a living, and met her husband when he sold her a Ford Mustang during a snowstorm. When not writing, Caroline backcountry camps, hikes, and cross-country skis with her family. She lives in Ottawa, Canada.

You can find her books on Wattpad at https://www.wattpad.com/user/MustangSabby.

Turn the page for a preview of

Available April 2022

Chapter One

Priyanka Seth was always a girl with a plan, and arriving hungover for a life-changing interview—*sans panties!*—was not part of it. Jumping into the backseat of a cab already loitering at the curb, Priya slapped a hand on the Plexiglas divider. "I need to get to Sutton Place then straight back to East Fifty-Third and Park before eight."

The driver lifted heavy-lidded eyes from his phone screen to meet hers in the rearview mirror. "You got a pair of wings in that purse?"

Opening her clutch, Priya frantically dug inside. "I have . . . seventy-seven dollars with your name on it if you can figure it out." She handed over the wad of mixed bills and the cab roared like a waking panther and charged—slamming Priya into her seat with an *oof.* While the car tore down the street, she unlocked her phone and scrolled through her contacts for the one person who could save her in her hour of need.

The line rang twice before Caitlin's bleary face filled the screen, all rumpled violet hair and sleepy dark eyes. "For the love of *Vogue—what!*"

"Cait! Oh thank *God*! Get up, get up right now. I'm on my way to your place. Meet me outside in ten minutes. It's an emergency. A Stiletto Sisterhood Code Red Emergency." If citing their code like a preacher would a passage from the Bible made her a touch melodramatic, so be it. Her life was on the line.

"Wait, slow down. I can't follow *stupidity* this early without coffee." Caitlin vanished in a flash of bedding and the creak of floorboards. "Where's the fire?"

"I'll explain when I see you, but I'm pulling a walk of shame to a last-minute interview, and I need to borrow a suit."

Caitlin's face smushed close to the screen. "You realize there's a height disparity between us? Like six inches? I'm good, but I'm not a wizard."

"No, you're Caitlin Choi-Emerson. Fashion guru. Savant of suits." As a self-taught stylist, Caitlin's brand was menswear made boldly female—with lush fabrics, daring cuts, and all the accessories. "If anyone can save me from this seventh circle of hell, it's you."

"Ah, flattery," she purred. "Well played. I'll see what I can dig up."

"Thank you. And Cait," Priya added with a panicked jolt before disconnecting, "something basic, okay?"

"Boo." Caitlin sighed. "See you in ten."

As the cab sped down the Upper East Side streets, mercifully empty on a Sunday morning, Priya combed through her purse for any other clues to fill in the missing gaps of last night's hazy memory. There was a receipt from the bar for almost three hundred—*holy fuzzknuckles!*—dollars, some spare change, and her lipstick cap but no lipstick. Of course it had to be her favorite *discontinued* shade.

No random numbers or drunken texts appeared on her phone, and by some miracle, all social media came up clear of damaging posts, but in her gallery there was a *video* . . . and given the thumbnail, it was absolutely NSFW.

Priya hugged the phone to her chest and closed her eyes with a fervent prayer before lowering the volume and hitting Play. Her voice slid out first. All heavy panting and hot gasps. The answering accompaniment of a man's laugh was smooth and wicked as he whispered something that got swallowed up in the start of a killer orgasm and ended abruptly with a partial view of his face. Vague and blurry as her memory, but it stirred a fleeting recollection of quick hands, a hot mouth. And something about an elevator . . .

True to her word, Caitlin stood waiting on the curb, dressed in yellow sweats, orange heels, and oversized sunglasses, a white garment bag hung over one arm.

Priya pushed open the passenger door and Caitlin slid in, draping the garment bag between them. "As requested."

"I could kiss you." Priya drew down the zipper and her joyful smile vanished with a horrified gasp. "It's *teal.*"

"And?"

"I said *basic.*"

"It's a solid." Caitlin dipped her chin, sunglasses sliding to the tip of her pixie nose. "No pattern. No texture. No *fun,* Basic."

"Didn't you have anything in black?" Priya sputtered as the cab pushed back onto the street, careening toward her certain demise. "Or navy? Charcoal?"

"What makes you think any of those exist in my wardrobe?"

"Oh my God."

"It's June, Priya, and with your complexion? This color is confident. Striking. This commands attention."

"Cait, this isn't a fashion editorial spread. It's an interview." Head in her hands, Priya groaned. "You had one job. One!"

"Okey dokey." Shrugging, Caitlin reached for the zipper. "Then don't wear it."

"No! Give me the pants . . . I'll make do."

Caitlin removed the trousers from the garment bag and handed them over. "Are you going to tell me what this is all about?"

Kicking off her heels, Priya slipped her feet into the pant legs and delicately shimmied the trousers on, careful to keep her skirt over top. "I went to the soft opening of that new Manhattan bar everyone's talking about. The one owned by that hot artist from Toronto."

"Pathos?"

"Yeah."

"Bitch!" Caitlin tossed Priya a glare sharp enough to kill a man at three paces. "We were supposed to go together when they officially open next month."

"Yeah, well, I'm sorry, but I got an invite from that guy from Stikemans I went to dinner with last week."

"Greg?"

"No, Matthew."

"Whatever. Stop talking before I shove you out of this cab."

"We'll go there for their brunch event—all-you-can drink mimosas. My treat, okay?"

Caitlin's scowl softened. Marginally. "Fine."

"Anyway. After inhaling enough tequila to flatline a frat boy, I got an email notifying me that my Monday morning interview was being shifted to Sunday at eight."

"Who sends out emails after midnight? Or requests an interview on a Sunday morning?"

"I'd call her Satan, but that somehow makes her more perfect." Sucking in a breath, Priya grunted. "Oh *no*. I can't fasten the zipper."

"I tried to warn you."

Twisting in the seat, Priya stretched out as flat as she could manage across Caitlin's lap, but there was nothing. Not even the barest ounce of give. "Why do these pants have no stretch?"

"This isn't off the rack, Priya." Caitlin leveled a baleful glare. "Lycra is tacky, and everything I own is tailored to *me*, therefore I don't need stretch."

4

Priya whimpered at the memory of her custom suit, the one that cost an obscene amount of money, pressed and waiting in her mom's apartment clear across town. "What am I going to do?"

"Reschedule?"

"This is Marai Nagao. Her calendar is always packed weeks — months out, even. I can't miss this interview." Especially not when there was a yearlong mentorship on the table. Some of New York's most successful lawyers and judges had been molded like raw clay by her hands. All kinds of doors blown open. "Might as well kiss my entire future good-bye."

Priya had already gone through three separate interview stages just to get this far. First with HR and then two more with senior partners. Nothing —nothing—was going to derail Priya from this moment. Not a brutal hangover or lost panties.

Shucking off the trousers, Priya folded them across her lap. "This is a disaster."

"We can salvage this." Caitlin spun a finger at Priya, taking in the trainwreck ensemble with a narrowed gaze. "The skirt's vintage Valentino, yes?"

A smile pushed at the corners of Priya's lips. Trust Caitlin to sniff out a label. "Yes."

"Classic A-line. Tasteful. Not a deal breaker for an interview of this magnitude." With a giddy wiggle of her shoulders, Caitlin plucked the jacket out of the garment bag and shoved it at her. "Put this on. It was meant to be a bit oversized, so it should fit."

Priya slid on the jacket—definitely a size too big—while Caitlin attacked her mane of thick black hair, twisting it up into a tight chignon, somehow taming it into submission with bobby pins and ChapStick, then added a silk scarf tied in a loose knot around Priya's neck for a final flourish.

"*Et voilà!*"

Priya frowned despondently at the picture Caitlin snapped on her phone. "I look like a hungover stewardess for a cheap airline."

"Do not insult my masterpiece." She chef-kissed her fingers. "I call it Tequila-Hoe-Chic."

"Hilarious."

"I thought so."

Priya removed the scarf and handed it back to Caitlin. "Less is more, right?"

"In the words of the great Coco Chanel, absolutely. You could use a bit of mascara to brighten those bloodshot eyes, though."

"Fresh out."

"Lipstick?"

"Lost it along with my panties, apparently."

"I'm sorry." Caitlin pushed her face so close to Priya's that she was all eyes and nose. "Repeat that for me but slower."

Priya hung her head. "I lost my panties in some guy's Fifth Avenue apartment."

Caitlin sputtered, blinked, and then doubled over in rib-cracking hysterics. "Stop," she cackled in a rasp that pushed well beyond laughter into out of breath. "Oh, it hurts. It hurts. I can't!"

Priya tucked her tongue into the pocket of her cheek. "Are you finished?"

"Almost." She straightened, eyes glistening with tears. "Oh wow. That's my workout for the week. Did you at least search the place before jumping into the cab?"

"Of course!" After tumbling ass-first out of bed when the alarm went off, Priya had hunted for her clothes like a deranged maniac, starting with the pale-pink pleated skirt by the foot of the bed and black Louboutin heels near the door with her purse on top and all her remaining cash, cards, and ID tucked inside. Everything was accounted for, except her underwear. Hot-pink lace—hard to miss and even harder to lose. Yet she had done just that.

And now she was minutes away from sitting down in front of her literal idol, bare-assed with tequila fumes wafting from her pores like expired perfume.

"It was a studio. Not like there were many places they could've gone. He—whoever I hooked up with last night—must've taken them."

"Ew." Caitlin's nose scrunched with a scowl. "He's a panty thief?"

"Apparently. But he had the decency to pay for a loaded breakfast before ghosting me while I drooled into the pillow." Not that she'd had time for anything more than finger-brushing her teeth. She'd snatched a pancake on the way out and inhaled it in the elevator, nearly choking on the damn thing. "I don't remember his name, and I'd barely even know what he looked like if it wasn't for the video."

"Stop." Caitlin flagged a hand like an officer halting traffic. Or a criminal. "First, you need to lay off the shots—think of the brain cells. Second, you own those pants now." She nodded toward Priya's lap. "Third, you have a *video*, and you're only just telling me *now*?" Her chin lowered to match her hushed voice. "Is it good?"

"Good enough that I wish my booze-addled brain had left the memory intact."

"Ah, tequila. She's a cruel bitch to us all, yet you gotta love her style."

"Miss." The driver rapped a hairy knuckle against the partition. "Your stop is up ahead. Where'd you want me to drop you?"

"At the corner would be great."

"All right, skank." Caitlin set her hands on Priya's shoulders as the cab jerked to a halt. "Best advice I can offer you is to keep your head high and pull your shoulders back. You are Priyanka Victory *fucking* Seth." She punctuated each syllable of her name with a heaving shake. "Founder of the Stiletto Sisterhood, queen of any room she walks into, a force to reckon with—goddess extraordinaire—even without undies. Shall I continue?"

Now Priya did laugh. "No, that's plenty. Thank you."

"Good. Because if anyone can turn a walk of shame into a stride of pride, it's you."

Caitlin slid out of the backseat first and held the door open as Priya struggled to steer herself across the sticky fake leather, and she felt a lick of sympathy for all those scandalized socialites who'd been caught with a lens up their skirts while exiting a car.

"Careful, Britney. Don't want to give someone a heart attack."

"It's not as easy as it looks." Sighing, Priya smoothed down her skirt, grateful there was no tunneling wind. The last thing she needed right now was an impromptu Marilyn Monroe moment. Torn between a laugh and a groan, she hugged Caitlin tight. "I owe you for this."

"Slay this interview and we'll call it even. Go get 'em, G.I. Jane. See what I did there?" She smacked a hand to Priya's butt. "Because you're commando." Laughing, Caitlin jumped back into the cab, blew a kiss through the open window, and sped off.

Head swimming, heart racing, Priya took a moment to gather herself. This was it. No turning back now. "Chin up," she whispered. "Game face on."